American Propaganda Abroad offers fresh and important insights into the little known and largely misunderstood role of the United States Information Agency (USIA): To offer foreigners a compelling, positive, but accurate picture of U.S. policies, country and culture. Benjamin Franklin first launched this function of propaganda in Britain and France during revolutionary times. Abraham Lincoln, Theodore Roosevelt, Woodrow Wilson and Franklin Roosevelt all proved themselves superb propagandists. From Harry Truman to Ronald Reagan, official propaganda has evolved through the cold war, the limited wars in Korea and Vietnam, detente and "glasnost." USIA propaganda is determinedly open and truthful, and, as such, fights deception, disinformation and other kinds of anti-American propaganda.

The author dramatically portrays the USIA's foreign affairs role and how foreign policy is born and transported overseas by USIA radio, television and wire services. Fitzhugh Green thus presents a vital facet of American international activity—one that too few citizens comprehend, though they may be prejudiced against it. Taxpayers will be well served to discover what USIA does with its annual budget of approximately one billion dollars.

AMERICAN PROPAGANDA ABROAD

AMERICAN PROPAGANDA ABROAD

Fitzhugh Green

93-1534

HIPPOCRENE BOOKS
New York

For information, address:
Hippocrene Books, Inc.
171 Madison Ave.
New York, NY 10016

Library of Congress Cataloging-in-Publication Data

Green, Fitzhugh, 1917-
  American propaganda abroad / Fitzhugh Green.
  216 p. 34 × 51 cm.
  Includes index.
  ISBN 0-87052-579-4
  1. United States Information Agency—
History.   2. Propaganda,
American.   3. United States—Relations—Foreign countries.
I. Title.
E840.2.G74   1988   88-21096
353.0089—dc19   CIP

Printed in the United States of America.

This book is dedicated to Edward R. Murrow, the noted CBS radio and television broadcaster and United States Information Agency director, 1961–63, "who gave his profession a standard of excellence and whose clarity, humanity and courage helped his country and the world to know what America at its honest best could be." These words are inscribed on a plaque in the park at 18th and H streets, N.W., in Washington, D.C., opposite the site of the original USIA headquarters where Mr. Murrow served as director.

He stood as a friend and inspiration to the author as well as untold numbers of USIA people searching always for the ideal way to speak up for America.

Contents

Acknowledgments

In my search for fact, words, wisdom, and analysis I profited from numerous valued friends and colleagues, none more so than Major General Chester Victor Clifton (ret.), whose guidance and generous gifts of time and imagination literally brought this book to term. I am particularly thankful to publisher George Blagowidow, a noted author himself, for his belief in my message. John Chancellor has given an important dimension with his kind foreword.

To give full scope to everyone who facilitated this book would total many pages. I should particularly mention those who opened their own and others' doors as well as their editorial views. The errors that may appear have survived in spite of all this contribution from Burnett Anderson, J. Gary Augustson, William Buell, Gerald Christiansen, Robert F. Delaney, Marilyn Dexheimer, Wilson Dizard, Clayton Fritchey, Peter Galbraith, Edmund A. Gullion, M. William Haratunian, Albert Harkness, Jr., Joan Palmer Hill, J. Allen Hovey, Jr., Jerry Inman, Leonard H. Marks, Susan Munroe, Joseph D. O'Connell, Jr., the late Yoichi Okamoto, Karl F. Olsson, Daniel P. Oleksiw, Claiborne Pell, Charles H. Percy, Michael Pistor, John E. Reinhardt, E. V. Roberts., Eugene Rosenfeld, Henry B. Ryan, Pamela H. Smith, Gordon Tubbs, Susan Walsh, William W. Warner, Dr. Nils H. Wessell, Granville Worrell, J. Burke Wilkinson, and Barry Zorthian.

Special aid in the form of research and busy keyboards has assured completion. Thanks are due to Trudie Musson, Randy Barrett, Katherine Guthmiller, Rosemary Cardona, Monica Loarca, and Joan Crawford, each of whom pitched in at critical moments.

Foreword

The United States was born with a decent respect for the opinions of mankind. The Declaration of Independence says "let the facts be submitted to a candid world." Half a century after the Declaration was signed, Thomas Jefferson wrote that it was "an appeal to the tribunal of the world," that its object was "to place before mankind the common sense of the subject, in terms so plain and firm as to command their assent."*

The mission of making the American argument in plain, firm terms is what this book is about.

Fitzhugh Green spent many years working in the vineyards of public diplomacy as an officer of the United States Information Agency. He has handled crises in Laos and conflicts in Israel; he was in the Congo when Frank Carlucci was, literally, stabbed in the back. Yes, Frank Carlucci. Green has watched the USIA as an official in its Washington headquarters where other kinds of back-stabbing are not unknown. He served as a staff aide in the U.S. Senate working on USIA legislation. He was a colleague of mine for two years when I served as Director of the Voice of America—an experience that opened my eyes to

---

*From an essay by Henry Steele Commager "American Primer," Mentor Books, 1968, p. 85.

the value and accomplishments of the USIA. He thinks public diplomacy is important, and so do I.

For a propagandist, and I use the word with pride, the United States is the best of clients—and the worst. Best because of its unmistakable virtues, worst because its vices can't be hidden. America has the most visible dirty laundry in the world. Other countries can hide their mistakes and cover up their faults. But an alert press and an active political system make that impossible in the United States. That's a special challenge to the communicators of the USIA, who must fashion their wares out of truth.

It doesn't always work. Green saw firsthand the difficulties of the American information and psychological warfare effort in Vietnam, and his criticism of this "longest crisis" in USIA's history is informative and unsparing. It can be frustrating. The demands of journalism and the disciplines of diplomacy intersect and clash at the Voice of America. Sometimes it works and few know it. The labors of USIA officers in countries half forgotten by Americans can make the difference between friends and enemies—which pays crucial dividends in times of crisis. There is world-wide success to report: 130,000,000 adults in foreign countries listen at least once a week to the Voice of America. The USIA is, indeed, a vast enterprise.

Is it worth it? Should something like a billion dollars a year be spent on public diplomacy? Green's answer is yes. So is mine. When the USIA began, the United States was the most powerful country in the world. There was enormous, world-wide interest in the lessons it taught and the examples it set. There was a great market for its ideas and great international curiosity about American life. But we don't live in the "American Century" any longer. The American story must be told to a new generation around the world that doesn't remember the years of unlimited American power. The United States is being tested by new forces of commerce and trade, new problems in the Third World, a new dynamic in its relations with the Soviet Union. The world has become infinitely more complicated; countries are interconnected in ways we could not have foreseen.

In my view, the USIA is uniquely equipped to further the aims of American diplomacy in today's world, and tomorrow's. The need is greater than ever before.

That is why I found this book so useful. American propagandists are the shoemaker's children of the information industry; they are good at promoting their country, but not themselves. Fitzhugh Green has shed a lot of light on one of our most important institutions.

—John Chancellor

Introduction

Not far from the White House in Washington stands the headquarters of a renowned export house. Its products are unusual
for an export company: ideas, opinions, beliefs, knowledge,
facts, figures, and, in a broad sense, culture. They are packaged
in books, films, pamphlets, magazines, television and radio
tapes, photos, paintings, exhibits, electronic signals, and
human brains; these latter belong to the overseas representatives of the organization. The profit and loss ledgers are virtually nonexistent because the products are distributed without charge and the only costs are for shipping, packaging, and
administration. This extraordinary firm is the U.S. Information
Agency (USIA). Its market consists of people anywhere outside the United States, with special focus on the channels to
mass audiences, such as media people, politicians, thinkers,
artists, and leading professionals of all kinds. Competitors
abroad are numerous and active, particularly the Soviet agencies. USIA's budget is only one of the largest, nearly a billion
dollars; its personnel number some seventy-five hundred.

USIA has operated as an independent government agency
since 1953, when President Eisenhower removed it from the
State Department. It has had ten directors under seven presidents of the United States. Each director has slightly altered
the agency's modus operandi and its philosophy. But the basic
aim has remained constant: to speak officially for the United
States government to the populations of all other countries, to
promote understanding of America as a political, cultural en-

tity, and to try to win support for America's foreign policy. The agency has always encouraged two-way communications with its clients, but President Carter formalized this spirit by ordering it to inform Americans about foreigners, in addition to telling them about Americans. When he did this in 1977 and renamed it the U.S. International Communication Agency/ (USICA), Carter thus transformed it into an export-*import* firm! (President Reagan restored the name USIA in 1982.)

Carter's act stirred up some criticism and controversy— nothing new. As long as this country conducts a program to inform and influence foreign populations, there will be argument on how to accomplish the task. But starting in prerevolutionary days, the task has been vital, unavoidable, and always evolving in form.

Right now the style and content of USIA's activities have shifted to fit the character of the present administration. This is normal and appropriate. The agency by definition must be mobile and adaptive. Surely USIA must reflect the tone of each president in explaining his aims overseas. It is doubtful that the USIA or any successor organization will achieve a perfect and ultimate formula. To find the right ideas and modes of expression for a changing nation in a changing world will continue to challenge the professionals in the USIA as well as each incoming president.

For these reasons, no other U.S. government agency needs such a high percentage of its careerists to be imaginative, broadly educated, personable, balanced, dependable, and, of course, skilled communicators.

I enjoyed serving USIA for sixteen years—fourteen as an officer in the agency and two more as a staffer for Senator Claiborne Pell (presently chairman of the Foreign Relations Committee) on USIA matters including the Pell-Rogers Act, which provided a career service for the agency. At USIA, I toiled in virtually every part of its mission: as assistant to the director of the press and publications; director of overseas posts in Laos, Israel, and the Congo (now Zaire); representative at the U.N. and director of the Foreign Correspondents Center in New York; graduate of the Naval War College; deputy director for personnel and training and for Far East operations— managing some fifteen hundred American and foreign employees.

These "hands on" jobs showed me, piece by piece, how USIA operates. They impressed on me why we must have such an agency. I want to share my enthusiasm for USIA's mandate, as well as the reason behind its trials and triumphs.

From my experience and research, I have tried to portray America's overseas information outreach since its beginning.

From the outset, America's story has stirred the minds and spirits of human beings everywhere. "Everywhere" of course meant Europe in the eighteenth and early nineteenth centuries. Then gradually in the Victorian period the ancient civilizations of the Far East began to know us through Commodore Perry's black ships and other visits and contacts.

Finally in the twentieth century, commerce and two world wars brought Americans closer to European colonies and ex-colonies in Latin America, Africa and Asia.

After World War II, when Europe shed its empires, the United States—which had encouraged this process—stepped more boldly into the picture. Indeed, between 1945 and the Vietnam war we became a dominant power and inspiration for people just released from their European metropoles.

During that era I participated in the so-called "nation-building" program by which the United States offered a sort of surrogate parenthood to the freshly freed countries. We parceled out technical assistance, military support, and training as well as financial aid. Technical assistance included advice on how to spur home populations to join their governments in converting colonies into self-sufficient sovereignties.

America's motivation was mixed. First, the program expressed our religious tradition of wanting to help others (not to mention our missionary habit of trying to convert others to our beliefs). Second, we had nervously watched the U.S.S.R. add the nations it captured from Nazi Germany to its own hegemony. Now the Soviets were as busy as we were courting the new countries. This twin interest of the U.S. and the U.S.S.R. was part of the tussle over whether democracy or communism would be ascendant in the post-World War II world.

Today, the struggle goes on, not just between communism and democracy, but between any form of despotism and democracy. As the world wrestles these mighty issues, along with poverty, military insecurity, and ruination of the environment, the welfare of humanity hangs in the balance.

America's role continues to be major, if no longer predominant. It is axiomatic that how the citizens of other countries perceive America will determine our ability to operate to our full potential.

Charles Z. Wick, director of USIA, likes to dramatize the situation: "Since 1945," he says, "the world has been a battleground for a 'war of ideas'. . . . The great traditions of the Western democracies, including the philosophies of Jefferson, Madison and Lincoln, have been . . . in combat against the ideologies of Marx, Lenin, Stalin and Mao."

This statement tends to oversimplify the case. But certainly from its inception the U.S.A. has had to battle for its independence, military security, and economic health. Since 1945, as Wick implies, our country has fought not only for itself but often for the freedom and well-being of all other nations.

The psychological component of these fights has always been important. Our forefathers knew this and embarked on this country's first overseas campaigns to inform and influence foreigners in our favor.

Today the power of public opinion over governments is growing because modern communications technology spreads ideas instantly to every nook and cranny of the earth. Not even the most repressive regime can keep the truth from crossing international boundaries.

So there is indeed a war, or at least a Babel of ideas among all nations, as well as the superpowers competing for attention and acceptance. Americans themselves need to understand how and why our government must act in this realm.

Although this nation demonstrates every day its ability to sell goods, services, and concepts, its people harbor a rather quaint and puritanical distaste for government "propaganda." Since in its pure form propaganda simply means advocating one's views to others, this prejudice should be rendered obsolete. It is no longer arguable whether we should use propaganda; the only question is how to do it in the best possible way.

PART I

Origins and Aims of American Outreach to the World

CHAPTER 1

U.S. Propaganda from Benjamin Franklin to the Cold War

THE U.S. INFORMATION AGENCY (USIA) rises from foundations laid over two centuries ago by two remarkable men.

For those who have forgotten, there are reminders in our London and Paris embassies that American diplomacy first flowered in those cities. In the hall outside the ambassador's office on London's Grosvenor Square hangs a faded painting of Benjamin Franklin, our pre–revolutionary envoy to England; pictures of all his successors continue from that spot. If you visit our Paris chancery, you will find Franklin's name cut into the marble wall of the lobby, near the Marine guard who screens you as you enter from the Place de la Concorde. Immediately below is Thomas Jefferson, followed by all the ministers and ambassadors since this illustrious pair.

Not so easily displayed is the fact that these early diplomats virtually invented "public diplomacy"—a term they wouldn't recognize. It's a euphemism for the word modern Americans abhor—propaganda. Call it what you will, these two geniuses excelled at publicity, selling, advertising, promotion, and psychological manipulation of the masses. They regularly courted English and French public opinion as part of their campaigns to win support for our new nation. And they did it without the large information and cultural staffs provided these days by

USIA. How these two men operated, the techniques they devised, the media products they created, and their personal traits provide an indelible blueprint for USIA. Even today, USIA officers can learn from them, despite the proliferation of communications media and differences in culture between then and now. After two hundred years, the principles they followed still apply.

Consider the length of their time abroad, Franklin's particularly. He spent fifteen years (1757–62 and 1765–75) in England and eight years in France (1776–84). By living so long in those countries Franklin grew comfortable with the people, and they with him. After the war for independence, Jefferson in turn became a household name in France. Both men proceeded on the premise that misunderstandings diminish in direct proportion to how well people know one another.

Second, these men were notable experts in a dazzling variety of disciplines. They were not simply mouthpieces for their government or super salesmen with the gift of gab. They knew what they were talking about on any significant topic of the time. They were Renaissance men. Between them they personified the best in science, agriculture, architecture, mechanical invention as well as literature, politics, and governments.

Third, they combined a natural flair for friendship with a shrewd selection of acquaintances among the host country elite in politics, science, the military, commerce, and the arts. Each not only sought but gained close relationships with leaders in these realms.

Fourth, they became powerful politically, gaining broad popularity in England and France which would have ranked them high in polls, had there been any then. Ultimately Franklin's fame spread until he was better known in Europe than any of his compatriots.[1] Jefferson's prominence steadily increased too, although he shunned self-promotion while arguing his country's causes.

Sure-footed in public relations, they ducked individual vendettas or taking umbrage when attacked personally. Franklin as usual coined a "how-to" adage: asked why he didn't fight back when the English king's council showered him with verbal abuse, he replied that mud comes off better if given time to dry; trying to rub it off while wet simply makes a more enduring stain.

A fifth principle guided Franklin and Jefferson: to act with sophistication and self-control whatever one's official goals.

While they were pushing the government and people toward a specific objective, they would fight hard, with exquisite timing and finesse. Then, after either winning or losing on the particular issue, they would change pace and reenter such non-political activities as philosophy, literature, agriculture, and science. Thus neither became an alien irritant by continuous harping on the same subject. They kept busy as members of the community, doing creative, interesting projects that led to easy, two-way communication between themselves and the populace. Then when it was time to seek public approval again, they could gracefully shift gears and start selling once more.

For example, when Franklin first sailed to England in 1757 on behalf of the colony of Pennsylvania, he began immediately to maneuver, talk, and write to win favor for the colonies. He exploited the available media with a mix of materials, such as a letter to the newspaper *Citizen*, written by his son, which he got placed by paying the paper a pound, or a series of books and tracts to illustrate Pennsylvania's grievances. He used "gray" propaganda freely—i.e., signing others' names to manuscripts he prepared. He even pioneered political cartoons.

But when he had triumphed in these efforts for Pennsylvania, he recommended his scientific experiments and treatises, played the harmonica—the glass version which Franklin perfected is now obsolete—the harp, guitar, and violin, and produced such a torrent of learned pamphlets and books that Oxford honored him with a doctorate.

Then in the 1760s Franklin went public again to spread an appealing view of the colonies as a whole. More and more he personified the "Voice of America."[2]

Franklin proved by his own versatility that he could act as both political advocate and cultural representative of the United States without either role harming or confusing the other. This point has been hotly disputed among the architects and critics of USIA. The argument has recently been settled in the Franklin mode, since he was himself a one-man information and cultural service. USIA now generates both information and cultural programs under one roof.

As England and the colonies became steadily alienated from each other in the 1760s, Franklin continued to speak out for strengthening the empire. When royal advisors suggested giving up Canada and taking over Guadeloupe, Franklin took the opposite stand. History underlines his sound judgment on this issue.

During the French and Indian War the American colonists stood with England against France and the French colonists of Canada. Franklin churned out some anti-French propaganda. It was pure fiction. He concocted and distributed a chapter from a nonexistent periodical; it "revealed" that France was covertly trying to persuade American colonists to defect from the conflict.

Up to the eve of the revolution, Franklin kept airing the idea that England could hold on to the American territory just by treating the inhabitants fairly. Like a good propagandist he repeated this theme, varying the form, as his feverish pen filled thousands of pages. One of his best tracts was a scourging satire, "Rules by Which a Great Empire Can Be Reduced to a Small One." A British magazine, *Public Advertiser*, carried the piece, in which Franklin recounted the bumbling moves of the colonial ministry which had most infuriated the American colonists. His language transcended that of the homey philosopher and scientist to which the English had become accustomed. He was on the march now, wielding his literary sword: " . . . suppose them [the colonists] always inclined to revolt, and treat them accordingly. . . . This means like the husband who uses his wife ill from suspicion, you may in time convert your suspicions into realities."[3]

Did Franklin actually influence the English by his prodigious output? He thought so, claiming before independence that "the general sense of the nation is for us; a conviction prevailing that we have been ill used and that a breach with us would be ruinous to this country."[4]

Franklin learned, as have all public diplomatists since his time, that moving the populace on an issue doesn't always bring the government along the same path, even in a democracy. Still, he was making an impact. There he was in England, like Iranian "students" demonstrating against the Carter Administration for befriending the Shah in 1979. One might have expected Franklin to be imprisoned or deported, especially since war was imminent. He wasn't though, because the king's ministers realized that the people were not only pro-American but pro-Franklin. To hurt or remove him would doubtless push their already unpopular administration into a corner. They rebuffed his petition against taxation without representation, but they never threatened his personal liberty or safety.

Having done his best in England to preserve the empire, Franklin went home in 1775 to help lead the revolt against it.

After starring in the tumultuous events of the next two years, he recrossed the Atlantic to seek an alliance with France. In Paris he plunged into months of official advocacy coupled with public diplomacy. Now that England had become the enemy, Franklin showed no reluctance in switching his considerable prowess in propaganda against his lifelong motherland.

The French proved susceptible to his publicity as well as to his negotiating skills—enriched by "the mesmeric quality of his simple friendliness and beaming smile."[5] Within months Franklin gained the treaty of alliance, and France soon poured men, ships, and money into the American war against England. This Franklin triumph ensured the survival of his fledgling country. The French saw the alliance in their own vital interest as well, for it represented a vast improvement in the power balance with England. In numerous speeches and articles, Franklin stressed this advantage to the French citizenry.

Near the end of the Revolutionary War, Franklin hectored his former mother country with a spoof about the Seneca Indians. He was a brilliant hoaxer, and this particular story turned English sympathy against its own government. Franklin thus foreshadowed, perhaps invented, the tactic that is known today as "disinformation." Right in the midst of peace discussions he secretly arranged to circulate in England a false "Supplement to the Boston Independent Chronicle."[6] This "supplement" reported in straight journalistic style that the New England militia had intercepted eight large packages of American scalps sent by the Senecans to impress the English king with "our faithfulness in destroying his enemies." The packages contained, according to the supplement, 43 scalps of soldiers, 98 of farmers, 88 of women, 193 of boys, 211 of girls, and 29 of infants "ripped out of their mothers' bellies." Atrocity stories have become standard fare in most of the world's wars since Franklin, and he even admitted to John Adams that the accusation might be inaccurate—but only in form, not in fact, since fighters on the English side probably scalped even more victims than the supplement suggested.

When England surrendered, Franklin deserved credit for the fierce psychological warfare he had waged—in infinitely greater quantity than touched on here.

Still in France in 1781, he immersed himself in multifarious studies and writings in science and philosophy. Long since the most famous American on the continent, Franklin drew even closer to the French. He became a favorite of intellectuals, including the legendary Voltaire, and many scientists. The Masons elevated him to Grand Master of a Paris lodge. He became so respected, liked, and integrated into French life that he could comment on anything and be believed. When he spoke, people listened, and he seldom disappointed or bored them. In 1783 on seeing the first balloon ascension in France he scoffed at the belittlers of the feat by saying, "A quoi bon l'enfant qui vient de naitre?" (What good is a newborn baby?)[7] John Glenn used this quote before the joint session of Congress after his first orbit of the earth, but wrongly attributed it to Michael Faraday, the English scientist who lived a century after Franklin. Franklin went on to predict that balloons might transport by air an invasion force of soldiers—as the Germans did when they landed troop gliders on Crete in World War II.

Franklin didn't waste the attentive audience he had created. He set up a printing plant near his house in Passy and kept it humming with leaflets and brochures to correct false impressions about his own country. Perhaps the best was "Information to Those Who Would Remove to America." In it, he counseled "immigrants who believed that Americans were rich but ignorant, ready to welcome scholars and artists from Europe, waiting for European persons of family to come and fill offices which were above the capacity of natives. . . . These were all wild imaginations . . . The truth is that though there are few people so miserable as the poor of Europe, there are also very few that in Europe would be called rich."[8]

"Our country offers to strangers nothing but a good climate, fertile soil, wholesome air, free governments, wise laws, liberty, a good people to live among, and a hearty welcome. Those Europeans who have these or greater advantages at home would do well to stay where they are."[9]

This was a superb pamphlet. Never has the USIA, with thousands of employees and hundreds of millions in the budget, produced a better one. Its humor, credibility, style, salability, and candor still sing in the reader's ear.

When Franklin quit France after eight years, the citizens agonized as if losing one of their own patriarchs. They would miss his deep involvement in their lives, his brilliant writings, and his presence as an original thinker. He was beloved for his unfailing courtesy with people at any level, his facility with the language (though imperfect, "his French to which even his incorrectness almost always gave an added force or grace"),[10] and his total honesty. Yet though he penetrated French minds and hearts so deeply, Franklin never altered his coloration. He wore proudly his homespun clothes, a plain manner of speaking, and loyalty for the country he represented. USIA personnel overseas should benefit from his example.

Thomas Jefferson replaced Franklin as minister. He got off to a fine start, since his reputation as a governor, scientific savant, and architect preceded him to Paris.

Within weeks he proved himself a wily public relations man. Franklin was still on the high seas headed home. A troublemaker in Paris floated the rumor that on landing in America Franklin would be stoned for fomenting the revolution. Jefferson retorted that if this were true, Franklin would doubtless be pelted with the same stones that were thrown at the revered Marquis de Lafayette.

Like a new father, France was curious about the new country it had helped break away from its rival, England. There were misapprehensions as to what was really going on. News was sparse and faulty. Supposition supplanted fact. So Jefferson turned his office into an American information center—the forerunner of USIA's present centers which dot the globe by the hundreds. Jefferson's biographer, Dumas Malone, lauds him as a promoter of the truth, a "Minister of Enlightment. What he was most anxious to do was spread correct ideas about America."[11]

For five years in Paris, Jefferson corrected wrong impressions whenever he found them. His book, *Notes About Virginia*, painted the only available picture of American society. Unlike the prolific Franklin, Jefferson wrote only this volume. Contemporaries judged it a masterpiece of revelations about America.

This book dealt with many issues that plague USIA officers today: racism, for example. Jefferson couldn't easily change French prejudice that blacks were inferior when his own country owned them as slaves at the very moment of declaring its liberty from England. He did, however, defend the Indians as superior humans despite their primitive social level, denying that they "were deficient in sexual ardor and lacked domestic affection."[12]

By counseling Frenchmen who wrote about Americans, he greatly reduced the spread of misinformation. Also he stimulated and supported American writers whose books would be read in France and elsewhere in Europe. He imported texts of key American documents on liberty, including the law he had introduced for religious freedom in Virginia, and sent them around to intellectuals and political leaders.

Jefferson's influence kept increasing until even the French political leaders sought his advice. When the groundswell of revolt rose, personalities like the Marquis de Lafayette and national assemblymen asked his guidance on their draft of a new constitution. What surer evidence of French confidence in Jefferson could there be? And when he had returned to Virginia, what clearer proof of his fascination as a friend than the steady stream of French visitors until his death in 1826?

Following the illustrious Franklin-Jefferson deeds in Europe, Britain gave the U.S. a practical lesson in propaganda. This concerned the Monroe Doctrine. American school children are taught simply that President James Monroe promulgated this policy in a message to Congress on December 2, 1823. There is more to the story. It began when England's Foreign Secretary George Canning tried but could not induce U.S. Minister Richard Rush to agree on a joint declaration: That Britain and the U.S. would not claim former Spanish colonies in the Western Hemisphere and would not view "with indifference" the transfer of any part of them to any other power. The idea was to forestall aggression by France. Monroe took George Washington's "no foreign entanglements" speech one step further: The U.S. wanted no foreign interference in the New World by Europeans. Britain resisted the temptation to boast that the Monroe Doctrine kept the peace for one hundred years mainly because the British fleet guaranteed it— though that is a fact.

Chester Bowles, undersecretary of state for President John F. Kennedy, told another version of the doctrine's conception: that Canning had sat down with young President Monroe, both men in shirtsleeves (this was strictly Bowles' touch, given his penchant for informal diplomacy), and hammered out Monroe's text for the Congress. This incident demonstrated, said Bowles, how best to influence other countries: Give them your thought and let them claim it as theirs. England got what she wanted, Bowles emphasized, and let the world believe that the doctrine was Monroe's invention.

After Monroe, America ventured only spasmodically into propaganda for the next century. There was a brief flurry in the Civil War: President Lincoln himself engaged in a widely reported correspondence to court the support of British labor unionists in his fight against slavery.

Pro-South Britain paid little attention. Indeed the British repeatedly broke the Union naval blockade with supplies for the secessionists and shored up the rebels in many other furtive ways.

Historians agree that propaganda by William Randolph Hearst, originator of "yellow journalism," stirred up a war mood in 1898. His papers spread the notion that the Spanish blew up the U.S. battleship *Maine* in Havana harbor. What actually caused the explosion is still shrouded in contradictory assessments by the navy and chroniclers of the incident.

No government information service existed to handle such stories at home or abroad during this period of "Manifest Destiny." But two powerful publicists advertised both themselves and their country to the world at large: the dashing colonel of cavalry, Theodore Roosevelt, by his flashy charge up San Juan Hill, and Commodore George Dewey, by his laconic "You may fire when you are ready, Gridley,"[13] on Manila Bay.

As president, propagandist Roosevelt dramatized his "speak softly and carry a big stick" policy: In 1907 he dispatched the "Great White Fleet" on a globe-girdling, goodwill trip. He had multiplied the navy in size and power and flexed American maritime muscle for all the nations to see. He ordered sixteen battleships and a flotilla of torpedo boats first to round Cape Horn and proceed to San Francisco and then to continue forging west. The fleet visited every principal port en route, until sixteen months later they made their final landfall at Hampton Roads, Virginia. Among other objectives, Roosevelt was implying that the United States could now enforce the Monroe Doctrine with its own navy.

How these glamorous warships, gleaming in white with gold and brass trim everywhere, impressed foreigners can only be imagined. Roosevelt intended, as did President Kennedy later with his Peace Corps, to show voters how he boosted the U.S. image abroad.

Accomplishing the circumnavigation by so many ships with no serious mishap was a feat that no other navy, not even Great Britain's, could claim.

Roosevelt cited another plus—doing good deeds along the way. The "Great White Fleet" stopped in the Mediterranean, for example, to assist victims of an earthquake at Messina,

Sicily. Such "civic action" programs are now part of any modern military unit's duty when on foreign soil—to win acceptance for itself, whatever its mission may be.

When Woodrow Wilson, who won reelection by promising to keep out of war, took America into World War I, he founded his country's first official government propaganda program: the Committee on Public Information (CPI). Until then American overseas propaganda had been one-man performances. Franklin and Jefferson had to act on their own in any tactical situation, because guidance from America wouldn't arrive for weeks—sailing vessels had to deliver it. They had no daily telegrams or calls from USIA to tell them what to say and how to say it as they would today. Indeed, "after not hearing from Benjamin Franklin, the U.S. envoy to Paris, for nearly a year, President Washington said, 'We should write him a letter.' "[14]

Abjuring the word "propaganda," Wilson replaced it with the softer "information" in the new agency, lest it remind Americans or foreigners of Germany's crude, mendacious, but effective programs. Yet it was doubtless the hard-hitting German style that led Wilson to build CPI.

CPI consisted of the secretaries of state, war, and navy. President Wilson instructed his political ally and friend, George Creel, to head this group. Creel hired a stable of brilliant professional communicators to create and transmit CPI messages. The Creel Committee, as it became known, had three functions: motivate Americans to enlist in the military forces, to produce munitions, to buy bonds; paint America positively in the perceptions of allies and neutrals; and weaken the enemy.

If anyone, even today, questions the domestic impact of CPI, he has only to ask educated Americans why we fought World War I. Inevitably he will hear that it was the "war to end all wars," to "save the world for democracy," and to put down the Kaiser who started it all anyway, the greedy imperialist. Creel virtually brainwashed the American citizenry.

CPI's strength overseas is harder to measure, but the volume and vigor of its propaganda campaign is not: It reached every inhabited continent except Africa, in those days mostly a colonial extension of Europe.

Creel displayed America's newfound mode of mass production as he designed his overseas facility. He installed three faucets which poured forth a steady stream of "information":

The Wireless Cable Service—this radioed thousands of

words daily, directly and by cable relay, to large, nonhostile cities.

The Foreign Press Bureau—this mailed photo and text features to dozens of countries.

The Foreign Film Division—this turned out scores of its own films and also capitalized on Hollywood's new preeminence, so that reluctant theater owners, even in German-owned houses in neutral countries, had to take CPI's propaganda or be denied commercial films and go out of business.

This great gusher would have splashed on bare ground at the foreign end of the pipelines without the skilled agents Creel sent abroad. They opened offices, made useful contacts, and soon could plant CPI output where it could do the most good—in the hands of opinion-molders. Foreign journalists, publishers, politicians, and academicians often used CPI information as their own, rendering it all the more credible. Indeed when a target audience receives a propagandist's thoughts through the hand or mouth of one of its own spokesmen, that is the ultimate technique.

Creel picked his agents carefully; being overseas they would have to act on their own with very little control from Washington. He drew them from the top drawer of writers, film producers, public relations experts, and even ambassadors in our own embassies. Creel sought the criteria of talent and VIP status that characterized Franklin and Jefferson—although he had to settle for something short of their magnitude. He could afford to, since his agents were fed voluminous ammunition from home: news in thousand-word takes, films by the hundreds, innumerable feature stories, and every week more than fifteen hundred photographs for window displays, plus captioned photographs and mats for newspapers sent to thirty-five countries. CPI also printed photos on broadsides called "news pictorials" which could be mounted in store windows or on buildings, much like present-day "wall newspapers" in China.

Additionally, six hundred fifty local branches of American exporters agreeably erected displays of CPI products in their retail outlets. Edward Bernays, CPI's chief for Latin America, tapped many more U.S. companies for help:

Ford, Studebaker, Remington Typewriter, Swift, National City Bank, International Harvester, and many other corporations were persuaded by Bernays to exploit their Latin American branches as veritable CPI outposts. Pamphlets and other publications were distributed to customers, and posters and photographic displays filled windows. Advertising was sometimes given or denied to Latin American papers in accordance with the editorial attitude toward the war.[15]

The cooperation of business with government can be useful to the nation. Other countries frequently profit from the practice, particularly present-day Great Britain, Germany, Holland, and Japan. But since the heyday of the Creel Committee, American government propagandists have not always found the business sector so willing to play this game. There were two explanations for Creel's ability to accomplish his task: first, it was wartime; and second, he was the president's personal choice, took occasional direct orders from the president, and reported to no one else.

When American soldiers joined the fight against Germany, Creel's operatives went into psychological warfare, or "trench propaganda" as it was known in World War I. At first the Americans merely assisted the Allies, but gradually they assumed the initiative.

To reach Germany's troops and population, CPI had to drop propaganda by airplanes, guns using shells packed with leaflets rather than explosives, and balloons. Sometimes the airmen objected to these arrangements. "The flyers who have been required to carry bundles of papers with bombs are usually filled with disgust by the idea and dump their load overboard as soon as they get out of sight of their starting point, often into French trenches or No Man's Land."[16]

Creel's people also circulated anti-German stories to neutral countries where they would surface as rumor or articles in the press. Some of the stories would be repeated among the Germans, thus hurting morale; the citizens didn't realize the stories were emanating from Creel's "disinformation" machine.

In a storm it is impossible to determine which raindrops cause the cloudburst. The Allies fired billions of real bullets, but certainly the Creel Committee contributed to the final collapse of the Germans. How much can only be determined subjectively, since no impact surveys were made during its short life.

Whatever CPI's overseas effect, Congress was suspicious of Creel's close relationship with Wilson and frequently accused Creel of advertising his boss with greater enthusiasm than his country. Creel retaliated with sarcasm and insult. The feud eventually boiled over, with name-calling between Creel and his critics, despite protests in his favor by the president. In 1919 Congress shut down Creel's funding, and the CPI disappeared without a trace. As a result America had no department of international information in the years between the two world wars.

America turned isolationist as war-mongering dictators shook Europe and Asia into the fateful imbalances that sped the tragedy of 1939–45.

The Soviet Union spread subversive propaganda in Europe, America, and Asia. Self-absorbed in its boom and bust in the 1920s and 1930s, the United States paid little attention as the Communists funded front organizations and disseminated their revolutionary literature openly and covertly. The United Kingdom responded with cool, factual programs of the British Broadcasting System. The Dutch and French national radios spoke for their official positions too, especially after Mussolini and Hitler Fascists caused more harm than the Communists, with military incursions into Ethiopia, Albania, Sudetenland, and Austria.

Although Americans shunned the thought of propaganda, they were enthralled by a wizard in the art, Franklin D. Roosevelt. In 1940–41 he subtly massaged the population with soothing explanations as he moved the country toward a war footing. Even as he successively managed the imposition of a national draft, shut off strategic exports to Japan, transferred fifty American destroyers to Great Britain, and molded the United States into an "arsenal of democracy," Roosevelt persuaded our citizens he was doing the right thing.

Roosevelt's own powerful phrase in response to the Pearl Harbor attack—"This is a day that will live in infamy"—instantly changed attitudes from peace to belligerence. Thanks to the president's manipulative genius, Americans readily accepted the need to fight with every means at hand—including propaganda—to defeat the Axis.

In 1941 the president established a Creel-like domestic information committee, with the innocent label "Office of Facts and Figures." Its first task was to give Americans gently the details of lend-lease to the British and other "defense" activities. To lull the public, Roosevelt put a poet, Archibald MacLeish, in charge. Simultaneously the president created an agency called "Coordinator of Information" (COI) under lawyer William "Wild Bill" Donovan to concern itself with foreign intelligence and certain covert duties. Donovan then designated Robert E. Sherwood, playwright and Roosevelt speech writer, to initiate a foreign information service under COI. Sherwood wrought no miracles at the outset, but in February 1942, under the impetus of war, he made history: He broadcast America's first overseas radio propaganda. The signals went from the U.S. to Europe over the facilities of eleven private, short-wave radio stations. He called this program the "Voice of America." The name has stuck and often been copied by other countries and even by clandestine stations like the recent "Voice of Iran" from Baku in the Soviet Union.

In June, Roosevelt amalgamated all public information into the Office of War Information (OWI). OWI generated its domestic programs out of Washington and foreign ones out of New York. There were at least two holdouts from OWI. First, Nelson Rockefeller persuaded the president to let him continue independently of OWI the information and cultural programs he had set up for South America. These were called the Office of Coordinator of Inter-American Affairs. Second, William Donovan was allowed to shift his black propaganda into the newly founded Office of Strategic Services (OSS). "Black" propaganda is the name given to activities which, if the source is revealed publicly, will threaten the national security of the perpetrator's country. Ultimately OSS succeeded the Coordinator of Information. Roosevelt put Elmer Davis, the famed journalist and novelist, in overall control of OWI. Davis, like Creel before him, was told to report directly to the president, but unlike Creel he never had much access to the White House after he assumed office. He suffered some of the same criticisms that had plagued Creel from both the press and Congress; indeed by the war's end Congress had cut funds for his domestic program to a trickle. Congress charged that OWI was soft on communism and did too much touting of the president and his New Deal. Politicians and the public detested Goebel-like propaganda inside America. They still do.

Dismayed but not daunted, Davis overcame bickering by prima donnas like Sherwood and others and built a varied and often successful overseas propaganda campaign. He set up twenty-six outposts in Europe, Africa, and the Far East. These took the multimedia output from New York and planted it with local writers, speakers, and activists best equipped and motivated to exploit it for the Allied cause.

These posts also sowed disinformation among neutral news

media so that the stories would resurface, at least by word of mouth, in Germany, Italy, and Japan. The posts were named U.S. Information Service (USIS).

Some of the material was poorly selected. For example, Vice President Henry Wallace insisted that every person in the world should drink a glass of milk every day. This revolted Italians, who don't like milk as a beverage. They complained that his prescription would make them ill if they had to comply. Pictures and features protrayed Americans as so rich and comfortable that the war-burdened Allied populations were convinced that we were making no sacrifice toward winning the war.

Despite such pecadillos, the OWI won respect from the enemy. When Italy surrendered, the Japanese government warned its people that the Italian collapse "could partly be ascribed to British and American propaganda aimed at the disintegration of the home front."[17]

When OWI supplemented the weak short-wave signals from the United States with a 50-kilowatt transmitter of medium and long waves, the results began to improve. When Italy stopped fighting in September 1943, the Italian Navy was steaming around the Mediterranean, its exact whereabouts unknown. For three days the OWI and other allied broadcasts beamed news of the cease-fire to every corner of the Mediterranean. Then the fleet obediently sailed into the British island of Malta. This massive, bloodless feat of arms has been credited in part to the radio messages picked up by the warships.

Wilson Dizard, a former USIA officer, recounts even more specific cause and effect from a joint U.S. Navy-OWI radio ruse. A German-speaking U.S. naval officer, Commander Robert Lee Norden, broadcast a regular program beamed at the German submarines at sea. Their crews were appalled by his accurate and amazingly detailed reports of the terrible losses inflicted on U-boats. A postwar admission by the Germans said Norden's commentary had "a crushing effect on the morale of German naval personnel."[18]

OWI always told its radio stories straight without bombast or vilification of the enemy. It resembled the BBC in this respect. OWI became more and more enthusiastic as the Allies landed in North Africa, and then Sicily and Italy. OWI formed combat teams and went right in on the beaches with the soldiers, participating in psychological warfare by the military units.

During the final Allied thrust through Europe, OWI's nonmilitary propaganda was spawned in London. By that time, OWI American civilians totaled more than three thousand in the various overseas branches. Although plagued with mistakes and mismanagement in its first year, OWI now was more and more accepted by its military comrades in arms.

In his report to the president at war's end, Davis summarized what had become the objective assessment of OWI, even by its debunkers among the generals and admirals. "Propaganda," he wrote, "is only an auxiliary weapon; it never won a war by itself, but properly used, it can powerfully reinforce the effect of military operations."[19]

After the Japanese surrender, Congress withdrew most of OWI's funds, and Truman terminated it in 1946. Still, he kept its remnant intact as he sought to install a permanent, peacetime U.S. information service. By the end of that year he placed it in the State Department, with sixty-six ancillary offices in our embassies abroad. The total number of people shrank from the wartime eleven thousand to three thousand, including Voice of America employees. They distributed bland news, and arranged an occasional cultural exchange. The VOA broadcast quietly on a greatly reduced schedule.

Then the peace that cost fifty million dead soldiers and civilians was undermined by the expansionist Soviet Union. Winston Churchill sounded the alarm in 1947 at Fulton, Missouri, about the "Iron Curtain" behind which free nations were rapidly vanishing. Gradually the United States began to take note of the threatening events in Europe. Truman reacted with aid to anti-Communist elements in Greece and Turkey as he launched the "Truman Doctrine." These counter-Communist moves culminated in diplomat George Kennan's "containment" policy in 1948. Kennan believed the free world should draw a perimeter around the Soviet Union and resist expansion beyond it.

Nobody "declared" the Cold War; it just grew, with the belated American resistance to Soviet imperialism. But the need had again arrived for an overseas propaganda mechanism to serve America's geopolitical strategy. No one yet had a clear idea of how to fill this need.

ENDNOTES

1. Carl van Doren, *Benjamin Franklin* (New York: Viking Press, 1938), p. 527.
2. *Ibid.*, p. 288.
3. *Ibid.*, p. 452.
4. *Ibid.*, p. 456.
5. Charles E. Thayer, *Diplomat* (New York: Harper and Brothers, 1959), p. x.
6. van Doren, *Benjamin Franklin*, p. 673.
7. *Ibid.*, p. 700.
8. *Ibid.*, p. 705.
9. *Ibid.*, p. 706.
10. *Ibid.*, p. 650.
11. Dumas Malone, *Jefferson and His Time* (Boston: Little Brown and Company, 1951), p. 103.
12. Ibid., p. 102.
13. Fitzhugh Green, Sr., *Our Naval Heritage* (New York and London: The Century Company, 1925), p. 291.
14. Speech by Charles Z. Wick, May 2, 1987, at Loyola Mary Mount University, Los Angeles.
15. James R. Mock and Cedric Larseon, *Words That Won the War* (Princeton; Princeton University Press, 1939; New York: Russell and Russell, 1968), p. 322.
16. *Ibid.*, p. 253.
17. Roger Burlingame, *Don't Let Them Scare You, The Life and Times of Elmer Davis* (Philadelphia and New York: J. D. Lippincott Company, 1961), p. 231.
18. Wilson P. Dizard, *The Strategy of Truth* (Washington, D.C.: Public Affairs Press, 1961), p. 35.
19. Burlingame, *Don't Let Them Scare You*, p. 231.

CHAPTER 2

More History—
Cold War to Jimmy Carter

FRANKLIN ROOSEVELT COULD NO DOUBT have pumped up U.S. propaganda needed in the Cold War. His natural flair extended beyond American borders, and he was personally popular in many of the World War II Allied nations. But Harry Truman, in his first two years as president before the Cold War, was neither knowledgeable nor inclined toward international communications. In Potsdam his sense of inadequacy among foreigners was evident as he tried gamely to replace Roosevelt in a face-to-face meeting with Churchill and Stalin.

For a time after Potsdam, Truman concentrated more on domestic duties than on international public diplomacy. Meanwhile our official propagandists struggled with their first peacetime role. Their titles kept changing in the process. Between 1945 and 1953 America's foreign information department repeatedly switched names. John Henderson's book on the U.S. Information Agency[1] gives a good account of this period. It reflects the differing perceptions of what Americans wanted from their overseas explainers and promoters—mostly that they not resemble in any way the propaganda excesses of the Nazis, Fascists, and Communists.

Still in the State Department where Truman had put them in 1945, U.S. propagandists enjoyed some momentum from their war days. In 1946, now called Office of International Information and Cultural Affairs (OIC), they operated 76 branches connected to U.S. diplomatic missions. Forty of these received the daily wireless file by radio teletype from Washington. Then the file carried some 10,000 words of news and features which included key pronouncements by U.S. leaders on foreign and domestic policy, as well as glimpses of the American culture and people. Additionally, 67 information centers and libraries were maintained and supplied with exhibits and film strips. OIC also mailed motion picture documentaries to its overseas posts. These films were acquired mostly from domestic commercial producers and amounted to some 50 different twenty-minute reels annually. OIC's field staffers, Americans and local nationals, simply served whatever people the tide of curiosity might wash up on the premises. The Voice of America (VOA) also broadcast with small discrimination as to who might be listening. It churned out a daily conglomeration of news and features similar in content but shorter than the wireless file and interspersed with jazz programs. The daily transmissions totalled 36 hours, in 25 languages.

"Radio in the American Sector" (RIAS) was formed in Berlin as a means for talking to the citizens in the American zone when the Soviet occupation forces took over the main Berlin station. It started as a collection of "public address systems mounted on trucks and driven around the shell-pocked streets of the conquered city"[2] announcing the day's news.

When it began to beam at the East Germans as well, its varied political and cultural programs acted as an impetus to the heavy flow of defectors to the West.*

The general tone of OIC's message to foreigners said that America and its institutions were friendly and honorable. OIC took no pains to find out how this approach was affecting the

---

*RIAS is still going strong. Gradually the West Germans have taken a larger role in the operations of RIAS until at present they provide most of the funds. It is now only titularly under U.S. control. Two USIS officers are assigned to RIAS in nominal charge; but the German government sets the policy, German professionals operate the station, and the Americans are merely figureheads. This status quo satisfies both West Germany and the U.S. and therefore will not likely be altered in the foreseeable future. RIAS has no relationship with Radio Free Europe, which does not broadcast to East Germany. In short, RIAS has become the business of the Germans. In 1986 Congress voted to establish RIAS-TV. It will reach audiences of three million in East Germany and two million in West Berlin.

recipients of its information products or how, if at all, it was advancing U.S. aims abroad. The State Department, which didn't take OIC very seriously, believed that its public relations campaign was harmless and vapid, though it might burnish the American "image" abroad. But the department's professional diplomats kept a fish eye on OIC (and its successor agencies, right up to the present) lest it damage official American relationships with foreign nations. These fears arose from the fact that OIC staffers were generally not trained in international dealings, as were the department's career foreign service officers. Furthermore, propaganda—under whatever name is used—is at best an imprecise and unpredictable activity.

The following year, 1947, brought another title and concept to America's not very prestigious public diplomatists: the Office of International Information and Education Exchange (USIE). The Cold War hadn't quite arrived, and the stress was on nonpolitical programs, particularly designed to reach out toward teachers and students in all nations, regardless of ideology. U.S. Senator J. W. Fulbright had initiated the student and professor exchange program in 1946; Fulbright scholars are still being exchanged today, over forty years later.

Although the agency kept evolving in name and form, the rank and file of its personnel remained constant. They consisted mostly of leftovers from the OWI. These were ex-journalists, radio announcers, and producers, and a smattering of public relations and advertising men (very few women in those days had jobs above the level of secretary or clerk). Also some foreign service officers were detailed to the agency in order to broaden their career development on the road to ambassador, as well as, no doubt, to monitor more closely what the agency was up to. Overseas, the agency's functions were directly subordinate to the ambassador or consul general; they still are.

Agency staffers during those years were considered mostly rather drab; the wartime stars among them had departed with Elmer Davis to private life in 1945. Even by 1954 Joseph Alsop, the famous columnist, warned me against joining the agency. "What are you thinking about?" he exclaimed. "Why would you want to work with all those dreary people?"

Nevertheless, Truman, who had begun to consider the agency important, now sought directors with enough charisma to influence the Congress. He wanted good advocates to keep money flowing into the agency during the country's postwar disinterest in foreign affairs. America had won the war; now the time had come to stay home and mind its own business—that's how many voters felt. No one could accuse America of isolationism. After all, it had masterminded the creation of the United Nations. With this mood in the nation, foreign information efforts commanded a low priority. They lacked any home-front constituency then, as now.

William Benton was the first Truman appointee to run the agency, with the rank of assistant secretary of state for public affairs. Although he came to Washington in 1945 as a polished advertising and publishing executive, his modest stewardship of the agency brought only diminished congressional appropriations. In 1947, Benton left the impoverished agency and returned to Connecticut, where he was eventually elected to the U.S. Senate.

Although Benton failed to bring home the budget bacon from Congress, he did run the agency smoothly. His legacy is its ongoing, basic organization that he soundly established. He named the agency's overseas chiefs, country public affairs officers (CPAOs), as they are still known today; their offices in each country were still labeled the U.S. Information Service (USIS) until Carter dropped the term in 1977. Reagan's administration has restored the name USIS.

President Truman replaced Benton with George V. Allen, a career diplomat and former newspaperman with a knack for international communication. His arrival coincided with the commencement of the Marshall Plan to rebuild the war-smashed cities and economies of Europe. Many have forgotten that Truman offered the Communist countries a share in the scheme. Moscow promptly rejected the gesture, both for itself and its satellites. "The Soviet Union then organized the Cominform, a propaganda-oriented successor to the Comintern, and set about to frustrate the Marshall Plan. A large-scale psychological warfare offensive against the United States was launched."[3]

With the Cold War now undeniably at hand, Congress woke up to its implications for the information agency. Congressmen began to feel that America should answer the floods of Communist propaganda against the free world. Representative Karl E. Mundt of South Dakota and Senator H. Alexander Smith of New Jersey had already drafted legislation for a strengthened agency; but it had languished in the Senate after passing the

House. Now these two authorized a joint committee to inspect the European offices of USIS.

Meanwhile, in Washington, Assistant Secretary Allen began to sharpen up the agency's response to Communist attacks. He ordered Charles W. Thayer, another professional diplomat skilled in public communication, to form a Russian language service to the Soviet Union. Thayer, a veteran of the Soviet scene, did so well in his new assignment that Allen promoted him to head the entire Voice of America within a few months.

Thayer humbly admitted it wasn't easy to expand the VOA's capability, either in the substance of its broadcasts or in the added technical equipment that was required. As a sample of his difficulties, he quoted a letter the VOA received from a community of exiled Cossacks living in Lima, Peru. They wanted to thank the VOA for its excellent shows in Russian beamed directly at them! Thayer investigated quickly and found that the transmitters were, indeed, aimed south instead of east.[4]

When the Smith-Mundt group returned from assessing the USIS functions in Europe, they redrafted their bill and achieved its passage in January 1948. They had argued in the Congress that Europe had again become a vast battlefield of ideologists in which words had to replace armaments and that the United States should aggressively carry this true story of Europe.

This argument was needed to persuade taxpayers they must pay for more government action; and the newly minted Smith-Mundt Act was going to cost more millions, $24 million in 1948, to be exact. Under this law, America possessed for the first time a statutory agency of propaganda in between shooting wars. The act required the agency to "promote a better understanding of the United States in other countries, and to increase mutual understanding."[5] between Americans and foreigners. In doing so the agency was to paint a fair picture of this country. Under its provisions the State Department set up two new offices, the Office of Information (OII) and the Office of Educational Exchange (OEX), both to be run as a single agency by Assistant Secretary of State George Allen.

Allen's agency met Cold War challenges by increasing budget, staff, and programs, though its output didn't change much. In explaining America, the agency went through a foolish exercise later dubbed the Green Bath Tub Era. Foreigners were treated to copious descriptions of America's prosperity in terms of millions of automobiles, washing machines, and bath tubs for every citizen. The idea was to contrast the benefits a democracy carries for ordinary people compared to the slim standard of living under communism. Unfortunately, this kind of material could only create envy and resentment among the deprived denizens of the Third World.

Meanwhile, Soviet propaganda intoned its prediction of inevitable Communist hegemony over all mankind. Yet despite communism's aggressive posture and widening influence, a hemorrhage of refugees fleeing the iron curtain revealed its weakness.

Shortly thereafter, the Soviets cut off access to West Berlin, and that city survived the winter of 1948–49 only by the great airlift of supplies provided by the U.S. Air Force.

The American information agency duly reported and exploited these events not only to Europeans but also among the young nations achieving independence in the Middle East and Asia. The Soviets were beginning to fear the VOA, it seemed, for they now jammed its signals to Moscow and other Soviet cities.

Then President Truman announced his Point Four program of technical assistance for the fledgling countries as one inducement to prevent them from embracing communism.

With fresh confidence after his surprising reelection in 1948, Truman asked the Congress to help him rearm America and also to improve its information program. He had already told the public he planned an international "Campaign of Truth"—he called it this to avoid the stigma of propaganda. To direct this fresh thrust against communism, Truman employed an Alabama journalist, Edward W. Barrett, to succeed George Allen, whom he simultaneously named ambassador to Yugoslavia. Soon the agency had swollen in size from 2,500 Americans and a budget of $24 million to 4,370 Americans and $47 million in early 1950.

Truman's new found competence as a propagandist impressed Barrett so much that he compared him favorably to Franklin Roosevelt in terms of "international information work."[6] By June 25, 1950, however, Truman's Cold War information machine had to shift gears again and participate in a hot conflict when North Korea hurled its forces southward.

The Defense Department requested that the information agency collaborate more closely with the American divisions that entered South Korea under the United Nations banner. It was an important suggestion since the ROK (Republic of Korea) soldiers' will to win certainly depended on the morale of their terrified home population. They had been overrun by the initial invasion and needed to be encouraged that the U.S.-supported United Nations troops could protect them from further assaults. USIS and U.S. military personnel did cooperate to this end and indeed are still doing so, as garrison divisions still stand guard in Korea almost forty years later.

There was little to boast about in the effort to win battles through influencing rather than killing the enemy. Part of the problem was the paucity of seasoned personnel in the agency. With the war the budget had jumped to $120 million and the agency had added thousands of staffers. Many were hired too hastily and trained too slowly, and confusion followed both in Washington, where the Congress was heavily critical, and overseas. Additionally, America's professional soldiers, like its career diplomats, distained the doings of psychological warriors, either in or out of uniform. They lacked faith in "psywar" action.

There was one noteworthy exception, I was told by an officer who had fought in Korea. He recalled how the U.S. artillery fired some leaflet-loaded shells set for high burst over a steep-sloped valley in North Korea. The surrender tracts floated gently down onto the forested ravine. Moments after they landed, one or two Chinese infantrymen appeared from the trees, picked up the papers, and studied them. Sure enough, they started in the direction of the U.N. command headquarters. The leaflets promised a safe conduct to the rear and good treatment as a prisoner of war until peace could be restored. Minutes later, he observed from his artillery post that hundreds of enemy soldiers were striding south. Finally, there appeared to be two or three thousand of them.

"What happened then?" I asked.

"Oh," he laughed uneasily, "we reloaded our guns with antipersonnel ammunition and wiped out the whole lot."

"So you would agree that psywar is effective?" I pursued.

"Why yes, you might say it can be devastating. . . ."[7]

Except for that bloody instance, the Korean War period lacked evidence that U.S. psychological warfare efforts influenced anyone, although the Soviets did complain of the VOA's "lies" when it reported the Soviet support of aggression against South Korea. The VOA also retained several research firms to determine the size of its listenership; it found that in France

600,000 tuned in to the English language broadcasts; in Sweden close to 800,000, or one out of every ten inhabitants; and in Norway's three major cities 46 percent understood its English programs. The less-educated audiences, particularly in East Germany, liked the VOA output more than the more literate people did; they appreciated the hard-hitting, anti-Communist theme.[8]

Back in Washington, however, Congress wasn't so sure the agency was anti-Communist enough and began to bore like a termite into its reputation. Other Communist gains in Eastern Europe and the Communist insurrections in Greece, the Philippines, Malaysia, and Vietnam had been proceeding for at least six years; and now it was becoming fashionable to look for Communists in the U.S. government. President Truman pooh-poohed the trend as a "red herring," but it was not to be stopped easily. Spurred by Senator Joseph McCarthy of Wisconsin, the Congress asked the agency's director, Edward Barrett, and his representatives the most insinuating questions as to their loyalty and competence. On one occasion, U.S. Senator Kenneth McKellar began a hearing by demanding of Barrett, "Are you a Communist?"[9]

Barrett persevered in enlarging the scope of his programs despite congressional carping. He added new USIS posts continuously until the total was one hundred thirty; he soon proclaimed that nearly a half-million foreigners were viewing agency films every year, and he steadily increased the VOA's number of broadcast hours and languages. Yet, the record shows no hint—except in some of the letters received by the Voice—of how many foreigners were converted during his regime into believers in U.S. aims or policies.

At his departure in 1952, the agency changed names again as the State Department melded its two offices, OII and OEX, into one, semi-autonomous International Information Administration (IIA).

Dr. Wilson Compton, a longtime lobbyist, became the first administrator of IIA and remained through the election of Dwight D. Eisenhower. The Truman administration evidently thought Compton's experience on the Hill might keep the IIA out of any more trouble. This logic was solid, but it failed to bring the desired result. Thanks largely to Senator McCarthy's persecution, the IIA grew into a campaign issue and, by the end of Truman's term, was wriggling in the grip of four separate congressional investigations, the most egregiously sensational being Senator McCarthy's. Reed Harris, a senior agency official, fought back frontally during the hearings in Washington and eventually had to resign for his courage on the stand.

Overseas a junior officer, Benjamin C. Bradlee (now executive editor of the *Washington Post*), resisted more cleverly and got away with it. In the fall of 1952, McCarthy's gumshoes, Roy Cohn and David Schine, were raging around Europe trying to discover USIS subversives and/or Communistic literature in USIS libraries. Bradlee decided to mousetrap Cohn and Schine when they came to Paris, where he was serving as press attache (USIS job) in the U.S. embassy. Since he was assigned to deal with the foreign and American journalists, Bradlee was able to engineer a press conference for the roving Senate staffers. Several dozen newsmen showed up, loaded for bear. They took a dim view of what the two young men in their early twenties were doing to American bureaucrats and to the reputation of anyone they suspected of communism.

When the conference got under way, Bradlee simply sat back as the host official and watched the British, French, American, and other reporters tease and torture McCarthy's men for almost two hours. For his part in this verbal lynching, Bradlee might have been criticized. In effect, he was using executive branch facilities to thwart the goals of a legislative study group. But no one in Washington complained when they read the anti-McCarthy, sometimes anti-American, copy which the conference generated in both U.S. and foreign newspapers.

Technically, Bradlee was innocent of any mischief since he had simply made it easier for congressional agents to explain what they were doing in Europe, something they wanted to talk about. The antics of McCarthy's men brought shame on America, but at least USIS Paris gained credibility by not trying to hide the dirty linen they insisted on waving before the European public. This incident unveiled Bradlee's judgment, flair, and convictions, which led to his becoming one of America's best-known newspaper editors.

Compton stayed on until Eisenhower's inauguration but then resigned under the congressional heat from McCarthy and others who kept finding fault with the agency. Eisenhower then appointed Robert Johnson, co-founder of *Time* magazine and former president of Temple University, to take over from Compton.

During World War II, Eisenhower had revealed an interest, unusual among army officers, in psychological operations. As a military history scholar, he doubtless had digested the Chinese dictum of antiquity, ". . . to fight and conquer in all your battles is not supreme excellence; supreme excellence consists in breaking the enemy's resistance without fighting.[10] Weakening the will of the enemy by propaganda in lieu of armed force appealed to General Eisenhower. During the campaign in North Africa, C. D. Jackson, a reserve colonel, served as his psychological warfare chief.

Knowing this background, IIA veterans perked up at the Eisenhower victory in 1952. His campaign pledge to improve the functions and status of IIA if elected was additionally encouraging. When he brought C. D. Jackson, then publisher of *Fortune* magazine, into the White House as a propaganda advisor, IIA senior officials were vastly cheered. They believed that Jackson would try to protect the agency and its management.

Their hopes sagged, however, when neither Secretary of State John Foster Dulles nor the president lifted a hand to ward off continuing congressional attacks on the agency's probity and performance. Hopes dropped further when Eisenhower's first selection to lead IIA, Robert Johnson, fell prey to Senator McCarthy's wild, unfounded, and unanswered allegations. No one contradicted McCarthy's charges that Communist sympathizers and homosexual security risks abounded in IIA. The agency's reputation worsened.

Morale in the agency sank deeper in the spring of 1953; its operations slowed, and the budget shrank from its Korean War high of $131 million to less than $50 million. When Eisenhower declared he would not get in the gutter with McCarthy, there seemed no escape from the agency's troubles.

Still the new administration was working to improve the government's overall information capability. President Truman had created the Psychological Strategy Board during the waning days of the Korean War in an attempt to orchestrate the government's miscellaneous international information programs, including the IIA, the CIA, and extensive promotion activities of the Marshall Plan and Point Four technical assistance administration. Eisenhower found this mechanism ineffectual, and he soon substituted the Operations Coordination Board (OCB). Among its duties were to centralize overseas propaganda efforts of the government and to direct them in an orderly manner. However, the OCB, like its predecessor, produced good ideas but was unable to implement them.

Meanwhile, the U.S. Advisory Commission on Information, which had been set up pursuant to the Smith-Mundt Act of 1948 as a sort of private watchdog of the information agency, was urging that IIA be divorced from the State Department and remade as an independent agency. President Eisenhower had simultaneously formed another group of experts in management and information to tell him what should be done with the messy situation in IIA and related agencies. This was the "Jackson Committee" headed by William Jackson, a New York businessman. C. D. Jackson (no relation to William Jackson) was a member. The Jackson Committee recommended an independent organization in its report of June 1, 1953.

IIA's Robert Johnson had completed a study of his own which also urged independence, and he spent his final months as administrator simultaneously fighting off McCarthy and preparing the agency for its separate status. On August 1, 1953, by executive order, the United States Information Agency (USIA) was born, free of the Department of State. Secretary Dulles and foreign service officers exalted to see this charmless foundling removed from their doorstep. They felt that at least some of the abuse heaped on the hapless agency was merited by the second-class citizens on its rolls and their mediocre performance.

More bloodletting was in store before USIA could make a fresh start under its first director, broadcast executive Theodore S. Streibert. For over a year, President Eisenhower, who had campaigned to "clean up the mess in Washington," did his best with a reduction-in-force (RIF) throughout the government. The RIF resulted in the departure of some individuals whose personal habits had worried the security division of USIA. I was acquainted with two of them whose reputations were wrecked by the RIF. Also:

> The new agency had to face formidable budget problems in its first year, including a 36 percent reduction in operating funds from fiscal 1953, requiring cuts in all activities and a personnel reduction of approximately 25 percent.
> To meet this severe cutback in operating funds, libraries were reduced from 184 in 65 countries to 158 in 63 countries and Voice of America operations were cut back almost 25 percent. The number of USIS posts was cut back from 255 in 85 countries to 217 in 76 countries. The wireless bulletin news file was reduced from 8,000 words six days a week to 6,000 words five

days a week. The agency had started with 2,820 Americans employed domestically, 1,526 overseas, and 8,531 local employees abroad—a total of 12,877. The total number of employees dropped to 9,281.[11]

Bolstered by Director Streibert's confident personality, employees accepted these adjustments as necessary. By the end of 1954 Streibert had restored morale.

Starting with little background in foreign affairs, Streibert tightened and improved the agency's operations. In Washington he put assistant directors in charge of each geographical area where USIS operated—Europe, Middle East–South Asia, Far East, and Latin America. Additionally, he named media chiefs for films, radio, press and features, and information centers.

For years the Voice of America had its headquarters in New York, and this isolation led to freewheeling actions independent of Washington's control. Indeed, there were times when the VOA spoke like a sovereign nation. Streibert moved the Voice to Washington and made it clear that he intended to run it as a part of USIA.

Streibert, in theory, took his orders from the president. In practice, he reported to the National Security Council (NSC). The agency advertised but did not formulate the national foreign policy—that was done at the State Department in concert with the NSC. As the years passed, however, Streibert was allowed to sit, as an observer, in the meetings of NSC and occasionally to make suggestions concerning the public impact upon foreigners of new policies under consideration. But the bluff and friendly Streibert never made the club of real insiders in the White House.

One anomaly remained. In Washington, the cultural exchange program (CU) remained in the State Department. Overseas, USIS cultural officers handled CU programs. This meant that the USIS cultural officer had two bosses—the country public affairs officer and the CU country desk officer back in Washington. This sloppy arrangement invited conflict.

Although the Senate eventually pulled McCarthy from his pedestal, others kept the witch-hunt atmosphere alive. Vice President Richard M. Nixon made one gratuitous contribution in a speech on TV. Backhanding Dean Acheson, John Foster Dulles' predecessor, he said, "Isn't it wonderful to have a Secretary of State in Washington who is not taken in by the

Communists, he is standing up to them?"[12] USIS did not carry this pronouncement abroad. I saw the broadcast at a dinner party mostly of Democrats; someone angrily switched off the set.

Still, the U.S. government did grow more anti-Communist as the Soviets' stepped up their imperialism. To counteract Communist influence, USIS posts were installed in more and more of the new nations born in the wake of colonialism.

Now that USIS belonged to a separate agency and there was a common target in the form of communism, the foreign service officers and information personnel grew more congenial. This was especially true in the hardship posts opening up in Africa and the Orient. A frontier bonhomie resulted from the shared difficulty in these developing countries.

Streibert left after Ike's first term. Arthur Larson took over, but he was doomed to serve only a few months.

Larson was soft-spoken, musical—he played the guitar and sang in a gentle tenor—and an intellectual. He had been a Rhodes scholar, dean of the University of Pittsburgh School of Law, and had written a handbook for modern Republicans called *A Republican Looks at His Party*. The president thought this broad-gauged man would make a fine chief of USIA. However, his hope was smashed. Larson's book had some scathing passages about Democrats, and Senate Majority Leader Lyndon Johnson ambushed Larson when he testified for a USIA budget increase in 1957. Larson further aggravated Johnson and other Senate Democrats by delivering a pro-Republican speech in Hawaii before the hearing. The senators responded by allowing the agency only $96 million, some $50 million below what the president had asked for. Eisenhower had to exert damage control; he kicked Larson upstairs as a temporary White House assistant.

In Eisenhower's second term, George V. Allen once again took the reins of the information agency. Allen was a wise and clever bureaucrat and extremely articulate. The return of this five-time ambassador added prestige to USIA's improving status. Allen built on the sound management structure left by Streibert, and he shrewdly enlightened USIA employees on the nuances of their task. For example, he stressed that USIA's value would always be tied to the policies it was given to push. He said, ". . . 90 percent of the impression which the United States makes abroad depends on our policy and . . . not more than 10 percent . . . is how we explain it."[13]

The trouble with Allen was, as Thomas Sorenson put it, "he would have been more effective had he believed that the agency should persuade, not just inform. He was America's chief propagandist, but he did not believe in propaganda."[14] Clearly, Allen shared some of his fellow foreign service officers' coolness about "selling America abroad." He wanted USIA output to resemble the detachment of "an independent, reputable news agency with stories that could be published by anyone."[15] He concentrated on long-range improvements in exchange programs, the Voice of America, and in ensuring that USIA accurately reflected policy delineations of the State Department.

The U.S. Advisory Commission on Information, upset by the worldwide impact of the Soviets' first spacecraft, *Sputnik,** didn't agree with Allen's soft sell and demanded a better brand of propaganda:

> The United States may be a year behind in mass technological education. But it is thirty years behind in competition with Communist propaganda . . . each year sees the Communists increase their hours of broadcasting, their production and distribution of books, their motion pictures and cultural exchanges and every other type of propaganda and information activity. . . . We should start planning to close the gap in this field before it widens further."[16]

Career diplomat Allen kept his politics to himself, and Congress dealt with him equably until the campaign of 1960, when a USIA poll again roiled the senators. Candidate John F. Kennedy contended that a USIA poll proved the United States' image was blemished abroad. Kennedy and other Democratic senators asked for a copy, but Allen refused. He thought that publicizing the poll would damage the country's overseas reputation still further. He pleaded that the agency should stay free of politics. Finally, the White House ordered him to release the document, but he remained adamant, indeed insubordinate. His toughness protected the agency until the election.

---

*Sputnik I, 184 lbs., launched as man's first orbited object in 1957; U.S., now behind, launched its first orbiter *Explorer I*, 18 lbs., three months later in 1958.

By 1960 the agency had grown larger and stronger as the contest with the Soviet Union heated up. USIA was engaged in continuing country-by-country struggles for public approval of American and democratic policies rather than those of communism. Nikita Khrushchev had proclaimed Soviet interest in supporting "wars of liberation" in whatever part of the world they might occur. A Kremlinologist, Harry Rositske, emphasized that "the main covert vehicle for expanding Soviet influence in the Third World will continue to be wars of national liberation."[17] USIA was, and still is, limited to overt programs in warning the free world not to be taken in by the Soviets' putatively unselfish aid in these "wars."

USIA's efforts to persuade other countries from going Communist were often on a global scale, like the campaign to celebrate "People's Capitalism" in the United States; or the "Open Skies" proposal, to goad the Soviets into opening their country to aerial inspection pursuant to any arms-limitation agreement; or the U.S. Marines' landing in Lebanon to save that country—at its entreaty—from a dangerous insurrection.

USIA popularized some of Eisenhower's own favorite schemes: the People-to-People committees to engage private Americans in collaboration with foreigners in activities of mutual interest; the Atoms for Peace exhibit to show that America was trying to harness atomic power to run utilities, ships, and medical treatments; and the Food for Peace Program through which America gave away mountains of surplus food to reduce one cause that impels needy nations to war. These high visibility, "showcase" projects never really caught fire in the minds of foreigners. They were Yankee-style activities that had political sex appeal in the United States but overseas went unnoticed as a gentle rain in the night.

Kennedy's vaunted Peace Corps stirred a similar lack of enthusiasm abroad, although it sounded wonderful to Americans. It suited America's long-held tradition of helping "little brown brothers" elsewhere—our missionary heritage of offering love and friendship to strangers. Nevertheless, President Kennedy's brother-in-law, Sargent Shriver, often had to lure foreign officials with the prospect of more millions in grants and loans before they would agree to "request" the legions of untrained do-gooders that Shriver wanted to send them. This is not to say that the Peace Corps volunteers were not sincere and industrious and doing their utmost when assigned, nor that the USIS posts and ambassadors didn't recognize their conscientious endeavors. But the Peace Corps didn't accomplish much of a practical nature. How could it? The corps too often fielded amateurs who were to lead amateurs, except in the teaching of English. Since 1969, more professionals have been added. Now the volunteers are comparable to other technical assistants of the U.S. Agency for International Development (AID) and such others as West German, Israeli, and United Nations personnel.

When the Peace Corps volunteers first went abroad, Sargent Shriver warned them to give USIS posts a wide berth to avoid speculation that his people were "propagandists." Yet, one purpose of the Peace Corps was propaganda, in the sense that the volunteers sought to enhance relations between Americans and foreigners. They served on the U.S. government payroll. Even though they called themselves volunteers, to pretend they were something else than official Americans was a refinement that often escaped the foreigners among whom they lived and labored.

As for USIA, Eisenhower passed on to Kennedy a useful study on international communications needs. Eisenhower had commissioned Manuel J. Sprague, a New York businessman, to head an inquiry on how to upgrade official propaganda. Sprague's group recommended more training, more extensive exchanges of persons, and a sharper focus on Latin America and the emerging nations of Africa.

Kennedy accepted these guidelines but rejected Sprague's advice to retain the Operations Coordinating Board (OCB) and promptly put it to death. This move dismayed USIA's senior staffers. They had counted on OCB as their link to the president. They were seldom listened to either in the National Security Council or in the high level deliberations of the Secretary of State. One Sprague idea found favor with USIA: any department concerned with making policy should consider the potential effect of that policy on foreign public opinion.

In short, USIA should have a hand in the formation, as well as the selling, of policies. Nobody, for instance, had told USIA that the high-technology U-2 plane was making stratospheric flights deep into the Soviet Union to gather intelligence. Yet when the Soviets downed one of these U-2s, USIA and everyone else in the Eisenhower administration had to hustle to explain away the embarrassing event.

President Kennedy held true to his campaign pledge for a stronger USIA. He invited the renowned broadcaster and folk hero of the liberals, Edward R. Murrow, to direct the agency. Murrow humbly agreed to do his duty, though he had to absorb a salary cut of some $200,000. His CBS boss, William Paley,[18] warned him to stipulate his acceptance on access to the president. Murrow tried to extract this guarantee, emphasizing— obviously with the U-2 drama in mind—that as America's global PR man he wanted to be brought in on the take–off as well as the crash landing of the administration's new projects, programs or policies. Kennedy and his aides said they concurred.

Murrow's appointment raised Americans' admirations for their propaganda machine. Most had never heard of USIA, or if they had, they didn't much respect its mission or performance. For example, one People-to-People chairman, Mark Bortman, always insisted on identifying his USIA collaborator, myself, as an officer of the State Department. Bortman would do this despite my patient reminders that the officer belonged to USIA. Bortman couldn't bring himself to admit in polite society that he was cooperating with the lowly USIA! Then one day I literally had to save him from drowning in the Mediterranean when I was PAO in Israel. Only after that did he take USIA seriously.

USIA personnel have always had trouble clarifying what their agency is and does; but during Ed Murrow's reign all the employees had to say was we work for Edward R. Murrow. Interrogators would nod knowingly, though they still were in the dark as to exactly what USIA meant or did. My colleagues and I frequently ran into this ignorance of the agency on speaking and recruiting trips as well as with otherwise well-informed Americans.

During Kennedy's brief and tumultuous presidency, USIA prospered with increasing responsibilities abroad. In Africa it opened posts in over two dozen freshly independent countries—Kennedy's "love affair" with Africa meant a flood of money and staff for us in those posts. I was running the program in the ex-Belgian Congo, now Zaire; in Latin America USIS branches were strengthened to win acceptance of Kennedy's "Alliance for Progress."

USIA featured prominently in defusing reactions to the Bay of Pigs fiasco and announcing the triumphant resolution of the Cuban missile crisis. Bruce Herschenson, USIA's talented moving picture chief, produced hard-line propaganda films. One, *Five Cities in June*, sneered at the obviously inaccurate

Russian portrayal of their space exploits and touted the brilliant U.S. space achievements. When I screened this film at the U.S. Mission to the U.N., the Soviet guests left the theater in a huff, understandably irritated over the space commentary. Herschenson's celluloid obituary for Kennedy, *Years of Lightning, Day of Drums*, made a great splash among foreigners. Hearing this, Congress enacted a special exception to its taboo against distribution of USIA products to Americans and allowed the film to be seen in this country.

Thomas C. Sorenson, brother of the president's speech writer Theodore Sorenson, has written a forceful account of the Kennedy and Johnson handling of the USIA called *The Word War, the Story of American Propaganda*. Sorenson extols both Kennedy and Murrow. He served as a USIA deputy director, having risen slowly through the ranks until the White House elevated him to this key job. He believes American propaganda came of age during the Kennedy era. USIA did take a giant jump from the alternate obscurity and tribulation of its history before 1960. As Murrow's vigorous lieutenant, Sorenson merits some credit for the agency's improvement.

With Murrow, the agency unabashedly strove to advance American objectives abroad. Although USIA honored the truth in all it said, including VOA newscasts, it avowedly sought to influence foreigners. Whether USIA reached the ripe maturity alleged by Sorenson is debatable. One wonders how it compared to the wonderful one-man programs two hundred years ago under Franklin and Jefferson. Murrow himself perhaps was in their league. He openly called himself a "propagandist." This statement constituted an abrupt turnaround from George Allen's dictum that USIA should mainly emit a stream of bland information about the United States and its policies.

But Murrow was disappointed not to be brought into the presidential inner circle. In fact, neither Kennedy nor Johnson permitted him the access he had asked for. At the very outset, for example, he was not privy to the disastrous Bay of Pigs adventure. Yet he did attend Secretary of State Dean Rusk's daily staff meetings. Lucius D. Battle, then assistant secretary of state for cultural affairs, told me that Murrow never spoke up in those meetings unless called on.[19] In short, even where he had access, this once glamorous TV star seemed too modest to exploit it. Tragically, cancer forced Murrow's resignation from USIA and premature demise. A notoriously heavy smoker, Murrow laughed at his illness in his final days at

USIA. He made no bones about nicotine's toll on him, saying drolly, "I'm smoking more now but enjoying it less," or as he appeared shaking and white at his last staff meeting, "There is no question about it, cancer is bad for your health."

Lyndon Johnson entered the presidency with mixed feelings about USIA. While vice president, he had often complained that the agency failed to drum up the crowds and press coverage he expected on his official visits abroad. Yet after Kennedy died, he liked the way USIA touted his doings and in particular the pictures it took of him. For still photos, Yoichi Okamoto had no equal in Johnson's mind and eventually he expropriated Okamoto from the agency for exclusive assignments to record every presidential activity.

After producing an agency documentary on the new president, USIA's motion picture chief, George Stevens, Jr., recalled a quaint detail: USIA cameramen shot Johnson from various angles as he sat at his desk one evening in the Oval Office. While the cameras whirred, the president scratched his fountain pen across white sheets of paper. Stevens wondered if he might be writing a speech and surreptitiously peeked over his shoulder. He saw that every page was covered only with . . . Lyndon B. Johnson, Lyndon B. Johnson, Lyndon B. Johnson, Lyndon B. Johnson.

Johnson named two able directors of the agency. The first was Carl T. Rowan, a prize-winning newsman, former deputy assistant secretary of state for public affairs and ambassador to Finland. With Rowan, a black, at its controls, Johnson signaled that the agency spoke for America's multiracial society. USIA people responded to Rowan's sure leadership, but he returned to journalism after Johnson was reelected.

Johnson then selected a lawyer and friend experienced in the broadcasting field, Leonard H. Marks. It was reported that he told Marks, "Keep that agency out of the newspapers and off the TV screens." But Johnson did back Marks's all-out attempts to gear up USIA for the Vietnam war. Nevertheless the agency's participation in that marathon of disappointment and disaster was dogged by failure. (See chapter 12.)

In 1968, President Nixon chose TV executive Frank Shakespeare to direct USIA. Agency personnel shivered at how they would fare under Nixon. On a trip through Africa as vice president, he had complained about "corn-balls" in the embassies. As president, however, he was kind to USIA.

He liked Shakespeare, who was a "quick study" and mastered easily the myriad names of countries, their leaders, problems, and unique characteristics.

As media advisor during Nixon's election campaign, Shakespeare had acquired a knack for portraying the president and his ideas. Shakespeare harbored no doubt that USIA's function was to win support for American goals. He ran the agency with care that Nixon's policies were sold unequivocably abroad. At one point, he reacted toughly to a Soviet move in the Middle East without approval of the State Department. This was a no-no. USIA is supposed to promote foreign policy, not create it. His initiative took the form of a policy directive to VOA and USIS posts. Secretary of State William Rogers dealt with this challenge to his authority quietly, and it didn't recur.

To avoid such gaffes, Shakespeare seasoned his own meager foreign affairs experience by hiring Theodore Weintal. This former Polish diplomat and veteran *Newsweek* reporter became Shakespeare's personal assistant. Shakespeare joked that Weintal was his liaison with the Congress of Vienna. Shakespeare was known as a hard-driving, shrewd, rather cold man who operated USIA competently. He has continued his interest in the agency in his recent assignments as ambassador to Portugal and the Vatican.

Shakespeare left after Nixon's overwhelming mandate for a second term. James Keogh, who had earlier done speechwriting at the Nixon White House, took Shakespeare's place. Keogh, one-time *Time* magazine writer, presided quietly over USIA during the complicated furors of the Nixon-Ford administrations. Keogh saw to it that Nixon's astonishing downfall was described with dignity and accuracy for a bewildered world.

By fall 1976, USIA was entering another period of obscurity. The Vietnam war was over, Watergate had subsided, and a national leader with no background in foreign affairs was packing his bags in Plains, Georgia. The prospects for an expert information agency in close touch with the president hadn't been so bleak since Harry Truman took charge in 1945.

ENDNOTES

1. John W. Henderson, *The United States Information Agency* (New York, London, Washington: Frederick A. Praeger, 1969), p. 39.

2. Wilson P. Dizard, *The Strategy of Truth* (Washington, D.C.: Public Affairs Press, 1961), p. 83.
3. Henderson, *Ibid.* p. 39.
4. Charles W. Thayer, "Diplomat" (New York: Harper and Brothers, 1959), p. 189.
5. Thomas C. Sorenson, *The Word War* (New York, Evanston, London: Harper and Row, 1968), p. 26.
6. *Ibid.*, p. 26.
7. Told to the author by a Naval War College classmate, January 1962.
8. Robert W. Pirsein, "The Voice of America," Ph.D. dissertation, Northwestern University, 1970, Evanston, Illinois.
9. Sorenson, *The Word War*, p. 27.
10. Sun Tzu, *The Art of War* (Harrisburg, Pa.: Military Service Publishing Co., 1944).
11. Henderson, *The United States Information Agency*, p. 54.
12. Nixon speech, in an aside in August 1953 during a CBS radio broadcast.
13. Dizard, *The Strategy of Truth*, p. 187.
14. Sorenson, *The Word War*, p. 116.
15. *Ibid.*, p. 105.
16. Thirteenth Report of the United States Advisory Commission on Information, January 1958, p. 9.
17. Sorenson, *The Word War*, p. 117.
18. William S. Paley, *As It Happened* (Garden City, N.Y.: Doubleday and Co., 1979), p. 296.
19. Lucius D. Battle, interview with author, January 1982.

CHAPTER 3

Changes Under Carter

BY 1976 USIA'S JOB DIFFERED FROM THE PAST. Until then, the America it advertised was the first superpower of the twentieth century. The United States had swept over its enemies of World War II with a display of overwhelming weaponry capped by the atomic bomb. We had bulldozed other countries into launching the United Nations and then dominated it for twenty years. We had contained Russian aggression with the American-made alliances—North Atlantic Treaty Organization, Central Treaty Organization, and Southeast Asian Treaty Organization. We had led U.N. forces to stop the Chinese/ North Korean attacks against South Korea. We had mounted what Robert F. Kennedy called "counterinsurgency" to repel Communist subversion in scattered places like Greece, the Philippines, Laos, and the Congo, with a mix of military, economic, and propaganda advice and hardware. We had established primacy in trade, manufacturing, music, the arts, and sciences—especially the space race. Despite black and hispanic tensions at home, we still ranked as the globe's most desired haven for refugees and other immigrants. Anything America said tended to influence hundreds of millions of people. We were sovereign in the kingdom of the free world and the envy of the Soviet empire.

But when Jimmy Carter reached Washington, he perceived that the American president could no longer snap the whip as ringmaster of the non-Communist nations. Vietnam, Watergate, civil disturbances, moral erosion from drugs, increased crime, and a loosening of social restraints had worsened the weakness. Carter's apologetic approach to foreign relations hastened our tumble from supremacy. Now America had to suggest rather than command, negotiate rather than demand, and accept rebuffs in the international arena.

Noting the country's diminished fortunes, Carter altered the USIA significantly. He analyzed its role in the context of current circumstances. He was moved somewhat by recent studies, which urged changing the agency for the nth time since its inception. Americans and their government have treated the information agency the way some homemakers handle living room furniture—no arrangement suits for very long. Carter revisualized the organization in line with his personal tastes. He wished it to be an instrument for better relations with other peoples. As a born-again Christian, he wanted U.S. citizens and aliens to have better feelings for each other, more Christian love. USIA's objective of "Telling America's Story Abroad," proclaimed by the signs that adorned the agency's headquarters building, didn't appeal to him. It seemed too nationalistic, and soon the signs disappeared. The president decided that the agency would have a "second mandate"—to tell Americans about the world.

He also renamed the agency. Henceforth it would be the United States International Communication Agency (USICA). This would signal that America no longer had a one-way propaganda agency to speak for it. Instead, it would be a sort of information bellows which could puff in as well as out. As the refashioned agency told foreigners more about the U.S. and vice versa, Carter reasoned, mutual understanding would increase and the chances for peace would rise proportionately.

The agency obediently adopted this second mandate and assigned personnel to implement it. USICA's good gray bureaucrats should have pointed out two discrepancies in the new concept:

First, efforts to show Americans how other parts of the planet live have been going on intermittently ever since World War I. They were given more scope by the Fulbright exchanges, the People-to-People committees of the Eisenhower era, and the Department of Commerce's U.S. Travel Service, which woos tourists to America. Foreigners, too, have taken initiatives, particularly the numerous information programs of their embassies and consulates in the U.S. They furnish press releases, pamphlets, books, and lectures to enlighten America about their home countries.

Second, the USICA, which (under its various names) has always complained of a shortage of funds and people to accomplish its original mandate, was poorly prepared to take on a far heavier load.

USICA handled this anomalous second mandate with a technique not unknown in government. It announced a plan to study the problem and simultaneously took a tiny, tentative step forward, hoping to look good at the White House. Also it began to promote foreign study chairs at universities around the country. Agency officers talked up the idea among colleges overseas. U.S. schools shared the financing of international language and cultural courses to enrich their own curricula at a bargain rate, for the originating foreign governments and/or educational institutions also bore some of the cost.

The results were modest; the agency was not sure how many academic exchanges were triggered.

The second mandate, like numerous other Carter innovations, never really matured. This was regrettable because there is good rationale for Carter's proposal. Americans do remain vastly ignorant of foreign nations and their value to us in terms of trade and military security. William Watts of Potomac Associates, a Washington think tank, cited as an example:

A majority of Americans believes that the People's Republic of China is one of our fifteen largest trading partners. A majority says that Indonesia is not a major supplier of oil and petroleum products to the United States. A majority also believes that the United States still provides major economic aid to South Korea.

The majorities are wrong on all counts. . . . More than three Americans in ten do not know that the Philippines was once an American colony. . . . Given the fact that more than 20 percent of the world's population now lives in China, that Japan has emerged as one of the world's economic superpowers, that the Korean peninsula remains one of the most dangerous flashpoints anywhere, with the direct interests of China, the Soviet Union, Japan and the United States all involved, and that Asia contains some of the world's most rapidly developing economies, in Singapore, Korea, and Taiwan, for example, it ill behooves us to remain so uninformed and parochial.[1]

But should USICA have tried to educate Americans about other nations? Probably yes. For USICA to achieve its basic mandate—to win understanding and acceptance by foreigners—requires close comprehension of their languages, mores, and politics. Franklin and Jefferson gained these insights in England and France. To the extent to which USICA fell short of this knowledge, it already failed in its basic mission and was bound to fail in the second mandate as well.

USICA was only sketchily equipped for the second mandate. Its experts were fully engaged in exporting information. To explain the culture, policies, and actions of one hundred twenty-five nations to the U.S. people would take more hundreds of staffers and a budget easily quadruple that of the USICA's allowance from Congress. As a practical possibility such an expansion was unlikely. All the agency's directors have favored more exchanges of political, professional, and academic leaders. Foreign visitors import fresh information about their homelands. While they're in America, USICA routinely facilitates opportunities for exchangees to speak, write, and appear on broadcast media.

Also, private organizations like foreign affairs councils, public issue groups, and universities could be expected to swell the audiences for these foreign spokesmen.

Finally, the ongoing foreign information services of embassies would help to enlighten Americans on what is thought and done elsewhere.

One way or other, Carter's dream for stronger two-way tides of knowledge between Americans and foreigners will come true.

Carter reshaped the agency in several other ways, most of which downplayed any semblance of a sales mechanism. In his statement of mission to the director, Carter wrote: ". . . the agency will undertake no activities which are covert, manipulative or propagandistic. The agency can assume—as our founding fathers did—that a great and free society is its own best witness, and can put its faith in the power of ideas."[2]

At USICA's inaugural ceremonies on April 3, 1978, Vice President Mondale seemed to countermand the president's proscription against propaganda: "We not only seek to show people who we are and how we live: we must also engage others in the delicate, difficult art of human persuasion, to explain why we do what we do."

In brief, Carter's Reorganization Plan 2 of October 11, 1977, ordered the new agency to encompass the former USIA and the State Department's Bureau of Education and Exchange. USICA's director would report to the Secretary of State. Yet in tune with Carter's reluctance to delegate anything, he would also report to the president. "Who's in charge here?" one might ask. Can one man serve two masters?

The first director of USICA, John E. Reinhardt, said simply, "We shall strive for the most collegial relationship with the Department of State . . . our sister institution. Our work, and our mission, are different but closely related."[3]

Switching the agency's name raised a drumfire of irritation and controversy. Agency officers felt they had poured their professional lives into giving USIA a sound reputation which now would be lost. But the president had added to the agency's mission, and he believed its name should reflect that fact. At first it was slated to be the "Agency for International Communication," but officials saw that its acronym was CIA spelled backwards. Even the final name ICA misled foreigners, for there is an active organization called "International Christian Aid." The old name had its shortcomings too. In French-speaking countries the word "information" may connote intelligence activity. But since the new name ICA was set and the new stationery and outdoor plaques were ordered, a reversal would have cost an estimated $157,000. While he was director, Reinhardt had the last word: to change back would only bring "incalculable confusion," he declared. He retired before the actual change—under Reagan—at a cost not yet announced.

Reinhardt ran the USICA with a calm and steady hand throughout the Carter administration. He was the first career information officer to become director, and the second black. His broad experience ranged from cultural affairs to area supervision of USIS posts in the Far East and Africa, plus stints in Nigeria as ambassador and in the States as assistant secretary for public affairs. All this fitted him to be USICA director. With a careful touch, he guided the agency through growing pains which were complicated by President Carter's troubled conduct of foreign relations.

Reinhardt, calm and deliberate, was noted for attention to detail and loyalty to people under him. He never forgot these qualities as he led his agency through major realignments.

To begin with, USICA was shrinking. Congress was cutting its budget, but Reinhardt did not object much. To taxpayers this may be unbelievable. No arm of government ever takes cuts lying down, not even under recurrent pressures to economize. But Reinhardt stoutly insisted that the agency had enough people. When President Eisenhower moved USIA out of the State Department in 1953, it housed 12,000 employees. About two-thirds were citizens of countries where USIA had its 225 branches. Now the total was down to 8,500 and falling; half were American, and half of these staffed the Voice of America. Reinhardt was content with the employees on USICA's payroll and reordered agency priorities so as to use them more cost effectively.

"I boil our actions down to three categories," he explained to me in an interview, "the Voice of America, exchanges of people, and all else." By "all else" he meant libraries, wireless file, films, TV and radio tapes, pamphlets, magazines, and exhibits. "We need more money for the first two categories; radio, because the Soviets outperform us in broadcast hours three to one; and exchanges because the president has told us to increase the flow of knowledge about other countries into America and exchange of persons is the best way to do that."

The moderate Reinhardt judged that a $20 million increase for exchanges from Latin America and Africa was needed; Senate Foreign Relations Committee member (now chairman) Claiborne Pell thought $150 million would be more like it.

Reinhardt was also frugal about films: "The Public Broadcasting System, business and private foundations have ample collections of documentaries we can acquire." By acquire he meant get them free or on loan.

I pursued the question of the agency's mission: "But aren't you doing more than just communicate? Aren't you trying to persuade other populations to accept our point of view?"

Reinhardt had stated that, through USICA, America entered the "marketplace of ideas." Surely one doesn't enter the market without wanting to buy and sell, especially the latter. Reinhardt answered:

> Through selection of material even Walter Cronkite is a propagandist because he and the network pick what they'll talk about. On the Voice the news is independent of politics except for the selection of stories. We will mention what's going on that's significant, but we're not going to emphasize Billy Carter's pecadillos. Persuade yes, but manipulate no. I'll agree our government should be prepared to do so, particularly in self-defense, but USICA is not the mechanism.[4]

USICA's and the nation's performance overseas suffered during the Reinhardt incumbency from the administration's refusal to take him into its policymaking counsels. He was odd man out when the top chieftains met, like his predecessors.

Still, although Edward Murrow had wanted to be closer than he was to the president and secretary of state, his ideas were sometimes sought and used, as in the Cuban missile crisis. President Johnson endorsed the agency's advisory role. Johnson didn't seek his friend Leonard Marks's views very often, though in 1968 he asked him whether the U.S. should bomb Hanoi docks where Soviet ships were tied up—the reply is not available. Director Marks also attended Secretary of State Rusk's early morning meetings. Marks, a gregarious and efficient man, was popular in official and nonofficial Washington.

Although Carter decreed that USICA's head should report both to him and the secretary of state, Reinhardt was given virtually no contact with either man. Indeed he seldom saw the inside of the National Security Council—not even during the head scratching over how to handle public reaction to the Soviet seizure of Afghanistan or the Iranian impoundment of American embassy staffers. Reinhardt was frustrated; he had built a coordination staff to help him develop policy advice and public diplomacy recommendations for the president, the secretary of state, and the National Security Council. But the staff's output went begging. Edward Murrow's hope that the agency would routinely be brought in on the take-off as well as the crash landing of policies and actions was still unrealized twenty years later.

The agency's trials are noted in Ambassador Charles W. Yost's* book, *The Conduct and Misconduct of Foreign Affairs*:

> USIS (the agency) faces the dilemma of hewing strictly to the official line and therefore lose credibility, or reflecting diversity of behavior and opinions and incur the wrath of the White House, State and Congress. [Consequently] over 25 years the agency has expanded and contracted like an accordion with disastrous effects on morale and effectiveness.[5]

Over the years each succeeding director has tended to remold the agency until its style and substance satisfy him—

---

*Yost's career included being ambassador to Laos, Syria, and the United Nations.

occasionally to the agency's detriment. Democratic elections are designed to produce change and improvement in response to the people's choice. The trick is to recognize what is good and what is rotten and not hurt the first in dispensing with the second. Reagan's director, Charles Z. Wick, faced a particular challenge when he began. The agency had been totally reconstituted under Carter's Plan 2 only four years earlier and still had not fully convalesced from that surgery.

ENDNOTES

1. William Watts, *Americans Look at Asia* (Washington, D.C.: Potomac Associates, 1980), Introduction.
2. Jimmy Carter, "Memorandum for Director, International Communication Agency," The White House, March 13, 1978.
3. John E. Reinhardt, "Remarks at Inaugural Ceremonies of the International Communication Agency, Departmental Auditorium, Washington, D.C., April 3, 1978," p. 8.
4. Quotes are from the author's interviews with Reinhardt in 1979 and 1980.
5. Charles W. Yost, *The Conduct and Misconduct of Foreign Affairs* (New York: Random House, 1972), pp. 166–67.

PART II

USIA Washington

CHAPTER 4

People

IN 1963, USIA DIRECTOR EDWARD R. MURROW called me into his Washington office: "This agency has some good people on its rolls. We need more like them. If we're going to improve our performance we've got to upgrade our personnel—all the way from clerks to senior officers. The best communicating device yet invented is a human being, properly trained, properly motivated and with inherent skills including charm. Do you agree?"

It was hard to contradict Ed Murrow, especially in this subject. The agency had suffered a talent shortage ever since the Office of War Information let its galaxy of star communicators quit after VJ Day.

"Well," he said, exhaling a gray cloud from his thirty-third cigarette that morning, "I want you to find and stock this agency with top quality performers, in whatever openings we have. Please start now!"[1] I agreed to do my best.

Alas, Murrow's fatal illness postponed the assignment. Finally, in 1965, under Acting Director Donald M. Wilson, I, with a small temporary staff, began the search. We called it the "Hot Shot" campaign. We wanted to locate men and women who had proved themselves, or shown strong potential, in advertising, television, international radio, the print media, and even the Peace Corps. We did discover a dozen or so "hot shots" and were able to circumvent the bureaucratic roadblocks and hire about half of them in a few months.

Also, we lubricated machinery for bringing in junior officers through the USIA portion of the State Department's foreign service examinations. We had to speed induction of new employees. It was pointless to attract a flood of applicants and then allow them to wait bumper to bumper for months or years for an answer from the personnel department. The two worst traffic-stoppers were security clearances, which are necessary to screen out subversive or perverted undesirables, and the rule that to employ someone by "lateral entry"—i.e., at a rank commensurate with his job elsewhere—the position must be exposed in the Federal Register so prior applicants for civil service can have first crack at the opening.

Security clearances can be expedited by a "Crabtree," named for a legendary political appointee who had his papers rushed through the FBI review; however, this version costs more because more FBI investigators must be used. In these post-Watergate times, candidates for elective office must also be checked for financial conflicts of interest or other closet skeletons.

Our recruiting extended to college campuses, where we painted the agency as a fascinating career opportunity. We sent officers with charisma and stellar records to give spiels to the students and placement officers. Our people had to compete with the high pressure "body hunters" from big corporations, as well as from the State Department and other government agencies. At that time there were forty-six divisions of the federal government with foreign programs. The count is still rising.

We also prospected among marketing firms and the mass media. We were aided by a list of contacts known to senior agency officials like Acting Director Wilson himself, who was on loan from Time, Inc.

As we started our drive, some two thousand young hopefuls were taking the USIA section of the semiannual written exams offered by the State Department. Those who passed then had to submit to an oral test. If they negotiated both, they had to wait until the agency got ready to swear in a new class of junior officers. Survivors of this gauntlet entered the agency at the rate of about fifty per year. Currently, three thousand take the annual initial test, of which some thirty-five to fifty eventually join the agency.

Before the Hot Shot program and other executive search schemes could gain much momentum, the Congress in 1966 reduced USIA's budget once more. This, de facto, ended Ed Murrow's blueprint for remodeling USIA.

Simultaneously, the Senate Foreign Relations Committee struck another blow at the agency. It sat on seven hundred sixty nominations which would have converted "career reserve" officers into genuine foreign service officers like those in the State Department. Years earlier George Allen had established the Foreign Service Career Reserve (FSCR). He encouraged USIA officers to take special examinations, both written and oral, to give them the designation FSCR. The idea was to create a cadre of officers who could be ready for admittance into the FSO corps through a blanket act of Congress.

President Johnson was persuaded in 1966 to submit names of FSCR officers. His action was ignored by the Senate. Some of the FSCR officers were not upset. They thought that becoming FSOs would deflect their growth into a truly professional service of public diplomatists or propagandists. Once FSCRs become FSOs, they reasoned, they would be maneuvering solely to rise to the rank of ambassador. The foreign service officers' disdain for the agency's work was felt by FSCRs, and many wanted to rise above it. Charles S. Whitehouse, an ambassador in three different embassies, still teases his USIA friends about the value of agency activities: Anyone who believes that USIA can change foreigners' minds on vital issues, he laughs, would believe that you can stop pregnancy by rubbing vanishing cream on a woman's belly! Former FSO Senator Claiborne Pell still refers to agency officers as those "tickety-tick" men because he visualizes them at typewriters preparing news stories and propaganda. Ambassador G. McMurtrie Godley used to claim their only valid function was to dish up press releases on decisions made by the State Department or ambassadors.

Curiously it turned out that Senator Pell became the hero of USIA officers who wanted a separate career service. In the spring of 1966 he began to weigh the idea. His own view was that the FSOs should remain a small elite group whose concentrated excellence should not be diluted by the "tickety-tick" men. Some FSCRs were convinced that agency officers should fear dilution of their ranks by the proposed integration.[2] In fact, this move would have been one more step away from the career specialization that USIA needed to be a proficient propaganda agency. Despite critics who eschew the term, a composite definition of propaganda for current dictionaries and experts in the subject looks something like this: Any organization or movement engaged in the propagation of particular ideas, doctrines, practices, etc., for the purpose of helping an institution (the United States in USIA's case) or a cause (the principles in which Americans believe, and the U.S. foreign policy, in USIA's case). This definition jibes with most of the numerous statements of mission under which the agency has labored. Certainly USIA's mission requires more than a generalist FSO striving toward an ambassadorship.

When Senator Pell introduced his bill to form a career organization of foreign service information officers, the purists for propaganda were pleased. The FSOs were relieved, among other reasons, because they considered it would have been unfair competition to bring in through lateral entry officers who had risen faster through an easier promotion system (this assessment was probably accurate). Agency officers who had set their caps on becoming FSOs were disappointed, and some of them complained. So did USIA Director Leonard H. Marks, until he saw the sense of the senator's bill. Then he pitched in with his general counsel Richard Schmidt to help the senator advance the legislation. Marks and Schmidt were indefatigable advocates. They smoothly lined up the necessary backing of the Bureau of the Budget and Department of State. Then Marks began to ply his own brand of magic with key senators and congressmen. Wayne Hays, chairman of the House Subcommittee on Foreign Affairs, told his fellow committee members they might as well give Marks the millions he asked for since Marks would simply go back to the office and write a check for it.[3]

But Senator J. William Fulbright, who headed the prestigious Foreign Relations Committee, was no pushover for Marks's blandishments. Fulbright had outspokenly opposed international propaganda in our government.* When he coldly queried Marks on the meaning of propaganda, Marks replied respectfully, "If I say you are chairman of the Senate Foreign Relations Committee, that's a fact; whereas if I say you are the finest chairman in the history of the Senate, that's propaganda."

Fulbright shot back: "No, you're wrong—that's a fact!"

Ultimately, neither Fulbright nor any other senator or con-

---

*When I recently told Mr. Fulbright I'd like to get his present view for this book, he growled (with a grin), "It wouldn't be worth your while." He's still negative on the subject.

gressman took exception to the legislation. No one on the Hill got very excited either since no constituents cared enough about USIA to pull their tail feathers. In fact, the sentiment boiled down to "if Claiborne Pell wants this done, he knows the subject, and I'll take his word for it. He's got my vote."

President Johnson signed the Pell-Hays Act the following year. Wayne Hays cosponsored it in the House. By 1968, Johnson had obtained Senate confirmation for over seven hundred careerists to become foreign service information officers. Agency morale soared at this recognition of its professional status, despite the vicissitudes Vietnam was causing many junior officers at that time.

Meanwhile Senator Pell, a thorough man, wanted to ensure that his reshaping of the propaganda agency improved its professional capability. He appended a statement with the final bill which made four points: First, the FSIOs should be chosen out of a communications background or bent; second, that they should be trained as public diplomatists; third, that they should be promoted on the basis of excellence in their specialty; and fourth, that they should be selected out if they failed to perform well. This guidance is part of the legislative history of the act. It implies that the Senate may keep an eye on USIA to assure compliance.

Career officers are the mainspring of the agency. The senator's precepts should be followed in the development of each officer as with line officers of the army and navy. In the agency's overseas posts they hold the leading positions of country public affairs officers, who run the post, and cultural and information officers. In the United States they fill the top slots in media and management except for a few presidential appointments like director, deputy director, or associate director for the Voice of America, program management, education and cultural affairs, and management. Career officers can aspire even to those exalted chairs if the president so wishes, as when John Reinhardt became director in 1977.

For a mutual broadening of experience it has also become customary for the State Department FSOs to be given an occasional tour in the agency, as well as for agency officers to serve in the State Department or in an embassy.

Superficially, the FSIO experiment went well. There were no major administrative snarls, and the system continued uninterrupted until the new Foreign Service Act of 1980: this created a single foreign service system into which both FSOs and

FSIOs were to be integrated. In the revised system, the public diplomacy specialty continues to exist. Men and women interested in becoming career public diplomatists may still do so, but all officers are called FSOs.

The USIA should review the record of its careerists in light of the precepts laid down by Senator Pell. The extent to which they have not been adhered to has weakened the agency progress toward professionalism.

Starting with recruitment, the agency has done very little lateral entry hiring and so has depended on the written and oral tests and the judgment of boards of examiners who choose junior officers. There is little evidence that they have selected candidates with much background or particular interest in international communications. Generalists is the word to describe most junior officer trainees that enter the agency.

As to training, it, too, is general. It begins with a brief orientation in Washington. New officers can take language and geographic area courses in the Foreign Service Institute run by the State Department. The agency provides on-the-job training in Washington and overseas. At midcareer, they can take a year of graduate study in international political science or be assigned to one of the four war colleges—National, Army, Navy, or Air Force—or the Senior Seminar. All of these are designed to broaden knowledge among military and civilian officers in international affairs. These enviable assignments go to people who already have shown the potential for flag rank in the military or as ambassadors and leaders in other agencies. Ideally, alumni meet again later in real-life situations to cope with global strategy matters in the National Security Council—for which they will have practiced together in mock sessions at the war colleges.

All of this education produces urbane senior officers who can mesh easily with their opposite numbers in the military and other agencies. But it fails to redress many officers' lack of any specific expertise. Very few can write an acceptable press release or pamphlet, tract, book, or even a speech; produce a film, radio or TV broadcast, or tape; operate a library; conduct or orchestrate a multimedia tactical campaign to promote a key news or policy item to the population of a foreign community. Yet agency officers are put in charge of these specialties and are counted on by ambassadors and (rarely) the president and secretary of state to advise on whether an action or policy by our government will "sell" overseas. Experts in one or more facets of media can usually learn to manage headquarters offices or overseas posts if they possess or can pick up administrative capabilities. But a generalist who has never achieved excellence on any subject will probably never be more than a mediocre manager in the USIA, even for the cultural exchange division which might appear to require only the attention of a responsible adult.

Promotion results from the perusal of personal records by a board of USIA, State, and public members and the ranking of all officers in each class. Those at the top are usually recommended for promotion; those at the bottom can find themselves selected out. What criteria do promotion boards look for? Intelligence, industriousness, managerial ability, language facility, and related factors are considered. But performance ratings do not indicate whether the officer has demonstrated a knack for getting across ideas to foreigners; nowhere can the board learn if the officer knows how to inform and/or influence foreign populations. About the best a rating officer does in this respect is to mention that an officer is good at "personal contact."

Why do these ratings omit judging whether the ratee is a persuasive communicator when the mission of the agency is to inform and promote? One reason is the nagging nervousness about admitting that our propaganda agency is that. Another is the difficulty of expressing and assessing this kind of ability. It's a very elusive quality, particularly if the rating officer doesn't know what to look for. "There is no formula for culture, no rule for ideas, no manual to guide the delicate interplay between one of our officers and the people he is trying to interest and influence,"[5] said former Director Carl T. Rowan. Edward R. Murrow clarified the issue by saying "no switch clicks, no light goes on when a man changes his mind."[6] So how can a rating board know if an officer caused that mental process in the foreigner? Not easily.

Nevertheless, as in the business sphere, the officer abroad is the last stop in USIA's portage of ideas and information from America to the world. In commerce, the advertising, merchandising, and wholesaling come to naught if the retailer can't get the product across the last three feet of his sales counter to the customer. Similarly, USIA's numerous products on paper, film, or tape don't reach the foreigner we want to influence without the final vital thrust by the officer on duty in that country.

What about firing underachievers? Again, how does the

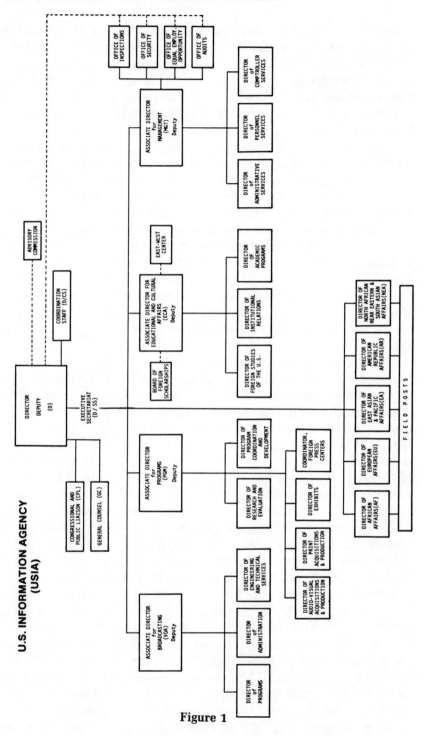

Figure 1

agency pinpoint an individual's worth in more than just personal conduct or slickness in impressing his superior? Deputy Director Henry Loomis profited by the selection-out process early in the Nixon administration to streamline the quality of personnel. In fact within a year or so after the act was passed, the agency underwent four reductions in force. Yet neither he nor the directors since 1967 used to law to improve the hiring, training, or promoting of good officers. These key elements of maintaining a career service for public diplomacy have been relatively neglected.

Nevertheless, officers remain the small elite, about 10 percent of the total agency. The agency has slowly dwindled from the twelve thousand employees on its rolls in 1953, a remarkable record for the federal government whose agencies often grow fatter and more ungainly with age. The final chapter will explain how USIA can grow leaner and more muscular still.

In Washington the nonofficers do the technical and clerical work. There are also the political appointees who usually number only a dozen or so at most. They include the very top management plus a few of the special assistants and associate directors. Director Wick has met criticism for bringing in more, both in Washington and overseas.

Technicians handle the VOA's radio, motion picture, and TV equipment in this country and, in the case of the VOA, its transmitter and relay facilities abroad.

Additionally, the agency has a stable of reporters who file stories for the VOA and the wireless file. Then there are magazine, pamphlet, and feature writers. Add radio, TV, and motion picture producers and directors, as well as radio news and commentary broadcasters. Finally, there are an occasional singer or poet, exhibits experts, cartoonists and other artists, research specialists, translators, lawyers, and accountants. Also there are printing professionals that operate USIA's regional production centers in Mexico City and Manila. All of the above are civil service employees. They are vital to USIA's mission.

Taken as a whole, the agency's staffers are livelier and more diverse and imaginative than most bureaucrats. The nature of their mission is doubtless responsible. They may affect attitudes and decisions all over the globe; their agency can be a force for peace among nations—that's heady motivation.

As one recruitment pamphlet explained: "[the agency is] charged with encouraging a broad exchange of ideas between

Americans and people of other countries so that each side better understands the other's policies and intentions and the culture and institutions. . . ."7 This approach may tempt idealistic Americans to serve USIA. The pamphlet should have added that the agency needs persuasive communicators.

Businessmen know that a firm's personnel can be an asset that doesn't appear on the balance sheet. The same holds true of the sometimes brilliant, often dedicated, people in USIA.

ENDNOTES

1. Edward R. Murrow, interview with the author, March 1962.
2. "Time for USIA to Turn Pro," article by author for *Foreign Service Journal*, July 1966.
3. Leonard H. Marks, interview with author, October 1981.
4. *Ibid*.
5. From USIA booklet of Carl Rowan's quotes, 1965.
6. Statement in agency press release by Edward R. Murrow, August 1962
7. 1980 USIA recruitment pamphlet.

CHAPTER 5

Products

USIA SPENDS CLOSE TO A BILLION DOLLARS annually to export messages to foreigners. These go forth in such numerous forms as magazines, pamphlets, photo-text features, radio tapes and videotapes, books, and exhibits. The agency calls these products the slow media, in comparison with the three fast media: the Voice of America with its hour-by-hour signals to five continents, the live TV broadcasts of Worldnet and the wireless file with its daily budget of news and features teletyped to USIA posts in one hundred twenty-five countries.

USIA's total output must be carefully selected and prepared, for it pales in size before the never-ending Niagara of nonofficial information about America that goes abroad from the private sector with no nudge from or reference to USIA. It begins with the latest happenings transmitted by a wire service like Associated Press or United Press International as well as by their counterparts, Reuters, Agence France Presse, and Tass. It also includes millions of personal and business telephone calls daily via satellite and undersea cable; telegrams, mailgrams (to Canada only), books; intelligence data ghosted out by spies; reports by foreign embassies dispatched by diplomatic pouch; stories by foreign journalists and other writers; political and economic assessments sent home by foreign business representatives; motion pictures, television and radio tapes and cassettes sold overseas; scientific papers and translations of American books (a wide enough choice exists among the more than forty thousand titles printed every year).

Even the U.S. government competes with USIA for the eye

and ear of alien populations. The Department of Defense's Armed Forces Radio and Television Services beam programs to its military personnel on guard in twenty countries. A shadow audience of many million citizens in those countries listens in to the news and entertainment intended for our GIs.

The semiofficial Radio Free Europe and Radio Liberty broadcast to iron curtain countries and the Soviet Union respectively. Although these networks are replaying accounts of happenings and pronouncements from the nations they broadcast to, they are American stations and therefore affect attitudes toward the United States.

Finally, personal contacts add countless more impressions about America on the consciousness of foreigners. The list is long: tourists from the United States—over four million annually, not counting those going to Canada; students, both American and foreign (there is a constant average of one hundred forty thousand studying in American schools); Americans on business or professional tasks; American military men and women stationed abroad; religious missionaries; and members of charitable organizations like HOPE, CARE, IVS (International Volunteer Service), and CARITAS, the Catholic relief service. These persons travel, write, talk, and otherwise express their views and knowledge of America to people everywhere.

Can we characterize these untold trillions of individual thoughts spread about the United States as good or bad? The only measurable indication registers "good," for the total of emigrants to the United States exceeds those of all other nations. Annual immigration averaged over four hundred forty thousand from 1974–79.[1] No other nation comes close to this figure. Presumably these foreigners still want the personal freedoms and economic opportunity they have sought here since the founding of the republic.

Whatever the reactions may be, America's open society spews forth information about itself as if from myriad firehoses turned on full blast at the rest of the world. Why does USIA bother to point its tiny stream of words and pictures at the same audiences? One answer is that the lion's share of non-USIA outpouring goes to the two dozen or so industrialized nations. Far less attention is paid to the Third World. This is why both Western and Communist propaganda focuses on Third World nations. They are relatively less educated and knowledgeable than other nations, often not yet married to either the Soviet or non-Communist alliances, and therefore worth wooing.

A second answer is that USIA fashions its slow media materials for opinion-molders or other targeted groups in each country. The agency operates on the principle that, when a politician, college professor, newspaper editor, or columnist reads a speech, pamphlet, or other message that a USIS minion has steered into his hand and he agrees with the contents, he will then speak or write about it to his countrymen. His credibility is bound to exceed that of USIA or any other foreign source of facts or attitudes. When this sequence occurs, then USIA has proved its worth.

USIA Washington creates or collects a variety of products and ships them to its overseas posts for this purpose. Simply put, they range from publications and press kits to films, radio tapes, videotapes, and books.

By any measure, USIA has grown into a formidable publishing company. Take magazines, for example. It produces and distributes 10 of them and some commercial bulletins in 20 languages. The articles consist largely of reprints from the best American periodicals. Each is created by a separate staff at USIA headquarters. Most are printed at regional plants in Manila and Mexico City, and a few are printed at USIA's biggest overseas posts. Using the euphemism of private publishers, USIA's magazines may be said to have "controlled circulations." This means they are giveaways; all except for the Russian language monthly, *America Illustrated*, which sells exactly 62,000 copies in 80 Soviet cities at 50 kopeks each. We have agreed with the Soviets to a reciprocal distribution in the United States at $1.25 per copy of their English language magazine, *Soviet Life*. Barely 62,000 Americans buy *Soviet Life* each month. *Soviet Life's* newsstand sales are sticky, and its direct mail campaign for subscriptions doesn't do much better. Otherwise *America Illustrated* would be allowed a far higher circulation in the U.S.S.R. Each new issue disappears faster than rain in the desert, and the pass-along readership approaches a half dozen per copy.

America Illustrated has for a generation been the most notable of USIA's general magazines. Its contents are governed by the U.S. embassy's country plan for the Soviet Union, which describes our policy aims in that nation. Each issue also carries variations and development of five worldwide themes which USIA reflects in all its media output: economics and trade; political and social processes in the United States; arts and humanities; science and technology; communications and media.

To economize, USIA reduced *America Illustrated* from *Life* magazine style and size to the dimensions of *Time,* but kept *Life's* style without advertising. A poll recently asked readers to give their reactions on a postcard inserted in each copy. Those who sent postcards, and the Soviet government insisted they pay the postage, were given six prints of well-known American paintings. More than two thousand replied, a substantial return rate as polls go. They overwhelmingly endorsed the kind of format and stories in *America Illustrated.* This is nice news, though it doesn't easily translate into how many minds the magazine changes or how many new friends it makes for America. Still, the magazine's amazing popularity endures, month after month. The agency claims that long queues form at kiosks when the latest issue arrives and even longer queues at agency exhibits when rumors say that *America Illustrated* will be handed out free, first come, first served. The agency reports that an American embassy employee got work done on his bathroom by promising the plumber a copy and that copies on public display were thumbed through so much that they became double and triple their usual thickness, necessitating heavier coated paper and more and thicker binding staples than usual for a magazine of its size.[2]

Other principal publications originating in Washington are *Topic,* produced six times a year in English and French for sub-Sahara Africa; *Dialogue,* a quarterly concerning American culture and ideas in French and Spanish, with additional language versions published by field posts; *Economic Impact,* a quarterly in English and Spanish; *Problems of Communism,* an intellectual bimonthly in English which has enjoyed a thirty-year span of popularity among Sovietologists in most major countries. It is now available to Americans as well, through the Government Printing Office by special congressional action. Pamphlets, leaflets, printed exhibits, and posters are also shipped to USIA posts in more than one hundred countries. USIA furnishes all these materials overseas free to carefully culled lists of foreign citizens in key "target" categories.

USIA's continuous press service from Washington mails features, byline articles, reprints from American publications, and photographs to all posts. These materials serve as background for U.S. mission personnel abroad, for distribution to foreign opinion leaders, and for broadcast and print media. An ancient and modern example of the latter would be the "wall newspapers" in China. These large broadsides carry illustrated news and features stories. They are pasted on retaining walls, sides of buildings, or any fencelike structure near human traffic for passersby on the city sidewalks. They are reminiscent of an advertising device prevalent in the United States of the 1920s and 1930s. This was usually a two-foot-square frame identified as the offering of some purveyor of goods or services. Each week the advertiser would place in it some unique news photo, such as a car wreck, Lindbergh landing in Paris, a bathing beauty in Atlantic City, or President Coolidge giving a rare smile in the Oval Office.

USIA also delivers the wireless file five days a week. This radioteletype network sends five regional transmissions of policy statements and interpretive materials to one hundred fifty-nine USIA branches abroad. Each regional transmission of the wireless file averages twelve thousand to sixteen thousand words in English. There are also Spanish, French, and Arabic language variations.[3]

The wireless file takes shape under conditions that resemble any daily newspaper. USIA's press people read stories from their own reporters, several top dailies of the United States, and the AP and UPI wire services (whose receivers are rented by the agency), as well as official press releases and statements from the White House, State Department, and other parts of the executive branch. From this vast batch of information, five or six journalists select and rewrite items for the wireless file. They sit before their typewriters at a circular table open at one end, called the central desk. At the open end, known as the "slot," one person edits what the others compose, and a copy clerk takes the final product to the teletype operator nearby for transmission overseas and to the newsroom of VOA to check facts. Another copy goes to a battery of translators for the language versions.

The wireless file is the single most important, complete, dependable, and verifiable pipeline of information between USIA Washington and its field offices. The wireless file sets the record straight when there is a crisis to explain, an accomplishment to tout, an enemy propaganda attack to refute, or extra dimensions needed on a personality, event, or the character and customs of the United States. It is the irreducible minimum to which USIA can be shrunk for budgetary or other demands and still remain a useful arm of America overseas.

USIA's next most vital component is the Voice of America; indeed, its staff and director would challenge any claim that the wireless file could rival it. Details on VOA appear in chapter 7.

USIA has set up what amount to mini-overseas branches in both Washington and New York to offer its products and assistance to foreign correspondents covering the United Nations and the U.S. government and any other event in this country. For example, the centers frequently organize special trips to watch a space shot at Cape Canaveral or observe a U.S. Navy carrier. Representatives from media giants tend to bypass this service, for they can find their own means for covering, writing, and transmitting stories. Still, the centers often bring in a VIP speaker from either the government or private sector; and these occasions draw not only the impecunious foreign journalists but the rich ones as well.

USIA's film and television service both acquires and produces videotape programs and films for distribution through its posts. The agency is doing its limited best to exploit opportunities in these two media.

Hollywood no longer plays god for the moviegoers of the world. A decade ago, only 10 percent of the thirty-five hundred commercial films made worldwide came from America. The trend is worsening. Today, censorship and protectionist legislation obstruct American film exports. A few blockbusters like *Jaws* and *The Godfather* won enormous popularity, and they alone made up half of the total foreign sales of American films during their heydays.

As to television program exports, they amount to less dollar value than films. But ". . . their overall impact may be greater, given the greater frequency of audience exposure. Over a quarter of the world's population watches TV daily on 300 million sets. Usually their viewing diet includes American lightweight comedies or drama."[4]

Television now saturates the globe. Virtually every country enjoys the medium, though it is seldom free from control by the state. In Asia and Africa all networks are government run, except in the Philippines, Australia, New Zealand, and Japan. In the Soviet Union and its satellites, television has become the latest propaganda instrument of autocratic regimes. In Latin America, every nation has a government network or a private "tame;" one which doesn't resist the ruling administration. In Europe, every government operates at least one national network; Luxembourg broadcasts all over Europe.

There is now a trend, however, toward one or more commercial networks in each country. Italy has literally scores of stations, many of which were formerly illegal "private" units. They have now all been ruled legitimate pursuant to a recent supreme court decision against the government monopoly.

This is the confused foreign television market USIA tries to penetrate with its TV and film output. In 1980 the agency created over seventy videotape programs in its own studios, and purchased many more copies of news-oriented shows from the U.S. broadcast networks.

USIA produces fewer than twenty films in all categories each year, but it acquires more than two hundred films and videotapes from private U.S. sources. USIA screens films for audiences overseas and sometimes distributes them also through foreign media and commercial theaters.

Additionally, USIA provides foreign TV stations with news clips of events in the United States, as well as with special film coverages. USIA's efforts are predictable, but the acceptability of its materials, of course, is always speculative. While comparative figures are hard to come by, it may be that USIA achieves the best penetration of foreign TV networks by being generous with its facilities in Washington, both human and technical. Agency personnel often help foreign TV correspondents get news clips from various American sources and allow them to use USIA's studios free of charge to compose broadcasts for their home audiences. Programs transmitted under these circumstances are more likely to be aired than products identified with USIA. Furthermore, USIA people have the right to hope that these correspondents are more apt to present a fair and favorable picture of America when they are enjoying our aid and equipment. Since 1983 Director Charles Wick has personally organized and launched a new series of live programs called Worldnet. Described in chapter 17, Worldnet has brought USIA into the mainstream of international TV broadcasting.

Since World War II, books have been the agency's most widely used staple. In the 1940s and early 1950s, they became a burning political issue. After the book-burning Nazis were defeated, the agency set up libraries in Germany to emphasize the intellectual freedom of democracy. They were called

"Amerika Haus" and grew to be a favorite of the dictator-weary people. Then our own neo-Nazi Senator Joseph McCarthy sent his amateur sleuths David Schine and Roy Cohn to Europe. There they ferreted about USIS libraries, including an Amerika Haus, for Communist subversive books they alleged were on the shelves. To appease McCarthy the agency repeatedly revised its criteria for selecting books to be shipped from Washington to the libraries.

In Sydney, Australia, the USIS library officer watched these directives with growing alarm. Finally, when he saw the latest set of instructions on what books were sanitary, he removed the books that had just been labeled offensive and ceremonially set fire to them on the street in front of his library. News media around the world had a field day with the story. This offbeat gesture expressed the disgust felt not only by other agency staffers and foreigners but increasingly by the American public. Their antipathy helped spur Congress to rid itself of McCarthy's sinister behavior.

Shortly after the Senate condemned McCarthy, I was hired and was being conducted through the USIA. When my guide brought me to the information center service, now called the Office of Cultural Centers and Resources, I was curious to see how the McCarthy furor had affected people who screened books for our overseas libraries. There were several rooms in a row where readers did this task. Entering the first one, I saw a single desk piled high with books. Two small shoeless feet were tucked motionless among them. My eye traveled from the feet up the potato-shaped body to the old lady's gentle face that gazed with closed lids at an open volume on her lap. After witnessing an identical scene in the next two offices, I said to my guide, "I guess they're a little tired from all the trauma." The guide nodded sheepishly. The whole agency showed its fatigue in those days.

Since then the agency has awakened to its book opportunities. USIA now maintains and/or supports libraries in American centers, reading rooms, and binational centers in 88 countries. The libraries display about 1.6 million books and 22,000 periodical subscriptions, which are used by 9 million visitors annually. The agency focuses on materials that will enable foreigners to learn about the United States, the American people, and U.S. history and culture.

In the mid-1950s, USIA experimented with encouraging or underwriting publishers to produce books that would strengthen its program. Louis Fanget conceived the arrangements with publishers, and they continued until Congress eventually intervened because USIA was disseminating its own books, in effect, without publicly acknowledging it was doing so.

Fanget and his aides, Donald McNeill and William W. Warner (later a Pulitzer prize-winning author), followed a regular procedure. For example, they would think of a book that could explain what the Soviets had done to hurt the freedom of its people; then they would offer Frederick Praeger or other publishers an advance to commission an author and publish his work for foreign markets, even if the topic would not normally sell abroad. USIA would let its branch officers choose titles they could usefully give away as part of their country campaign.

Thousands of books from Praeger and Franklin Press and other publishers flowed into dozens of countries. There they were either donated by the USIA posts or, in some cases, sold through local retailers. Field officers liked these results and admired the fact that a government agency could stimulate the appearance of so many good books. Vienna-born Frederick Praeger's enterprise and energy contributed to the program's success as did the willingness of Fanget, McNeill, and Warner to slash red tape.

However, in retrospect, Praeger eyes the program with slightly less enthusiasm. He recalls that USIA had a tendency to "discover unspent money for the current fiscal year, and they would call me to try to spend it before the appropriation ran out. A poor way to do things. . . ."[5]

Louis Fanget grew disappointed too. He testified in 1961 before the House Subcommittee on Foreign Affairs under John Rooney that the quality of the book donations program was uniformly deficient because the budget was too small. We would spend peanuts on our vital book program, he said, in the days when the Soviets at parties would offer caviar and champagne.

"The agency never had clout in Washington," explains Warner, "especially with Congress. Therefore the program was chronically starved for funds. Occasionally we could buy two or three thousand copies of anti-Communist books and offer them to our field officers. We would guarantee Fred Praeger a large advance order, to assure publication plus adequate quantities for overseas markets, along with foreign language rights."[6]

In one case, Warner recalls that "the CIA helped us out with funds for a projected anthology on worldwide Communist strategy and tactics. The money was funneled through *The New Leader*, an anti-Communist monthly organ of the American Socialist Party." Warner adds that *The New Leader* was worth CIA's support since it was well regarded by Socialists throughout the developing Third World.[7]

USIA's present books support program has evolved from its days of gray propaganda (the term used when the name of the originating agency does not appear on its products) to a very busy "white" (totally overt) program. The agency now assists American and foreign publishers in turning out an average of three million copies a year of full-length trade books, textbooks, adaptations, condensations, and serializations in English and twenty-five other languages.

The agency also collaborates in a major way to boost the U.S. publishing industry's exports. It creates and implements promotional campaigns, including international book exhibits, to encourage the use of American books abroad.

Recently, there was some talk about reviving the information media guarantee (IMG) program which began as part of the Marshall Plan and lasted into the early 1960s. The IMG was a bureaucratic device that allowed countries with a foreign exchange shortage to buy American books and other information materials, including motion pictures, maps, and magazines, and to pay in their local currency. The local funds that built up from this source belonged to the United States; however, they were tapped for spending on scientific, cultural, and educational projects which the United States and the host country could agree on. IMG achieved its greatest success per capita in Israel where a reservoir of some $6 million accumulated before any of it was spent. Robert M. Beers, IMG's outstanding manager for many years, reminds us it will not recommence, since the foreign exchange imbalances no longer exist.

USIA's exhibits used to appear only occasionally and then were often criticized for not meeting professional standards. There were some outstanding large traveling exhibits such as "Atoms for Peace," which drew thousands to it during the late 1950s. It proved unexpectedly fortuitous in Israel when the 1956 Four-Day War caused the U.S. embassy to send all but a few to safe havens in Rome and Athens. The U.S. Air Force planes waiting to transport the exhibit to its next engagement were countermanded to remove the fleeing diplomats and their families. We who stayed watched with mixed feelings when those planes left.

Now USIA sustains a heavy production schedule of thirteen major exhibits a year, including solo exhibitions and participation in international trade fairs and special international promotions. Public exposure often exceeds a half million at solo events. Itinerant tours of major shows have sometimes provided the only vehicle for presenting Americans to the provincial cities of Eastern, iron-curtained Europe. USIA also circulates about seventy-five smaller exhibits through the posts during an average year.

How many agency products should a post have for maximum strength? What if budget were no object, and the public affairs officer could order anything he could imagine for his country program? Would he ask for five-, ten-, or a hundredfold what the agency allows him at present? The answer is as various as the target groups in each country, what is brewing in the political cauldron, the size and quality of the national communications infrastructure, and most of all how ingenious the officer and his team are in achieving country objectives.

A USIS post differs from a commercial marketing organization in the same way a guerrilla force differs from a fully equipped, marching army. The more a post can live off the existing channels of information and not infuse them with USIS brand-name products, the more penetration of public attitudes the post may accomplish. The public affairs officer should try to transfer program facts, logic, and policy into the minds of editors, leaders, teachers, writers, artists, and politicians. If one or more of these individuals express such thoughts as their own in books, articles, lectures, exhibits, films, and electronic tapes, the results may be more useful than any USIS-packaged material, however grand and expensive.

ENDNOTES

1. *The World Almanac and Book of Facts; Providence Journal Bulletin,* 1975.

2. Tony Bowman, deputy editor of *America Illustrated*, draft for agency booklet, 1971.
3. From USICA Fact Sheet, May 1981.
4. *Ibid.*
5. Frederick A. Praeger, interview with author, May 1981.
6. William Warner, interview with author, May 1981.
7. *Ibid.*

SHORT DESCRIPTION OF AGENCY PUBLICATIONS

Dialogue
A quarterly intellectual journal which presents a wide choice of articles drawn from U.S. publications and is designed to appeal to a worldwide audience with a discriminating interest in ideas, social problems, literature, and art. The magazine features high-quality color artwork and photography on approximately half of its pages. It is circulated in some seventeen languages.

Economic Impact
A quarterly in two language editions—English and Spanish. Its primary emphasis is on explaining the U.S. economy. Its second major concern is U.S. policies and trends that affect world economic developments. Articles include reprints from commercial journals and magazines, reports, conferences, and features commissioned from economic authorities.

Problems of Communism
A bimonthly journal of original commissioned articles by leading specialists in the current affairs of the Soviet Union, the People's Republic of China, and related states and political movements. Circulated overseas through USIA posts and in the United States (with special legislative authority).

English Teaching Forum
A professional quarterly edited for a worldwide audience of English teachers, administrators, and education officials. It contains original articles by American and foreign authorities. *Forum* is regarded as

the leading professional journal on the teaching of English as a foreign language. In 1979, Congress passed legislation authorizing distribution in the United States.

Topic
The agency magazine for sub-Saharan Africa, published six times a year in English and French. The magazine is used by forty posts in sub-Saharan Africa and by several in North Africa, Europe, and Latin America. Distribution by USIA posts is free to selected audiences in positions of responsibility in their respective countries. *Topic* explains U.S. policy positions, highlights achievements of American society, and underlines the continuing American support of African economic and social development.

Al-Majal
A monthly in Arabic, published in Tunis and distributed to selected addressees in seventeen Arab countries. *Al-Majal* features articles on development and technology transfer, economic subjects, and U.S. society, particularly as they relate to U.S.-Middle East relations. It frequently carries texts on U.S. policy positions regarding the area.

America Illustrated
Published in Russian and distributed monthly in the Soviet Union under an exchange agreement. Most of the copies are sold at kiosks and through subscriptions. The American embassy in Moscow also distributes copies. Its contents, with high-quality color illustrations, include articles on American foreign policy, life, culture, and institutions.

Span
A monthly magazine edited and published by USIA New Delhi for India. Distribution includes post-selected readers, paid subscriptions, and newsstand sales. Content consists of commissioned articles by Americans and Indians, staff-written stories, and reprints from U.S. magazines on current affairs, policy positions, bilateral relations, and Americana, all of them closely related to post objectives. *Span* has been a frequent winner of Indian awards for magazine excellence.

Trends
A Japanese-language bimonthly, distributed free to members of Japanese cultural, intellectual, and professional leadership groups. The editors choose content to interest a select Japanese audience in themes important to post objectives, including U.S. perspectives and policies on bilateral security and economic relationships. Some articles on American arts are written by Japanese critics and academics. Some are related to important visitors or special USIA events. The magazine has won Japanese awards for graphics and content.

Interlink
Published by USIA Lagos for Nigeria. Copies are distributed free to

selected audiences. Contents concentrate on U.S.-Nigerian relations, leaving broader subjects to *Topic*. Local material is supplemented with articles commissioned or acquired from U.S. private-sector house organs.

Trade USA

Published by RSC Manila and distributed in East and Southeast Asian countries, and its Spanish-language counterpart *Vocera Comercial*, published by RSC Mexico and distributed in Latin America. Both are produced in cooperation with the Department of Commerce in support of U.S. trade opportunities abroad.

Pamphlets

The agency produces a sizeable number of pamphlets and leaflets each year, in several language versions, discussing and illustrating various aspects of American society, history, institutions, international relationships, and policy positions. Stock items include the *Outline Series* of American government, history, geography, and economics; *Facts About America; A Handbook for Foreign Students; This Is America*. Other pamphlets, topical and short-lived in nature and published in response to posts' program needs, treat current major issues of international concern, worldwide agency themes, and special events (such as presidential visits) of importance to particular countries.

CHAPTER 6

The Fast Guidance Man

ALL WASHINGTON-GENERATED PRODUCTS OF USIA except books must faithfully reflect foreign policy. Each item, each story, each commentary must leave the agency accurately keyed to American policies they are designed to explain and promote. Policy is not just an additive; it also controls which stories will be carried, which omitted, and what elements will be stressed. A remarkable bureaucrat called the Fast Guidance Man sparks the entire process of inculcating policy into USIA's outbound products. Dozens of USIA and State Department staffers collaborate with him.

A typical day in the life of a Fast Guidance Man starts at 7 A.M. when he and his deputy arrive at the agency. He reads the night's cable traffic from embassies while his deputy peruses five newspapers—*Washington Post, New York Times, Wall Street Journal, Christian Science Monitor,* and *Journal of Commerce*—plus the Associated Press wire service, which they both keep an eye on all day to find events or statements which bear on U.S. interests abroad.

8:20 A.M.—He calls the State Department division of public affairs where a half dozen people have already scanned newspapers and wire services. They tell him what items they will ask State's geographic area offices for guidance on. He tells them what significant findings he has made in the cable traffic.

8:30 A.M.—The Fast Guidance Man meets with agency policy officers from the media geographic area and media divisions—TV, motion pictures, wireless file, and research. The Voice of America plugs in via conference telephone. VOA initiates the discussion by reporting which commentary and news analyses it will run. The day I wrote this, USIA featured Assistant Secretary of State for Africa, Chester Crocker. He had delivered a speech to the American Legion in Hawaii, giving what was the first policy statement on Africa by the Reagan administration in months.

The Fast Guidance Man mentions which half dozen or so of the fifty to one hundred telegrams he's seen are more significant; he then adds items that State has mentioned. It is then agreed by all that a background briefing by State's deputy assistant secretary for the Near East and South Asia is needed to share information on the Israeli prime minister's upcoming visit. This will enable the VOA to avoid being led astray by comments it may have seen in the press.

9:00 A.M.—Now the Fast Guidance Man briefs his supervisor, the associate director for press and publications, and the agency counselor (a new position created by Charles Wick) on what he has learned to date. He also gives these two a copy of the daily media reaction report which derives from cables from fifteen to twenty major U.S. embassies. Copies of this also go to three hundred senior government officials, beginning with the president, vice-president, secretary of state, secretary of defense, NSC advisor, etc. This report centers on bilateral and international issues of key importance which are covered in the foreign newspapers and broadcasts.

9:15 A.M.—The Fast Guidance Man briefs the director, deputy director, five associate directors, and four area directors on the principal developments so far. Since State hasn't made any new policy, he only suggests what may be coming later in the day.

11:00 A.M. to noon—The spokesman of the State Department holds a meeting at which his guidance book is reviewed—there is one copy for him and one for the Fast Guidance Man. It is typed in question-and-answer form and represents the guidance which the area people have produced on the developments of the day raised earlier by public affairs people and the Fast Guidance Man. Typical questions are: What does the department say about the bombing in Iran which killed the president and prime minister? The spokesman examines everything he wants amplified or clarified in the book, plus any questions he may have. As the meeting progresses, the Fast Guidance Man updates his copy of the book.

Noon—State's spokesman briefs the press. He may start with an announcement if he has one. For example, he has just stated our official protest made to the Soviet ambassador when a Soviet warship purposely collided with one of ours in the Black Sea. He coordinates details of this announcement with the White House and Department of Defense spokesmen in order to keep confusion out, even in the nuances.

After his briefing, the spokeman's immediate staff and the Fast Guidance Man conduct postmortems in which adjustments are made to the spokesman's book. Then a corrected copy is xeroxed for the White House and the Fast Guidance Man.

2:30 P.M.—He meets with the same group as at 8:30 A.M., this time with the VOA represented in person. Each participant gets a copy of the spokeman's book. Most have heard the noon briefing on the Monitrone (one needs only to call a given number and listen to the meeting live over the telephone). The Fast Guidance Man gives highlights for those who haven't heard. He goes over specifically those guidances which were used by the State Department spokesman. VOA can only quote what the spokesman actually answered, but the wireless file and other media are permitted to draw freely from any guidance in the spokeman's book.

3:00 P.M.—The Fast Guidance Man eats a sandwich. Then he and his deputy read wire services and the wireless file plus the cable traffic for the balance of the day. The staffers at the agency's twenty-four-hour continuous operations center keep their eyes peeled for significant developments at any time and mark them for special attention of the Fast Guidance Man.

Over the weekend the Fast Guidance Man or his deputy spends four or five hours checking incoming material to avoid a pileup on Monday mornings.

The present Fast Guidance Man, Linder Allen, says relations between State and USIA are quite collegial throughout these complicated dealings and that State even takes some agency guidance along the way.

CHAPTER 7

The Voice of America

ON A DUSTY SIDEWALK IN BEIJING, an American wire service reporter noticed a relaxed Chinese youth behind dozens of people jostling each other to read the latest wall newspaper.

"How come you're so patient," asked the American in fluent Mandarin, "when everyone else is pushing?"

"I'm in no hurry," replied the youth. "I've already heard the news on the Voice of America."[1]

Despite the tiresome chant of some journalists and politicians that the U.S. is losing the "battle for the minds of men," despite those who whine that the Voice of America is a mere mumble among the sonorous tones of our adversaries and competitors for airwave supremacy, or perhaps because of them, the VOA can now point to a worldwide audience of tremendous scope.

Many listeners resemble that young Chinese, though available surveys still omit China. USIA research defines VOA listeners as adults who listen to its programs on a regular basis. This means individuals over fifteen years of age who tune in once a week or more. The profile of these adherents indicates they are educated, young, politically curious, and concerned for the world around them.

VOA surveys suggest that its listeners are heavy users of media and often examine a variety of sources to compare them for veracity. They regularly select VOA because they deem its coverage to be timely, accurate, and relevant. USIA concedes that it is not possible to provide a scientifically sound tally of VOA's worldwide audience, but in January 1981 it published

Figure 2
VOA Listenership Worldwide

REGION	ADULTS WHO LISTEN TO VOA AT LEAST ONCE A WEEK (IN MILLIONS)
West Europe/Canada	1.8
East Europe	31.2
USSR	31.8
Near East/North Africa	6.1
South Asia	17.6
Sub-Sahara Africa	14.9
East Asia/Pacific	3.9
China	15.8
American Republics	4.7
Caribbean	1.8
ROUNDED TOTAL	130 million

estimates from polling data and other "reliable information" which indicated a total of over 66 million listeners.[2] In 1987, the agency revised this total to 130 million,[3] as showed in Fig. 2.

These estimates refer to listenership during an average day; they don't show the expanded audiences resulting from special events and crises. The Apollo 11 broadcasts in worldwide English, for example, reached an estimated 450 million people. That number includes those who received the broadcasts directly and others who heard VOA coverage as relayed or rebroadcast by 1,374 foreign stations and networks, including 868 television stations.[4]

The Voice of America radiates out to millions of human beings over a huge international broadcasting system. It transmits over 1,200 hours of programing per week in English and 43 other languages via short and medium wave. The backbone of its content is news and news analysis interlaced with portrayals of American society, plus popular music, notably jazz. Additionally, the VOA produces and tapes programs of varying lengths which are lent or given to local stations in numerous countries. To get an idea of the volume of tapes acquired and/ or produced at the Voice, consider that there are nearly 90,000 recordings of lasting value filed in archives in Washington.

The Voice is a round-the-clock operation. It broadcasts 24 hours per day, seven days a week, from 27 studios located in Washington, and it relays abroad via transmitters in the United

States and 14 other nations. See maps in Figs. 3 and 4. One hundred twelve active transmitters in the U.S. and overseas generate a total of 25,515 kw. These figures represent large increases since 1980. In budget-trapped Washington today, VOA has led a charmed life, so far.

How does the United States compare to other international broadcasters? In numbers at least, the VOA summary in Fig. 5 gives some idea. These figures do not include anything like a Hooper rating of popularity or respect, not even total audiences enjoyed. Still they are one benchmark against which to measure VOA efforts.

In Fig. 6, thanks to BBC's external service audience research, are listed target areas of international broadcasters. Wired radio sets, which don't exist in this country, are hooked up directly to radio stations, usually government-controlled ones. They are most numerous in Eastern Europe where they provide dictatorships with a ready propaganda conduit to their citizens. This system is costly since cables have to be laid underground or overhead to each receiver.

In 1986 a BBC publication updated these figures as follows: 1,745 billion radios worldwide and 875 million TVs worldwide.

Although BBC predated World War II, the VOA took to the air in response to it, seventy-nine days after Pearl Harbor, February 24, 1942. In German language its broadcast included this statement: "Daily at this time, we shall speak to you about America and the war—the news may be good or bad—we shall tell you the truth." Since then the VOA's program content and treatment have often caused bureaucratic and political turmoil.

At that time, "the master of the airwaves was Nazi propaganda minister Joseph Goebbels. 'News is a weapon of war,' he said. 'Its purpose is to wage a war, not to give information.' The BBC promised all the news—the good and the bad. VOA spoke for a brash, younger America gung ho on a just war."[5] John Houseman, the actor, was the first director of VOA.

From its inception, the VOA's supporters, leaders, and staffers have bickered over its daily recipe. The same controversy has plagued the information agency as a whole, but the issue is sharper concerning the Voice, since it communicates constantly and directly with people all over the globe. Whatever else its freight, the Voice primarily purveys news. How should we phrase the news, news analyses, commentary and

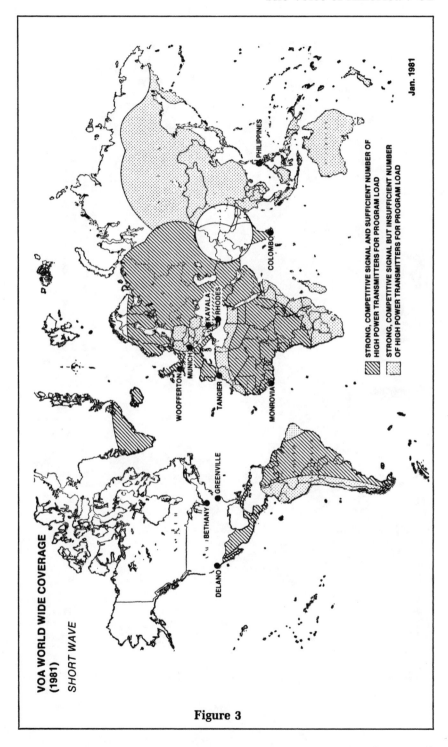

VOA WORLD WIDE COVERAGE (1981)

SHORT WAVE

STRONG, COMPETITIVE SIGNAL AND SUFFICIENT NUMBER OF HIGH POWER TRANSMITTERS FOR PROGRAM LOAD

STRONG, COMPETITIVE SIGNAL BUT INSUFFICIENT NUMBER OF HIGH POWER TRANSMITTERS FOR PROGRAM LOAD

Jan. 1981

Figure 3

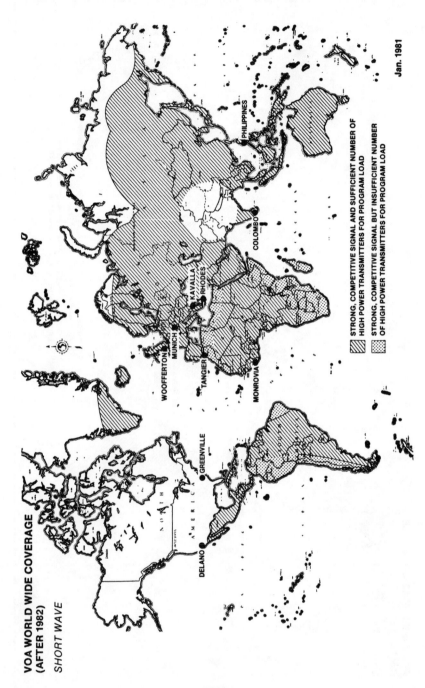

Figure 4

Figure 5
Major International Broadcasters—1986
(More Than 300 Hours Weekly)

BROADCASTER	LANGUAGES	HOURS WEEKLY
1. United States including	48	2368:34
RFE: 9— 635:49 (Radio Free Europe)		
*RFA: 1— 5:00		
RL: 12— 434:00 (Radio Liberty)		
VOA: 42— 1293:45		
2. USSR (all external services)	82	2259:17
3. China (all external services)	43	1411:05
4. Taiwan (Voice of Free China)	17	1098:25
5. West Germany (DW & DLF)	37	821:25
6. Egypt (includes Middle East Radio)	30	820:15
7. United Kingdom (BBC)	36	737:00
8. North Korea	9	534:55
9. Voice of the Andes (religious)	11	499:55
10. India	25	461:25
11. South Korea	11	458:30
12. East Germany	11	452:45
13. Albania	21	448:00
14. Trans World (religious with stations in Bonaire, Guam and Swaziland)	31	412:17
15. Cuba	8	380:20
16. Far East Broadcasting (FEBC) (religious)	21	368:40
17. Australia	9	345:20
18. Iran	13	323:45
19. Nigeria	6	322:00
20. Netherlands	7	316:20
21. Poland	11	319:40

Above information drawn from BBC monitoring schedules.
*Radio Free Afghanistan (RFA), since 1985 (prior data not available).

Figure 6
World Radio and Television Receivers

	POPULATION	RADIO SETS	WIRED RADIO SETS	TELEVISION SETS
Total 1979	4,193,000,000	1,260,400,000	202,500,000	512,800,000
Western Europe	414,000,000	250,000,000	966,000	130,500,000
U.S.S.R. and European Communist Group	377,000,000	116,500,000	78,160,000	102,100,000
Middle East and North Africa	188,000,000	38,600,000	—	10,700,000
Africa (excluding North Africa)	328,000,000	29,500,000	117,000	3,700,000
Asia and the Far East	2,280,000,000	233,500,000	123,266,000	78,500,000
Australia, Pacific, and Oceania	24,000,000	20,700,000	—	6,200,000
North America	242,000,000	476,000,000	—	146,000,000
Latin America	330,000,000	90,900,000	5,000	33,700,000
West Indies	10,000,000	4,700,000	25,000	1,400,000

JUNE 1980

BBC External Service
Audience Research

features? VOA managers must answer this as well as another nagging question: Does the Voice of America speak uniquely for our country? It is *a* voice from America, yet it is not the only voice with all the competitive sounds like Radio Free Europe, Radio Liberty, the Armed Forces Radio and Television Services, (AFRTS)* and Radio Marti (VOA's Cuba program).

When the Voice speaks, should its tone be that of a tribal chieftain, with total self confidence, total wisdom, total decency and truth, offering order, reason and biblical love to its listeners? Or should it be that of the town crier, eager to pass the word on anything or everything that happens, often the object of derision among the townspeople of the world? Should VOA exploit its ability to hopscotch over geographic and political boundaries to make friends and influence people a la Dale Carnegie, like some tailwagging dog? Or should it play the heavy and belabor the Communists incessantly with hard-line propaganda a la Radio Moscow?

If the Voice tried to fill all these roles, which at one time or another it has been tempted to do, it would not be a voice but a Babel. Instead, it has endeavored to pattern its programming and style after the BBC which has always separated factual news presentation from advocacy. The Voice has long fought for the right to deliver news without interference from the agency in Washington and in the field.

For example, in the Congo during 1961 and 1962, the official American line was to discourage support for secessionist Katanga. A Voice reporter did a newscast to highlight the struggle between the central government in Leopoldville and Tshombe's rebel camp in Elisabethville. As head of USIS Congo, I reviewed the correspondent's copy before he voiced it and had him remove a passage that clearly supported Tshombe. This was routine "policy guidance."

Senator Charles H. Percy, former chairman of the Committee on Foreign Relations, explained to me how he corrected this situation:

*In post-World War II Europe AFRTS used the VOA's newscasts. The result was increased credibility among VOA listeners, according to Major General Chester V. Clifton, Jr., U.S.A. (retired), who said that if the U.S. was telling its soldiers the same news, it must be accurate.

Voice of America

OVERSEAS RELAY STATIONS	PRIMARY PROGRAM FEEDS	NO. OF ANTENNAS	TRANSMITTERS MW & SW	TRANSMITTER POWER (KW)	TOTAL POWER KW	AGE YEARS	TARGET AREA/S
Judge Bay, Antigua	Commercial satellite from Washington	1	1 MW	1– 50	50	18	Lesser Antilles down to St. Lucia
Bangkok, Thailand	HF from the Philippines	1	1 MW	1–1000	1000	33	Southeast Asia
Selebi-Phikwe, Botswana	HF from Greenville, Bethany & Liberia	1	1 MW	1– 50	50	5	Northern South Africa and Southern Zimbabwe
Kavala, Greece	Commercial satellite from Washington	23	1 MW	1– 500	500	33	MW–Eastern Europe;
			10 SW	9– 250	2250	15	SW–Central, South and Western USSR; and Eastern Europe
				1– 250	250	15	(Used by Gov't of Greece)
Rhodes, Greece	Commercial satellite from Washington	8	1 MW	1– 500	500	33	Middle East
			2 SW	2– 50	100	23	
Monrovia,	Commercial	27	8 SW	6– 250	1500	22	Sub-Saharan Africa

OVERSEAS RELAY STATIONS	PRIMARY PROGRAM FEEDS	NO. OF ANTENNAS	TRANSMITTERS MW & SW	TRANSMITTER POWER (KW)	TOTAL POWER KW	AGE YEARS	TARGET AREA/S
Liberia	satellite from Washington			2– 50	100	22	
Munich, Germany	Commercial satellite from Washington	17	1 MW	1– 300	300	40	MW–W. Europe; E. Europe (Hungary, Czech, Poland;
			4 SW	4– 100	400	50	SW–West. USSR and Eastern Europe
Poro, Philippines	Commercial satellite from Washington	17	1 MW	1–1000	1000	33	MW–Vietnam
			6 SW	1– 35	385	33	SW–China, SE Asia and East Africa
				2– 100			
				3– 50			
Tinang, Philippines	Commercial satellite from Washington	39	15 SW	3– 50	3150	21	Eastern USSR,
				10– 250		18	China, Southeast
				2– 250		5	Asia, and Eastern South Asia
Quesada, Costa Rica	Shortwave from Greenville	1	1 MW	1– 50	50	18	Northern Costa Rica
Colombo, Sri Lanka	SW from Kavala and Philippines	19	4 SW	2– 35	80	33	India
				1– 10			

OVERSEAS RELAY STATIONS	PRIMARY PROGRAM FEEDS	NO. OF ANTENNAS	TRANSMITTERS MW & SW	TRANSMITTER POWER (KW)	TOTAL POWER KW	AGE YEARS	TARGET AREA/S
				1– 35	35	33	(Used by Gov't of Sri Lanka)
Tangier, Morocco	Commercial satellite from Washington	32	10 SW	3– 100	440	36	Eastern Europe and North Africa
				4– 35		41	
				1– 100	100	36	(Shared with Gov't of Morocco)
				2– 50	100	46	
Punta Gorda, Belize	Shortwave from Greenville	2	2 MW	2– 50	100	2	Northern Regions of Central America
Woofferton, England	Commercial satellite from Washington	37	10 SW	6– 250	1500	23	Western USSR; & Eastern Europe
				4– 300	1200	6	
TOTAL: DOMESTIC AND OVERSEAS		343	10 MW 102 SW		25,515	—	

The biggest problem for VOA in the last decade has been the intrusion of American ambassadors and State Department bureaucrats into the news broadcasting. For a time, VOA couldn't stand up to the pressure and had to take legitimate news items off the air when complaints were lodged. But I took the lead in putting the VOA Charter (first promulgated in the Eisenhower administration as a guideline) into law, and the problem has almost entirely gone away. It was, and is, my feeling that the news has to be honest if VOA is to have credibility with its audience.[6]

In short, Senator Percy made it illegal for the Voice not to adhere to its charter, which reads as follows:

VOA CHARTER

The long-range interests of the United States are served by communicating directly with the people of the world by radio. To be effective, the Voice of America (the Broadcasting Service of the United States Information Agency) must win the attention and respect of listeners. These principles will therefore govern Voice of America (VOA) broadcasts:

(1) VOA will serve as a consistently reliable and authoritative study of news. VOA news will be accurate, objective, and comprehensive.

(2) VOA will represent America, not any single segment of American society, and will therefore present a balanced and comprehensive projection of significant American thought and institutions.

(3) VOA will present the policies of the United States clearly and effectively and will also present responsible discussion and opinion on these policies.

Gerald R. Ford
President of the United States
Signed July 12, 1976
Public Law 94-350

Sponsored by:
Charles H. Percy (R.) Illinois
Bella S. Abzug (D.) New York

The charter's third "principle" offers the one avenue open to those who wish the Voice to "sell" American policy abroad. It says the "VOA will present the policies of the United States clearly and *effectively*"—that is the word which justifies advocacy. To present policies effectively calls for casting them in a favorable light, to persuade foreigners to accept them. VOA is permitted to promote policy; but when the sales pitch is added, it must be identified as commentary. Otherwise, it delivers policy as it evolves through the president, cabinet officials, and other spokesmen.

To help implement the charter, different guidelines were issued to VOA foreign correspondents. Now they perform like journalists, except that they report to the VOA news director. They acquire the news just like every other news hunter. No longer will they have special access to the U.S. embassy or any of its logistical perks like housing, commissary and post exchange facilities, classified documents, or diplomatic passports.

Have these changes bettered the VOA's quality? Program Manager Claude (Cliff) Groce claimed they have led to an acceptability and respectability heretofore only enjoyed by the BBC. In fact, says Groce, informal reports from the field suggest that the VOA has at last begun to overtake the BBC in the minds of listeners as the most preferred wellspring of news.[7]

As usual, no consensus reigns at present on the Voice's mission. A top Reagan diplomat speaks off the record of VOA's dilemma in Latin America. "What's happening," he declaims, "is that Radio Moscow broadcasts more hours than we do and tells the Latinos that the U.S. Americans are no good; that we are racists, economic imperialists, lovers of oligarchy and dictatorship. Then," the diplomat chuckles coldly, "the VOA chimes in with its compulsive drive to maintain credibility by telling the truth. It tells the same audience that has just heard what terrible people we are, that indeed we are terrible and categorically proves it by news stories of racism, strikes, plus repeats of anti-administration columnists and the like. So what does the Latin American peasant think?" the diplomat asks. "He doesn't give a rap for credibility; he's just interested to discover whether it's better to look to the Communists or American-style democracy as the key to his future."

VOA former deputy director, M. William Haratunian, was amused by this tirade:

> One of these days I am going to bring back that "peasant" that everyone talks about and put him under glass. Then I'll ask him

if he really does think we're terrible people for telling the truth about ourselves. I don't think peasants are stupid. They know when they're being snowed.

It is useful to compare our system with the U.S.S.R.'s. People were kept in the dark there for forty-eight hours after Alexei Kosygin died. They learned of his death from VOA, BBC, and other outside news sources. When President Reagan was shot in 1981, VOA went on the air live before we knew the end of the story. So when it came out well, the listener had to believe that Reagan really was okay. . . .

We are an open society and that is our way and to change will reduce our greatest strength.[8]

A veteran VOA broadcaster concedes that the charter, instead of clarifying the radio's assignment, had led to some confusion. One State Department official said that "VOA lives in a world of its own, trying to ignore the State Department, refusing to recognize that it is being perceived abroad as the voice of the U.S. government. . . . At best VOA misleads foreign governments. At worst, it endangers American lives and interests. I am not sure that VOA is worth all the trouble it's causing."[9]

Allegedly, morale is sagging among VOA staffers due to conflicting perceptions about their task. Longtime star newscaster, Lawrence E. (Larry) LeSueur, gives the lie to this charge. Edward R. Murrow hired LeSueur once for CBS in 1939 and again for the VOA in 1963. LeSueur says dryly, "Morale bad? Maybe so, but I haven't noticed anyone quitting."[10]

Former deputy director of the VOA P. Hans "Tom" Tuch describes as well as anyone how the VOA honors its charter without confusing or upsetting either its listeners or U.S. officials concerned about our national interest:

To attract listeners, we offer news, especially where it's not available in other forms. We keep news isolated from other programs and we won't take orders or counsel from anyone. Even someone like Mobutu Sese Seko [president of Zaire], who listens frequently to VOA and tells our ambassador in Kinshasa when he doesn't appreciate something he has heard, is told: We can't change it. This is a news operation and is run as one. The news itself dictates the selection of stories through the expertise of its editors.[11]

In terms that should assuage officials like the diplomat cited above, Tuch explained:

> We insert necessary background information to make the subject clearer. For example, if a strike is announced, we would add that unions have slush funds to support workers during strikes. Otherwise, in the U.S.S.R. listeners might think that American workers will starve. Or if our president declares some town flooded by the Mississippi a disaster area, then this doesn't mean that people are dying like flies and that utter chaos reigns. It only means that some federal assistance is pumped in so the people don't go broke paying for the flood damage themselves. So our writers must be experts in their subjects and the language translation must be exact too.[12]

It is quite possible to write the news factually but not objectively. The print and broadcast media do it sometimes, voluntarily or involuntarily. Take the 1981 air traffic controllers' strike. On several occasions, press interviewers tossed very tough questions at the secretary of transportation and other federal aides. Yet when querying the head of the union, they failed to raise one obvious point: How do you justify your members striking when they have sworn an oath not to? This omission left the distinct impression that such interviewers were siding with the union. On many topics in which the reader or listener is not an expert, the journalist may paint a slanted picture without the audience noticing it. Not so with some officials of the Reagan administration, who have contested the VOA's handling of the news. They believe numerous stories help the enemy and hurt the allies. Some examples are:

- A replay of American media reports that the VOA furnished arms to Afghan rebels. This angered several American embassies and the White House.
- When VOA described the departure of refugees from Vietnam, the American embassy in Manila worried that wrong handling of this topic might unduly encourage Indochinese to flee their homes.
- The embassy in Geneva objected to VOA's describing the Afghan Mujahadeen as "anti-government guerrillas" (because this term appeared to condone the Soviet puppet regime).
- A replay of excerpts from a commercial interview of Soviet spokesman Georgi Arbatov moved the embassy in Moscow to protest his being given air time on VOA.[13]

Like the complaint about broadcasts to Latin America, these incidents may have stemmed simply from a lack of knowledge among new appointees about VOA's function. VOA's house organ, *News Room*, warns that they have "already created a difficult psychological atmosphere which increased the danger of self-censorship, that almost self-conscious tendency to avoid the controversial, to play it safe, to lie low until the controversy blows over."[14]

One wonders if BBC supervisors ever heard such objections from Her Majesty's royal officers. Probably not. Somehow the calm, elegant, factual presentations never cast the United Kingdom in a bad light. They prove it feasible to maintain credibility as a news service without going out of their way to pick aspects of delicate issues that will make British subjects blush at home or diplomats tear their hair abroad.

One wonders, too, how the VOA protected its news output from the persistent mea culpa attitudes that characterized so many American broadcasters, politicians, and self-appointed oracles during the past fifteen years. By adhering to its charter, former Ambassador Edmund Gullion suggested in 1978, "It's just as well that the news is kept independent of policy. Otherwise it might be dominated under the present administration by evangelical or indiscriminate detente mongers."[15]

The VOA is presently well endowed with professional newsmen and women.* In Washington, it includes several dozen writers and a support staff plus a dozen or more correspondents covering the major news areas of the country. Overseas it has centered staff correspondents in the key cities of the world and drawn on foreign stringers (part-time reporters) for supplemental manpower. The danger with the latter is that there is always a trace of doubt about their loyalty to their own govern-

---

*Off and on, the Voice has been directed by stars of national commercial radio, such as John Daly of CBS News and John Chancellor of NBC News. They benefit VOA by bringing in techniques and touches of class learned in the major league of radio. For instance, Chancellor instituted a two-hour block of programming called the Evening Broadcast Service which beamed continuous news, features, and music. Patterned after NBC's Monitor Program, at VOA it was affectionately known as the New Sound. Its raison d'etre was that a listener to any twenty-minute segment could get completely updated on news, commentary, and features being offered that day. This endeavor earned good feedback abroad. Its style reflected Chancellor's axiom "think short and write short."

ments which could adversely affect their contributions to the Voice.

Nevertheless, Claude Groce responded strongly as to whether Americans or foreigners should narrate news, news analyses, and commentary. "It has to be the native immigrant from the country to which each broadcast is beamed, the more recent the better," he insists, "because any American accent at all will take away from the excellence of the program."[16]

BBC adheres to a similar policy. In fact, it normally limits contracts with narrators to five years. After that period the BBC observes that local nuances of accent creep into a foreigner's speech and the receiving audience is bound to spot the difference. Once a language specialist joins the VOA, however, he almost never leaves before retirement.

For years, the Voice has blamed the agency for treating it like a second-class citizen, not only by forcing it to stick to policy, but also for not providing needed language specialists. The Reagan transition team, under former USIA Director Frank Shakespeare, recommended remedial measures. Under Reagan, the VOA requested and the Congress approved a separate personnel office. The VOA wanted to fill hundreds of vacancies, most of them foreign linguists.

The VOA's reputation on the Hill has improved considerably since its early Cold War days. Referring to budget struggles with the Congress, VOA Director Charles W. Thayer recalled that "the Kremlin succeeded where the State Department failed. In . . . a single day in 1949 more than one hundred powerful jamming transmitters went on the air all over Russia trying to drown us out. . . . From then on Congress was more generous. . . ."[17] Congress had once directed that because "our programs to Europe and Latin America were being run incompetently, they should be farmed out in large part to private broadcasters, and they were—to NBC and CBS." Then there was a show produced that referred to the State of Texas as having been "born in sin." Not only Texas but Congress erupted, and Thayer was ordered to testify. He never had to appear since the senators themselves decided to forbid any more parceling out of the government's programming responsibility.[18]

Jamming the Voice has continued intermittently in the Soviet Union. In 1987 the Soviets stopped per an agreement with USIA's Charles Z. Wick. When actually jamming the U.S. network, the U.S.S.R. reportedly spends some $250 million worth of rubles to obstruct the VOA. The Voice has averaged only $80 million to operate worldwide each year. The technique is like heckling a politician's speech—drown him out with a louder sound. Similarly the jammer broadens noise or music on the same frequency with more power when the VOA transmits its program.

The Chinese jammed the Voice for almost thirty years after the 1949 Communist takeover. Then in 1978 the Sino-American rapprochement began to jell, whereupon the People's Republic stopped jamming, first on one frequency and then another, until finally all frequencies were clear. Since then VOA has freely broadcast in Chinese and English. Results have been dramatic. Prior to 1978, VOA promised that anyone who wrote in could have a free English teaching book. About five replies a year reached VOA's Hong Kong address. Then suddenly, requests by the hundreds began to pile up, and the offer had to be rescinded.

When former agency director John Reinhardt[19] visited the People's Republic in 1979, one Chinese official said he thought hundreds of millions of citizens were hearing the Voice. New York Times correspondent V. Fox Butterfield confirmed this impression from Beijing:[20]

But the biggest surprise was that these days, nearly everyone in China, it seems, listens to the Voice of America. Where once a Chinese who tuned to the station could be sent to labor reform camp, now students are ordered by their teachers to listen regularly to practice their English. Prince Norodom Sihanouk, the one-time ruler of Cambodia, startled a press conference in Peking by announcing that he wanted to thank the station for keeping him informed about events in Cambodia during his three years of house arrest. Later, a Chinese official recalled that in 1971, when former Defense Minister Lin Pao died in a mysterious plane crash in Mongolia after trying to assassinate Mao, some senior party leaders who had been purged in the Cultural Revolution learned the news only by listening to the Voice of America in their place of confinement.

The VOA is now busily strengthening its language programs elsewhere as well as in China. It has particularly made an effort in the whole Islamic world, from Indonesia to Nigeria; it has added languages like Bengali, Uzbek, Farsi, Dari for Afghanistan; Swahili and Amharic for Ethiopia. For the Caribbean, it is producing more English programs and transmitting in Spanish to Cuba's Radio Marti.

More and more people will be hearing not only VOA news, commentary, and Americana as the radio service expands into a truly global network. They are also likely to become faithful followers of individuals like Larry LeSueur and his fellow newscasters, Patty Gates and her breakfast show, and Willis Conover, who selected and aired American music via VOA for nearly thirty years. The Voice appears to be nearing its zenith with the clearest tone, most languages, and widest listening audience ever.

VOA staffers also note with approval that USIA's present chief, Charles Wick (whose name gives jokesters the chance to call the Voice "Air Wick"), has managed to institute a healthier relationship between VOA and USIA headquarters. This closer bond worries those who have long plotted VOA's complete independence, but it may present lapses into the disruptions of the past and enable VOA to pursue its charter comfortably into the future. Moving agency headquarters closer to VOA—just across 4th Street, S.W., in Washington—has made life simpler.

The VOA needed better hardware, too. Its transmitters were old, outmoded, and too low powered, and its auxiliary equipment was similarly obsolete. Furthermore, security protection was minimal; with terrorists at large, it needed to be reinforced.

Charles Wick has taken long strides towards physically renovating VOA. See chapter 17.

ENDNOTES

1. Claude Groce, VOA program manager, and others at VOA cite this story from a wire service reporter several years ago; they are unable to agree on his name.

2. Briefing book, office of director, Voice of America, January 1981.
3. VOA briefing book, 1987.
4. VOA briefing book, January 1981.
5. Charles Fenyvesi, "I Hear America Mumbling," *Washington Post Magazine*, July 19, 1981, p. 21.
6. Charles H. Percy, letter to author, April 13, 1981.
7. Claude Groce, interview with author, September 9, 1981.
8. M. William Haratunian, interview with author, September 11, 1981.
9. Fenyvesi, *Washington Post Magazine*, p. 24.
10. Lawrence E. LeSueur, interview with author, September 10, 1981.
11. P. Hans Tuch, interview with author, April 24, 1979.
12. *Ibid.*
13. VOA's newsletter, *News Room*, September 9, 1981.
14. *Ibid.*
15. Edmund A. Gullion, interview with author, 1978.
16. Groce, interview with author.
17. Charles W. Thayer, *Diplomat* (New York: Harper and Brothers, 1959), p. 191.
18. *Ibid.*, p. 190.
19. John Reinhardt, interview with author, 1981.
20. Fox Butterfield, "Inside China—More Than a Perspective Changed," (*New York Times*, Peking, January 21, 1979).

CHAPTER 8

Cultural Interplay

AT THE HEIGHT OF THE COLD WAR, *Porgy and Bess*, Gershwin's classic musical, played in the U.S.S.R. under commercial auspices. Truman Capote went along with the troupe to record their experiences. Two of his recollections reveal what it feels like on the front line of cultural exchange: First, some local reaction in the Leningrad newspaper *Smena*: "It testifies to the high talent of the Negro people. . . . The performance broadens our concept of the art of contemporary America, and familiarizes us with thus far unknown facets of the musical and theatrical life of the United States." Then a comment from one of the cast, "Sure it's nice they write okay things, but who cares? It's not what the Russians think. It's the stuff they're hearing about us back home. That's what counts."[1]

A private entrepreneur organized the *Porgy and Bess* tour with no financial or facilitative support from the State Department. The impressario's invitation for Ambassador Charles E. Bohlen and his wife to attend a performance marked the only contact with U.S. government officials. Yet Capote recalls that both in critical and popular reception *Porgy and Bess* impressed the Soviets most agreeably. Surely, the visit bolstered our national interest.

Americans often travel and expose their talents as artists, actors, and lecturers without government help. Perhaps this is one reason why official cultural and educational programs abroad have lagged behind those of other nations, both friends and adversaries. Why *should* the government try to replace or crowd aside private initiatives that are going well on their own?

In the last century, other governments decided they would stimulate such activities. France began the modern practice of international cultural salesmanship in 1883 when it launched the Alliance Francaise. The Alliance offered enticements to learn more about French culture through books, plays, and teachers of its language. Today, in America alone, France maintains two hundred thirty chapters of the Alliance. Germany followed suit with a section of arts and sciences added to its foreign office in 1896. This led to an exchange of American and German university professors starting in 1905.[2] Great Britain, with its global empire and vast network of trade, didn't feel the need to establish the British Council for Relations with Other Countries until 1935. In 1938 the United States government began its own modest cultural thrust among the Latin American republics, called the Office of Inter-American Affairs, under Nelson Rockefeller in the State Department.

In Washington's annual contest for bigger appropriations, a time-honored move is to cite what the competition is spending. During the 1981 Senate authorization hearings, the agency didn't have to use this ploy. The Foreign Relations Committee itself asked what other countries invest in cultural and information programs. The agency's answers suggest that America's official programs are feebler than they should be:

> It is estimated that the Soviets spend about $700 million for Radio Moscow's foreign service and $200 million for education scholarships to Third World students, academic exchanges, and international visitor programs.
>
> In comparison, USICA spent approximately $88 million for VOA broadcasting and $73 million on exchange activities in fiscal year 1980.
>
> Other major countries' expenditures in 1980, for all of their foreign cultural and informational activities, were as follows: France—$1.06 billion; West Germany—$880 million; United Kingdom—$440 million; Japan—$242 million. . . . The U.S. government spent about $511 million for comparable programs.[3]

The agency agreed with Senator Pell's opening statement that the Soviets spend some $2 billion on cultural and information activities. The agency added that the U.S. government, through its AID and information programs, sponsored only 3,523 students in 1979–80, but "it is important to note that an additional 250,000 foreign students are estimated to be studying in the United States, either on private scholarships or at the expense of their own government."[4] The 1980–81 figure is 311,882.

What the agency failed to mention is the astounding total of nearly one million "purposeful" foreign visitors in one year alone. For example, the General Accounting Office's (GAO) 1978 study on the subject describes purposeful, nonimmigrant travelers as all but tourists (or troops or government personnel) and points out that the bulk of purposeful travelers—businessmen, professionals, students, teachers, scholars, entertainers, etc.—enter or leave the United States under their own or other private auspices.[5]

The U.S. government sponsors only about 5 percent of this total, continues the GAO, those whose visits are deemed to merit financial subsidy because they are in the national interest. About sixty thousand persons a year are entered into USIA's computerized Exchange Visitor Information System. They include visitors sponsored by approximately nine hundred government agencies and private organizations under programs "designated" by USIA.[6]

These invited guests comprise only a fraction, however, of the more than six million foreign nationals who enter the United States for temporary visits in a typical year. Even that huge figure omits another half million people in such special categories as United Nations employees, foreign press, and foreign traders, plus untold numbers of Canadians who can circulate in the U.S. without visas.

With that horde of foreigners visiting this country every year, what is left for the USIA to do? Surely among those millions there are adequate numbers of opinion-makers from other nations, either actual or potential.

The trouble is that even the GAO was unable to deliver a comprehensive inventory of visitors. No one seems to know just how many of what categories from which countries come pouring into the country each year. The USIA concedes that the kinds of foreigners whom they would like to have the "American experience" may well be among the grand total of visitors. But the staff and leadership of the agency's associate directorate for educational and cultural affairs argue that they cannot just sit back and assume that this is the case. They have to make sure. That is the rationale for the agency's complex exchange program. It breaks into five divisions—academic, international visitors, American participants, private sector cooperation, and the East-West Center's cultural and technical interchange between East and West in Hawaii. Its purpose is to give citizens of other countries a better sense of what the U.S. stands for and why, as well as to give Americans a more accurate perception of other peoples—the so-called Carter second mandate.

The Fulbright Program still accounts for the most significant academic exchanges handled by the agency, guided by the presidentially appointed, twelve-member Board of Foreign Scholarships.

Numerous other agency programs aid scholarly exchange, including the Hubert H. Humphrey Fellowship Program. This exchange fund enables mid-career professionals from Third World nations to take a year of individualized graduate training at American universities.

The International Visitors program, which used to be known more appropriately as "leader grants," permits American ambassadors and consuls general to invite about sixteen hundred foreign leaders in government, labor, mass media, science, education, and other fields to visit their counterparts in the United States for periods of up to thirty days. About five hundred of these foreigners participate in multiregional studies and meetings on such topics as energy, food systems, environment, communications, and the role of women. The rest have individually tailored itineraries. These trips don't happen in a vacuum. The details of planning and follow-through call for vastly more help than USIA can furnish. Astonishingly, volunteers and ninety community organizations contribute their time and skills to fill the gaps. Many are members of the National Council for International Visitors.

Over the years, USIA and the State Department have brought hundreds of VIPs and thousands of future leaders to American shores. In 1984, the heads of state list totaled 42. In addition, 4,579 alumni of USIA exchange of persons programs held prestigious positions in government, academia, media, and other fields. Of that number, 698 held cabinet-level positions.

More recently under the American Participants Plan the agency annually sends some six hundred American experts abroad to give speeches and consultation in economics, foreign policy, political and social processes, the arts and humanities, and science and technology.

Private sector cooperation enables the agency to implement its now virtually defunct second mandate to inform America about foreigners. The agency furnishes small grants awarded competitively to selected, internationally oriented organizations in the United States.

Fortunately, John Richardson, who knows more about international exchanges than anyone, has assembled the best and most seasoned private associations of this sort. Richardson, formerly assistant secretary of state for educational and cultural affairs, is chairman of the Consortium for International Citizen Exchange. These open-hearted Americans beggar the government's total effort, although many seek government funds to help defray their expenses.

Statistics furnished by Richardson to the Senate Foreign Relations Committee in 1983 are overwhelming. He revealed that the consortium operates in thirty states and the District of Columbia and manages one hundred thousand exchanges annually between the U.S. and eighty other countries. Furthermore, the consortium enlists a half million working volunteers, sends citizens in exchanges lasting from ten days to one year, and represents almost six thousand committees and chapters. This work accrues expenditures of almost $200 million annually and involves some five thousand American communities. Key groups represented on the consortium's board are: the American Field Service, Experiment in International Living, Friendship Force, National Council for International Visitors, Partners of the Americas, People-to-People International, Sister Cities International, and Youth for Understanding. USIA gives grants to all these except for People-to-People International, established in 1956 by President Eisenhower, and the Friendship Force, founded in 1977.

Neither Richardson nor anyone else who feeds this mammoth effort can spell out evidence of its effectiveness in any practical terms. Americans' dedication has to be based on faith in the process; for no one has yet devised a measuring stick on the value of exchanges. They definitely do not bring sure-fire benefits to this country. So why do we bother? Bani Sadr studied in the United States and that fact didn't solve the Iran hostage crisis; Kwame Nkrumah matriculated from Lincoln College and that didn't prevent him from anti-Americanism when he was Ghana's leader. There are no guarantees that for foreigners to know us is to love and admire us or even to understand us. Familiarity breeds contempt and good fences make good neighbors, Americans are told as children. Why do we push so hard for exchanges? It is a hit or miss proposition, which can be spoiled when a visitor is mugged, ignored, or insulted.

Still, anyone who has administered exchanges either for the government or private sector has stories to tell which touch the heart and seem to justify all the labor and money devoted to getting people together. Take the professor in agricultural chemistry named William S. Clark who spent his sabbatical year from Amherst College in Hokkaido, Japan. Officially, that year of 1876–77, the Japanese made him vice-rector of the Sapporo Agricultural School. Unofficially, he created a legend during those brief months. This bluff New Englander spread an enthusiasm for Americans among the students and neighbors in Sapporo that has endured to the present. It is still remembered that he encouraged agricultural students and farmers to stop lagging behind the rest of Japan. He gave them pep talks that always ended with "Boys, be ambitious!" Even today on at least one patch of fruitful farmland near Sapporo, voyaging Americans are surprised to notice a well-kept, dark red New Hampshire-style barn.[7]

Foreigners must be similarly pleased in the United States— the French to see their gift of the Statue of Liberty still standing to greet them on arrival; the Egyptians to see their tall obelisk in New York's Central Park; and the Japanese to see cherry trees they donated in 1923 still blossoming each spring in Washington.

USIA cannot yet point to such showcase results. However, it tries to erect intellectual monuments in the minds and sensibilities of foreigners. Its Arts America program attempts to do this by assisting qualified artists and performing groups to arrange private tours overseas. This ideas sounds straightforward enough, but Livingston L. Biddle, former chairman of the National Endowment for the Arts (NEA), recounts a peculiar problem that bedeviled such a program when the State Department was running it. Some "quartet from Podunk," as Biddle put it, who weren't good enough to merit a grant from the State Department, would get booked to Athens for a limited tour arranged by an irresponsible fly-by-night agent.

There they would contact the USIS cultural affairs man and say, "How would you like to fund us around Greece for more appearances? You'll have us at a bargain rate because you don't have to pay our transatlantic fares." So the cultural officer would bite on this plan, only to have the "bargain" blow up in his face when the Greeks would ask, "Is this the best music the magnificent government of the United States can bring in?" The Greeks would sneer and the ambassador would gnash his teeth at this sequence which occurred with as many as 30 percent of the USIS-sponsored performing arts grantees to various parts of the globe.

Gradually, the agency grows more like the Alliance Francaise and British Council as it increases support of American studies and the English language in foreign institutions. It also provides liaison between American and foreign universities, academic associations, and scholars. It publishes *English Teaching Forum*, a professional quarterly for English teachers around the world. This magazine augments agency help for English language instruction at binational and cultural centers. More than three hundred fifty thousand foreign citizens now attend English-language classes at USIA-assisted facilities of one kind or another.

The aforementioned activities constitute the agency's major cultural and educational actions from Washington. They are complex, time consuming, and hard to justify in a cost-benefit ratio. Their impact on American foreign relations also tends to be blurred by the fact that other federal agencies also operate exchange and training programs—notably the Peace Corps, AID (Agency for International Development), the Department of Health and Human Services, the Department of Defense, and the National Science Foundation. Another score have more limited programs, or they are reimbursed by these five primary agencies.

Despite its idealistic, sometimes wishy-washy rationale for cultural and educational programs, the agency finds that more private sector collaborators and congressmen favor them than its informational and propagandistic endeavors. This is particularly true of exchanges. Some Senate Foreign Relations Committee members have urged the present director, Charles Z. Wick, to increase exchanges of persons, and he has done so. Senator Pell has said they should be multiplied tenfold.

One of the agency's most colorful critics, Ambassador Ellis Briggs, wrote that "the elaborate edifice of the United States Information Agency ought to be taken apart, with only such pieces salvaged and reassembled as experience has shown to be useful. Those should include more of the cultural and exchange programs than those of the lily-gilders and megaphone wielders."[8]

Until 1978, both official and unofficial American exchanges enjoyed popularity and freedom in most of the nations outside the Communist sphere. Then, in 1978, President Carter signed an agreement to pursue full-scale exchanges with the People's Republic of China. A flood of exchanges followed. They still continue. Most of them are privately arranged. Their progress has been rapid but rocky in some respects, due to the differences between an open and closed society.

There are some five thousand Chinese in the United States studying physics, engineering and other natural sciences. But the number of Americans in China has hovered between only two hundred and four hundred. Most of them are studying and doing research in musicology, linguistics, economic development, agriculture, and family life in China.[9]

The official programs are conducted by the Committee on Scholarly Communication and the National Science Foundation. In addition, numerous American universities have commenced their own collaboration with Chinese institutions.

Until recently, the Chinese who came to the United States were granted unlimited access to research sources. Contrarily, Americans in China were and still are blocked from copying documents, entering certain repositories of Chinese knowledge, and seeing certain experts. The Chinese responsible for the agreement's implementation have often had to beseech participating Americans to be patient until their national sociological and political patterns change enough for the exchange to be a truly two-way street. At the same time, the U.S. State Department has begun to tighten freedom of access to the Chinese.

Charles Wick encountered these obstacles when he first went to Beijing in September 1981 to expand cultural ties between the two nations. His arrival was marred by the Chinese refusal to allow the Americans to include thirteen abstract paintings in an art exhibit. The Chinese finally relented when the United States announced it would terminate the exhibit if the paintings were rejected.*

In toasts which followed the signing ceremonies, Wick said

---

*Indeed Mr. Wick did terminate another art exhibit in 1987 when the Chinese refused paintings of General Douglas McArthur and Golda Meir of Israel. These were provocative selections; and the point of cultural exchange is to improve relations. So USIA won an argument that should have been avoided.

bluntly, "Under our democratic processes we have freedom of expression in art, in literature and in the various sciences which I know are the hallmarks of that which you aspire to."[10]

Although Wick's remarks did not sit well with his hosts, they needed to be said. There is little point in weakly accepting an arrangement by which one side benefits disproportionately. As the New York Times' James P. Sterba commented, "Cultural problems remain the biggest day-to-day headache for Chinese officials trying to shield their population from the lack of freedom in China while opening themselves to the beneficial aspects of dealing with the United States.[11]

The Voice of America has already completed an equal exchange of three staffers with Radio Beijing, proving as Charles Wick was trying to do, that a fair exchange is no robbery. In the radio swap, the Chinese consulted with VOA journalists on how to fashion a professional news program. The VOA personnel concentrated on learning what effects years of isolation under the Cultural Revolution have had on the Chinese society and what the Chinese people are interested in hearing. Additionally, VOA staffers made notes on the changes in inflection of the language spoken today in order to update VOA broadcasts with the most modern accents.

Unquestionably, the exchange agreements will warm and enrich the recently reformed Sino-American relationship. The same would hold true if a real detente could be achieved between the United States and the Soviet Union. Yet in neither case should U.S. federal expenditure exceed token amounts as a trigger mechanism. Countless amateur and professional Sovietologists would leap at the chance to visit and probe into the vast reaches of the U.S.S.R. Businessmen, scientists, scholars, and tourists have already shown their eagerness by seizing every opportunity to travel, explore, study, or trade in the long forbidden territory of China.

Nonetheless, one recurrent embarrassment surfaces during return visits by official delegations or individuals from these and other authoritarian nations. They expect the U.S. government to arrange entertainment and housing, if not travel expenses. Why? Because that is how they host Americans in their countries, often royally, given a favorable political climate.

Washington federal agencies need only to mention this inequity, however, for as soon as it's understood it can be dealt with. Either the volunteer throngs of John Richardson's consortium or the National Council for International Visitors, for example, may furnish gratis both amusement and living quarters. Or these comforts can be economically purchased through a nonprofit, but self-sustaining institution like Art International in Washington, which already has opened its doors for this purpose.

Despite the biblical warning that it is dangerous to be a good Samaritan and despite the truism that no good deed goes unpunished, most Americans are generous to "visiting firemen." They can hail from out of state or from any nation in the world, the more exotic the better. Doubtless this American trait impelled young Senator J. William Fulbright to launch his famous exchanges. He believed that if a larger number of the world's people knew and understood people from nations other than their own, they might develop a capacity for empathy, a distaste for killing, and an inclination for peace.

Senator Pell lavished considerable eloquence on Fulbright's name, which led to "what an Oxford don has called 'the largest, most significant movement of scholars across the face of the earth since the fall of Constantinople in 1453.' Indeed," continued Pell, "since 1946 the Fulbright program has enabled some 45,000 Americans to teach and study in other nations, and some 80,000 scholars and leaders from over 100 countries to teach and study in the United States."[12]

Perhaps the Fulbright and International Visitors exchanges played Pied Piper to foreigners who wouldn't have come to America otherwise. Perhaps such federally funded invitations to share knowledge and mingle cultures released denizens of American and foreign ivory towers who would have stayed sealed in otherwise. Whatever and whoever broke the dam, the floodwaters of scholars, teachers, researchers, and future leaders in every walk of life flowed freely, for at least a generation following 1946. While USIS chief in Israel back in the late 1950s, I acted as American co-chairman of the Fulbright Commission in Israel and I discovered that virtually every candidate for grants could, if qualified, find private means to pursue his studies, or other academic projects in the United States.

Every year almost six million foreigners enter the United States on temporary visas, as well as hundreds of thousands of immigrants from every continent and more hundreds of thousands of illegal aliens from Latin America. An equal number of Americans venture abroad. Why then do legislators and executive branch officials want to expand exchange efforts? Why do some say, "No federal budget can claim a higher return on the dollar in terms of extending American influence and winning American friends?"[13]

The above figures demonstrate beyond the fondest hope of exchange advocates that foreigners in enormous numbers already pour into the United States to study, work, and live. Why must USIA or any other federal agency pay more people to come to America?

The logic is that the government can have a hand in selecting the visitors, deciding where they should go, whom they should see, and what they should learn. The government's grip is a loose one, of course, for the ambience of freedom that enhances any visit to the United States must not be tampered with. Nevertheless, official programs give the government "a voice it could not otherwise have in the organization of the transnational dialogue—in the choice of themes, establishment of standards, selection of foreign visitors and American 'specialists' and the encouragement of worthy but underfunded private initiatives."[14]

This rationale is persuasive for providing a few selected grants each year. It does not support the cries of zealots, both in and out of government, who would expand the present level of grants by many multiples.

ENDNOTES

1. Truman Capote, *The Muses Are Heard* (New York: Random House, 1956), p. 180.
2. Terry L. Deibel and Walter R. Roberts, *Culture and Information: Two Foreign Policy Functions* (Washington, D.C.: Center for Stra-

tegic and International Studies, Georgetown University, 1976), chap. 2.

3. The Senate Foreign Relations Committee authorization hearing April 21, 1981, committee report, pp. 185–86.

4. *Ibid.*, p. 187.

5. General Accounting Office Report to the Congress, "Coordination of International Exchange and Training Programs Opportunities and Limitations," July 24, 1978, p. 3.

6. *Ibid.*

7. Recollections from the author's visit to Sapporo in 1969; refreshed by USICA's Japan desk officer, Karl F. Olsson in 1981.

8. Ellis Briggs, *Anatomy of Diplomacy* (New York: David McKay, 1968), p. 102.

9. Robert Reinhold, "Troubles Plague U.S.—China Exchange Program," *New York Times*, August 16, 1981, p. 40.

10. James P. Sterba, "China and U.S. Sign Pact on Cultural Exchanges," *New York Times*, September 6, 1981, p. 3.

11. *Ibid.*

12. U.S. Senator Claiborne Pell, "International Exchanges and National Security," speech to National Council for International Visitors, March 20, 1981.

13. *Ibid.*

14. Briggs, *Anatomy of Diplomacy.*

CHAPTER 9

Nuts and Bolts of Global Public Diplomacy

THE MAN WHO TURNED PUBLIC DIPLOMACY into an academic discipline doesn't like the way USIA operates. Former Ambassador Edmund A. Gullion believes that it's wrong for USIS posts to pick information materials off a transmission belt from Washington. Posts should generate their own products, declares Gullion.[1] This is true. The man on the spot possesses the vital ingredient for communicating with the host nation. Only he has the needed familiarity with the people, culture, and institutions around him.

Gullion, who founded the Edward R. Murrow Center for Public Diplomacy at the Fletcher School, observed USIS in action throughout his twenty-five years of foreign service. He saw repeatedly that materials sent by Washington were usually off target.

Jacques Ellul, author of *Propaganda*, concurs: "A poster or article that evokes a response in one country may fail to do so in a neighboring one. From which it follows that one cannot export propaganda."[2]

America's first practitioners of public diplomacy, Benjamin Franklin and Thomas Jefferson, would have understood Gullion. They had to create their own pamphlets, booklets, policy statements, and news releases, given the absence of air mail, radio teletype, and telephone. Sea pouch and stagecoach hookups from America took over two months.

Now USIA manufactures, buys, or otherwise gathers and ships pamphlets, films, TV and radio tapes, exhibits, and other items. Franklin and Jefferson had no public diplomacy aides at their elbow or backup at home. They arranged their own travel. Even Franklin, the inventor, had not visualized the wondrous future in terms of a wireless file, Voice of America, television, countless media knickknacks, computerized research, or other technology to streamline programs and assess how well they were doing.

In contrast to those sparse conditions, USIA has heavy supply responsibilities. Although it has shrunk from twelve thousand to nine thousand employees in the past two decades, the agency is left with a complex array of people and functions to maintain at great distance. The director and associate directors from programs, media, and geographic areas supervise the agency's substantive activities. The associate directorate for management (MGT) supports them.

MGT shoulders the details of purchasing agency supplies and maintaining one hundred ten radio transmitters and relay stations, two regional printing centers in Manila and Mexico City, the wireless file, VOA, and TV panels and studios in Washington. It contracts for exhibits, books, printing of magazines and pilot model pamphlets, and it ships personal effects from Washington to the field and back for hundreds of field officers, staffers, and their families. USIA requires extensive logistical support behind each field man and woman in the front lines.

The administrative personnel usually stay in Washington, rising in rank at the same function. As a result, the machinery purrs so quietly that the average employee is no more aware of it than a first-class passenger is of the engines on an ocean liner.

The agency personnel office has to juggle a bewildering set of parallel recruiting, training, career planning, promotion, and retirement activities for the mixed foreign and domestic personnel services of the agency.

For almost a decade the agency has been systematizing old procedures to exploit advances in logistics, management, and communications.

Word processors using electronic mail concepts are tightening interoffice connections throughout Washington. Memoranda, letters, and fast media products can now be electronically sent in seconds among the agency's numerous buildings.

The agency is spending heavily to install these technological betterments since they will also speed the flow of information, texts, and agency products between Washington and the field. Progressively, as money is available to complete it, the new system will tie in USIS libraries and posts to the enormous computerized data base available in the United States.

Planners have dreams that one day any factual question asked at any USIS post, library, or binational center abroad will be answered almost instantaneously. Policy and guidance questions will receive equally fast response by tapping the agency computer's collection of past VOA broadcasts, guidances, wireless files, and agency magazines.

One intriguing element of these changes is the Distribution and Records System (DRS). The agency now requires each post to identify target audiences, by individual and institution, and record in the DRS each program used with them.

Procedures are straightforward enough. USIS enters into the DRS names of individuals such as a key journalist or politician or the president of a university. Under each individual the post lists all action taken to inform or influence him/her, with the date. Taking the journalist as an example, USIS records that on August 1, the public affairs officer gave him/her a book on President Reagan's economic plan; on August 15, the information officer invited him/her to dinner at the ambassador's residence; and on September 1, the cultural officer engineered a grant for him/her to go to the United States under the International Visitors program; and so forth. DRS thus forces the post to review its breakdown of priority audiences and to be sure it neither forgets one group or individual nor is too attentive to another.

Some old agency hands worry that these renovations of time-honored practices will dehumanize relationships with foreigners. It is impossible to translate into numbers, they warn, the impression some program may make on a person. For example, the newsman mentioned above might detest the book on Reagan, be snubbed by the ambassador's wife, or lose his job while on a grant to the United States. USIA's former chief of inspectors, Daniel P. Oleksiw, wonders if DRS might encourage officers to substitute quantity of actions for quality of accomplishment.[3] Such adverse reactions probably constitute standard bureaucratic paranoia in the face of change. DRS is a good reminder that a USIS post must pick its priority individuals and categories of people, concentrate on them, and not waste resources of time and software trying to please and inform everyone. As the wise father warned his overactive teenage son, "You can't kiss all the pretty girls."

The agency argues that automation is being used in the organization to free USIS officers from clerical, repetitive, and mundane chores so that they will be able to conduct more personal contacts. Many time-intensive tasks like producing multiple letters and guest lists can be done speedily on word processors. The aim is not to replace our officers, but to help them, the agency insists.[4]

The advent of systems technology in the agency began only in 1979. Much remains to be done. Former FSIO Alan Carter foreshadowed the trend with his "package program" formula: When planning an event, a USIS post should employ several media simultaneously, to increase the impact on local audiences.

Suppose a famous writer on environmental protection is due to lecture at a binational center in Santos, Brazil. The post should have copies of his/her book stacked in the lecture hall for distribution, mail pamphlets about his/her life and achievements in the same envelope with the invitations to the lecture, assemble an exhibit on environmental controls and place it in the lobby, set up interviews on radio and television with the local stations, and urge target VIPs to stage a reception at the center after the performance.

The Carter package program attempted to adapt American multimedia merchandizing to the purposes of USIS. The analogy must not be carried too far. Although it is logical to orchestrate a post's selling tools to exploit a visiting lecturer, or symphony orchestra, or exhibit on the virtues of capitalism, USIS planners must never see themselves as mass advertisers. They are in no position to saturate the market directly. If they tried to do so they would surely be met with cries of "the U.S. is drowning us in their propaganda!" They have to put points across indirectly, in most cases through that human transformer known as an opinion leader.

USIS posts are the concern of the ambassador and the area director in Washington. They are also subject to surprise appraisals of their performance, morale, and general condition by MGT's office of inspections.

A good inspector can spot problems missed by the area directors and their assistants on brief stops at the post. He huddles with the public affairs officer and other USIS staff to iron out whatever personnel and technical difficulties he has uncovered. Before leaving, he composes detailed recommendations on how to improve and correct deficiencies.

One weakness has plagued both the USIA and State Department inspection corps. They become a dumping grounds for officers who are hard to assign because they have crossed swords with a boss, are unpopular, or are in some way incompetent. The inspection office offers a handy disposition for such individuals, for the tours are open-ended and, whenever an appropriate full-time job is found, the inspector can be moved without much advance notice.

Fortunately, the average inspector is capable and industrious, as are the public members in the inspection teams: a qualified nongovernmental person often is added to the USIA group. Furthermore, the extra energy, courage, and imagination that may have led an officer into controversy can enable him to shine. Someone who is afraid to challenge the status quo or question higher authority probably won't do well as an inspector.

The inspection system provides vital oversight of programs and personnel by objective, knowledgeable critics. The function will prosper if it is considered a priority assignment like a Class A post abroad. The periodic critical review of operations merits the attention of the agency's best officers.

Research polls offer a more impersonal method to determine what USIS posts are accomplishing. Ever since the agency began, congressmen, presidents, secretaries of state, agency directors, and field officers have pondered the value of public diplomacy. It is at best an inexact science. What persuades a person or group to do something today may simply be ignored tomorrow. It is certain that, to paraphrase Abraham Lincoln, you can convince some foreigners sometimes, but you can't convince them all, all the time.

Nevertheless, there is a growing expertise in how to learn which USIA programs influence their target audiences and how much. Properly designed, such assessments can help the Congress and the executive branch to decide what programs should be modified, expanded, inaugurated, or eliminated.

But in the late 1970s, having concluded that program evaluation research had been overproduced and underused, the agency shifted most research money into foreign opinion analysis. A high level interagency group of foreign policy formulators sifted through this advisory research. They realized that past policy makers tended to ignore storm warnings that this kind of data may surface. For instance, there were ample clues from Cuba before the Bay of Pigs misadventure that Castro's popularity was running strong. If he had focused on this fact, President Kennedy could have foreseen that an invasion of ragtag refugees from Miami would not trigger a spontaneous rebellion on the island.

It is surprising that the agency gave up program evaluation in view of the heavy demand for it. The originating Smith-Mundt Act of 1948 required that the agency should include in its annual reports "appraisals and measurements, where feasible, as to the effectiveness of the several programs in each country where conducted." And, in 1978, the comptroller general noted that many members of Congress "have expressed a need for objective information and analysis to counterbalance the subjective, impressionistic, anecdotal, and self-interested information presented by the executive branch administrators, lobbyists, and self-interested parties."[5]

In 1978 the agency did a four-country survey on readership of its magazine *Horizons USA*, which is designed for elite readers who are concerned about international affairs. The survey revealed that, although 75 to 91 percent of recipients read the publication, they would prefer more emphasis on economics and political-security topics and less on arts and humanities. The study also found that unpredictable delivery (an average of 30 percent of the magazines weren't arriving) was causing readership to drop.

The VOA's Continuing Audience Analysis Program determined that in 1977, in urban areas of Java and Sumatra, 2.7 percent of the 9.1 million adult citizens listened regularly to the Voice. According to the study it ranked behind Radio Australia, BBC, and Radio Malaysia but well ahead of Radios Moscow, Beijing, and Japan.

A 1976 motion picture survey tested agency-sponsored documentaries shown in Bogota, Manila, and Beirut over a period of two years. Viewers considered the films worthwhile and credible, although often too superficial for the mental level of the audiences. The findings furnished critical insights which guided the agency on how to make more appealing features.

In 1976 the agency published its worldwide survey on the

placement of its television series *Vision*. The format of *Vision* is a half hour of reviews on contemporary American life and personalities. Evidently *Vision* found its way into a lot of dead-hour screening, but was eschewed during prime time in uncut versions. Since the price of *Vision* exceeded $750,000 in 1975 alone, the agency accepted the research division's suggestion that its TV products could be more easily marketed with shorter material that could fit in with other local programming.

A 1978 report on an agency exhibit in a remote Soviet city was based on the observations of the American exhibit staff. As might be expected, they found a strong, positive reaction. More than one hundred forty-five thousand attended despite Soviet government attempts to downplay the exhibit. Still, this prejudiced group conceded that the more sophisticated customers were disappointed not to see American agriculture displayed with authentic machinery, technology, and statistical data.

The agency is presently surveying the impact of its "Information USA" exhibit as it appears in nine Soviet cities. A thirty-page report on visitors' reactions and general attitudes is completed after each city.

In judging exchange of persons programs, a commonly cited gauge is the number of grantees who rise to top positions in foreign governments. Recently, USIA Director Charles Wick claimed ninety-four heads of state and hundreds of parliamentarians as alumni of the International Visitors and Fulbright programs. In 1976 a private consultant completed for the State Department an in-depth study of sixty recently returned grantees from Africa. The consultant offered thirty recommendations on how to improve exchanges through better selection, orientation, programing, and follow-up. Her report also contained a euphoric summation: "Something profound has happened to many of these people as a result of their American experience: In many instances they stand taller, they feel better about themselves and their role in their own societies. They certainly feel better about Americans, and are better prepared for continuing open dialogue with them." She concluded that in the International Visitors program "mutual understanding ... the somewhat vague objective of [the exchange] programs can be met."[6]

These samples of federally funded research on official products for public diplomacy reveal their own values and flaws. The above studies did yield evidence on the extent to which target audiences were reached and how they reacted to the products. They also raised meaningful questions for USIA as to whether products and programs should be improved, expanded, contracted, or canceled.

However, when the government hires a researcher or conducts an in-house critique of its actions, the result can easily be marred by the bias, conscious or otherwise, of courtesy, gratitude, or self-promotion. This type of error occurs especially when the survey respondents are government employees. Furthermore, cataloguing audience reactions and suggestions and measuring exposure can yield only partial answers.

To get the best research for planning public diplomacy requires constant awareness of its purposes. Certainly, the ultimate aim of public diplomacy is to influence foreign behavior: to get a foreign government to agree on a specific proposal, to vote in the United Nations to censor the Soviet invasion of Afghanistan, to participate actively in an alliance like the North Atlantic Treaty Organization. It is nearly impossible to prove that a USIA product or program merits sole credit for any such result. The behavior of people and their governments derives from the interplay of many forces, most of which lie beyond USIA's power to influence. Those forces are all variables. Attitude is only one, but it is the one that the agency can measure.

Early agency research demonstrated that in some situations changes in attitude can be assessed and attributed to specific USIA programs. Two examples are quite convincing. The first involved the agency's director, Edward R. Murrow, who in 1960 presented a televised defense of the controversial U.S. Polaris missile policy on BBC's show *Panorama*. The British Gallup organization then established that 8 million British adults had seen the program. Twenty-one percent, or 1.7 million, asserted that Mr. Murrow had left them with a higher opinion of the United States. Nine percent, or 700,000, indicated their opinion had gone down. This left a net gain of about 1 million viewers being more favorably disposed toward the United States.

A second demonstration of attitude-altering by USIA came from its survey of visitors to a 1960 exhibit in Berlin, "Youth USA." A random sample of three hundred was interviewed at the entrance to the exhibit and a comparable sample of five hundred at the exit. As the table in Fig. 7 shows, the exhibit

Figure 7
Youth in America

	BEFORE		AFTER
Number of cases	300		500
Very good opinion	20%		35%
Good opinion	50		50
Neither good nor bad opinion	20		12
Bad opinion	6		1
Very bad opinion	—		*
No opinion	4		2
	100%		100%
Net favorable	64		84
Change		20%	

*Less than half of one percent

worked a distinctly favorable change on the general opinion about American youth.

USIA's present research yields more sophisticated and realistic assessments. Gordon Tubbs explains that for most exhibits the agency looks for two results: Did the exhibit live up to what would be expected in the U.S.? Was there a short-term attitude change (positive or negative)? Tubbs said the 1986 U.S. space exhibit in Vancouver emerged positive on both fronts.[7]

Programs and products of the agency have thus been proven susceptible to measurement of their impact on foreign populations. So far, no one has devised a handy assessment kit for learning what personal contact has wrought on opinion-molders. USIS can only watch for the appearance of their articles, books, speeches, notes, or other actions in tune with American objectives.

Currently the USIA research office devotes a third of its resources to evaluate agency effectiveness abroad. For example, its ongoing "Five Year Plan" examines the size and performance of VOA audiences around the world.

Director of Research Nils H. Wessel heads a fifty-five-person department, of which some forty are skilled professionals, many with PhDs. They use survey research techniques annually in a dozen countries to learn who listens to the VOA regularly, what their demographic characteristics are, and what their favorite and least favorite programs are. With these data the VOA management can adjust its programing accordingly.

USIA also compiles foreign opinion research. This is essential for the agency to fulfill its advisory role among high policy formulators in Washington and in ambassadors' country teams session abroad. This rationale is somewhat diluted by the proliferation of such reports among federal agencies. Often five elements of an embassy may be reporting to Washington and the ambassador on foreign opinion: USIS, the Foreign Broadcast Information Service, the embassy's political section, the defense attache, and the CIA.

USIA researchers, however, devoted more than $1 million in 1987 to their principal mission: polling foreign public opinion on critical international issues to assist top U.S. policy makers. The National Security Council and White House staff frequently review these reports as they formulate strategies in public diplomacy.

With evident pride, Dr. Wessel states, "When President Reagan signed the INF treaty with General Secretary Gorbachev to eliminate an entire class of nuclear weapons, he could be confident that overwhelming majorities in key western European countries favored the treaty."[8]

Research is a tool the agency must not neglect, though it can never deliver complete answers. There are many instances where USIA effectiveness is scientifically measurable. Still much of the work on opinion-molders must be executed discreetly, and satisfactory observation must be perforce "by guess and by God."

ENDNOTES

1. Edmund A. Gullion, interview with author, September 1981.

2. Jacques Ellul, *Propaganda, the Formation of Men's Attitudes* (New York: Random House, 1973), p. 296.
3. Daniel P. Oleksiw, interview with author, September 1981.
4. J. Gary Augustson, interview with author, September 1981.
5. Congressional Research Service, *Executive Reorganizations: The U.S. Information Agency and Associated Programs*, Hearings, House Subcommittee on Government Operations, 95th Cong. 1st sess., July 14, 1977, p. 346.
6. Mary W. Brady with Georgette J. Garner, *An African View of an American Experience*, April 1976, p. 1. (A pamphlet—now lost).
7. Gordon Tubbs, chief East Asian Branch Research Office, interview with author, February 1988.
8. Dr. Nils H. Wessel, USIA director of research, interview with author, February 1988.

PART III

USIA Abroad

CHAPTER 10

A Typical Overseas Post—
Fiction

BENJAMIN FRANKLIN HOLMES STEPPED OUT of the TWA 747 and paused to see if he could spot Tad Jenkins in the crowd behind the chain link fence on the field. He squinted, blinked, and gave up. The equatorial noonday sun was too much for his eyes, accustomed to Washington in the winter. He fumbled in his pocket and pulled out dark glasses.

Now he could see Public Affairs Officer Jenkins' nearly seven feet of lanky, seersuckered height under an enormous straw hat. As he waited for an airline agent to open the gate, Holmes observed that many of the crowd were calling to Jenkins, jokes and hellos, anything to get his attention. His would be a tough act to follow, mused Holmes. After nearly five years in the Republic of Landrovia, Jenkins had become a kind of folk hero—nothing, though, to make a citizen jealous. Jenkins was too modest and full of humor to evoke any such dangerous emotion among the Landrovians. He was liked, that was all, and respected. Holmes had read the ambassador's comments in his fitness reports of the past three or four years. He knew that, although the post's budget had been reduced, Jenkins was still carrying on a many-faceted countrywide program. Even in Cleartown, the capital city, USIS had, under Jenkins' leadership, reached a big percentage of its three hundred thousand citizens.

USIS also operated four branch posts, two at opposite ends

of the great central valley for farms and factories in the towns of Coronado and Octobe, one at the seaport city of Starbeck, and the fourth in the mountain resort of Taglio, seat of the summer capital.

Back in Washington, USIS Cleartown had become known as USIA's typical overseas post. As such, it was a sought-after assignment, like sea duty for a naval officer. Once you became public affairs officer in Landrovia, you had proved yourself capable of rising to the top of the agency.

Holmes strode happily through the gate. As he shook hands with his friend and colleague, whom he would replace in a day or two, he felt his career had hit a high plateau.

"Holmes, you dog, welcome to the greatest country in the world outside our own! Now, give your passport to Edelwize here. Edelwize, let me introduce you to Mr. Holmes, the new PAO. Ben, you'll find that USIS can never do without Mr. Humphrey Edelwize."

The redoubtable Edelwize moved swiftly, followed by Holmes and Jenkins, without stopping at the customs and health windows. In the baggage area, he turned briefly to extract Holmes' checks for his three suitcases.

Waving frequently to a variety of men and women, Jenkins then ushered Holmes out of the terminal and into a small chauffeur-driven sedan.

"We're going to the Press Club, Kerry; and this is my successor, Mr. Holmes."

"Ben, we've got so little time, and since my plane leaves tomorrow at 5 P.M., I've packed your schedule pretty tight. It'll be easier to show you what I'm up to rather than just giving you papers to read."

"Now, can you freshen up at the Press Club and not change until dinner time? You don't look tired from your trip . . ." Jenkins paused hopefully.

"Nope, I'm fine," Holmes assured him. "Let 'er rip. I'd sure as hell rather learn by watching than dredging through the files."

"Terrific! Well I've arranged a dutch treat lunch—that's a bit embarrassing, but our entertainment allowance is at rock bottom. The point is to introduce you to the national journalist club members. That'll include some American newsies as well, plus the local Reuters and Agence France Presse people."

Holmes nodded. He knew that three members of the club

had already been to the states as International Visitor grantees, one each from the leading paper and TV and radio stations.

Jenkins slipped him the guest list and he studied it, noting the affiliations of each of the 30 odd people. Jenkins explained quietly, so Kerry (the driver) couldn't hear, which were pro-American, pro-Communist, and simply apolitical, which included most of them.

Lunch was low key—no lengthy toasts. A long cocktail period had allowed each a short exchange with Holmes. Thus began the long get-acquainted process which might go on for months. USIS dealings with these media heavyweights would be the post's priority. Although the PAO was boss, the day-to-day contacts would be handled by Fred Bakst, the information officer.

Holmes thought about the welcome lunches to come, from the Landrovia-America Friendship Society, the Rotary Clubs which would invite him to speak, and the American business club, with its many Landrovian members who were employees of U.S firms. These would all be more hail-fellow-well-met affairs but less important in terms of opinion-molder status. Later, he would be invited to address Moslem groups, if he became as acceptable to them as Jenkins. They were vital to his program.

Without waiting for coffee, Jenkins hustled his replacement back to USIS headquarters at the embassy. First, he invited the other USIS Americans into the PAO office. Eve Centurion, the PAO secretary, Holmes already knew. She kept the free-wheeling Jenkins' nose to the grindstone enough to get reports written and memos from the ambassador replied to. College grad Hope Jawarsky wanted to be an officer. At present, she was secretary for the information section. She hadn't shown restlessness yet. The short intense information officer, Fred Bakst, had been a journalist and amateur actor and had entered USIA in mid-career. He had caught on fast and was already on top of his job in Landrovia. He told Holmes about the post's monthly general magazine. Inadequate funds and labor troubles were hindering this project. He remarked that USIA's regional production center in Manila might take it on. Also, Bakst said, it might be better to sell the magazine for a nominal sum rather than give it away. If so, maybe people would take it more seriously. Holmes agreed but said he wanted some assurance the magazine could maintain its circulation of ten thousand if the Landrovians had to pay for it.

The cultural affairs officer, Hedrick Cutting, was a hustler. A middle-aged bachelor, he had made USIA his whole existence and no chore was too onerous for him to run a good program. He explained that private cultural events produced in the United States were furnishing the post a banner year. Impressarios with USIS help would stage an American Ballet Company tour in Cleartown and Taglio, visits of Dave Brubeck and Stevie Wonder, and a small production of *Abe Lincoln in Illinois.* "By the way," Cutting went on, "the binational center in Cleartown is staging a shadow play this evening and I hope our new PAO will not be too travel-weary to attend."

"Not at all," said Holmes

"I'd like to. It will be a first for me." Holmes had learned that the binational center was humming. It taught English to some fifteen thousand students. The center operated on the funds collected for this service. It had been in the black for years, with no help from the post, after the original grant for furniture and tape recorder booths.

Before the meeting ended, field program officer Grant Barantanian introduced the four branch officers who had come to meet the new PAO. Holmes liked the looks of this thirty-five-year-old veteran of the hardship posts in South Asia and Africa. He could run his section with little surprise. Holmes took this moment to say that the branch post at Octobe would close before the next fiscal year. To Holmes' relief, Barantanian already knew about the cut and had figured out how to deal with the disappointment this would cause in Octobe. He planned to turn over the contents of the post's library, including twelve thousand books, to the state university. This would coincide with a chair in American Studies to be furnished with the remaining counterpart funds.

Jenkins presented Holmes to the thirty-five national employees in the posh miniature motion picture theater. It had been constructed during the 1950s with counterpart funds. This was money generated when the United States sold its surplus wheat in return for Landrovian pounds, which at the time were not acceptable as foreign exchange. The government of Landrovia agreed that the funds could defray embassy expenses.

The Landrovian local employees clapped politely for Holmes. They knew English, having served USIS for many years. They also knew the post's operations, perhaps better than some Americans. But the shrewd ones had learned to keep their own counsel, unless drawn out by the American officers.

Watcham Woytan, the senior staffer, then stood up. The slender 50-year-old said that on behalf of his fellow countrymen he wanted to say how much they would miss Mr. Jenkins after so many pleasant years of his presence among them. Then his brown face turned dour. Was it true, he asked, that salaries of Landrovians in USIS would be frozen by the new administration? Holmes responded that he had heard the rumor and would oppose the freeze if it came up.

"It's almost four," announced Jenkins. "Hedrick and I promised we'd have you at the library by now, so we'd better hurry."

A statuesque woman, with hair like shaved ice, was pacing the sidewalk when Kerry opened the car doors. Her manner was frosty as she said, "We were afraid you weren't coming, Mr. Jenkins. I was very nervous, because you know I've got librarians from all over Landrovia here to examine our methods at the library. You do remember that USIA's regional librarian is here to give them a seminar this afternoon?" Her gray eyes looked up only a few inches at the giant Jenkins.

"Yes, I do, Mrs. Mussy," he said gently. "This is Mr. Holmes, who will take over from me tomorrow. Before we meet your visitors, I'd like you to show him the fine exhibit on American presidents you put up last week. I've been telling him about it. I think it's the best thing we've done for years."

Mrs. Mussy melted a bit, shook hands with Holmes, and ushered him proudly up the brick walk. Before he entered the large shuttered stucco building, however, a jeep screeched to a halt behind the PAO's car, and Bakst's local assistant rushed out. Breathlessly, he whispered to the three Americans that something had gone wrong and that the editor of the *Cleartown Courrieur*, Gabriel Bestoso, was waiting to see Jenkins.

Jenkins turned to the librarian. "I'm really disappointed, Mrs. Mussy, but Mr. Cutting will have to talk with the visitors on my behalf. Something has come up that I've got to deal with in the embassy."

Back in his office, Jenkins introduced Holmes to Bestoso, who said, "When you hear what is the matter I'm sure you'll be as angry as I am." The bulky, vigorous sixty-year-old lapsed into his own language and quickly described the letter he had just received. Then from his pocket he removed an envelope clipped to a single sheet of paper and handed it to Jenkins.

Bestoso declared, "This could be a scoop that would sell papers. On the other hand, I don't want to make unnecessary trouble for my American friends. But, if this is what it seems to be, I'm not sure what I think about you any more."

The Americans read the letter, which was postmarked in a neighboring, Communist-controlled country. It started out "Dear Harold," under the full name of the American ambassador to Landrovia, Harold J. Springer. It was signed from "your friend," George Schultz (Secretary of State). The letter contained racist slurs against the brown-skinned Landrovians, and alluded to plots and other secrets which the secretary and the American National Security Council had allegedly concocted to corrupt the Ministries of the Interior and Defense in order to oust the incumbents and appoint known American sympathizers.

"Gabriel," Jenkins began slowly, "I really appreciate your giving us a look at this before running the story. I can tell you right now that it is a forgery, put into your hands to ruin relations between our countries. It's full of inaccuracies. Let me show you: first, the secretary of state calls our ambassador by his nickname, 'Pete.' Nobody uses his Christian name, 'Harold.' Second, any of our secretaries would see that the letter's margins don't conform with our rules; third, if such a letter were actually written by us it would have to be classified 'Top Secret, Eyes Only,' not merely 'Confidential' as this one is.

"Now, Gabriel, this really is a bombshell. I ought to show it to the ambassador. I need his views. Can you wait a couple of hours before you decide whether to publish it?"

Bestoso nodded. "You have just about convinced me, but I would like to hear what your ambassador thinks. I'll hold the story till 6:30 P.M. Call me!"

Minutes later the ambassador gathered his country team—the chief political officer, the top defense attache, the deputy chief of mission, and, of course, Jenkins and Holmes. Jenkins brought a half dozen copies of the letter, which he had personally xeroxed to keep the matter at a "need to know" level.

The officers had a field day. In minutes they had found a total of eleven errors. The ambassador agreed that Jenkins should take Bestoso through the mistakes which proved the letter was fraudulent.

By 5:30 P.M., at the newspaper's office, Bestoso was chuckling with Jenkins and Holmes at the inept forgery. "I ought to write an editorial scolding the Communists," he said.

Jenkins suggested that he not do so, since some readers might think that it was a pro-American whitewash of a real letter. Bestoso agreed.

As Kerry drove Jenkins and Holmes through the rush hour traffic back to the embassy, Jenkins explained why they had to see the CIA station chief, Appleton.

"He says he has some peculiar information for me and that he supposed you might as well come too. This is probably as good a time as any to give you my theory on our relationship with the CIA here. I know they're not going to let us in on any of their covert stuff. But just in case it involves any actions we're taking, or people we contact, I keep Appleton up to date. This way we can avoid duplication or foul-ups between us. We lunch together every Tuesday, and sometimes he actually clues me in on certain attitudes, or developments that we need to do something about."

Appleton was a rollicking extrovert who threw an Australian boomerang for relaxation. Holmes' immediate impression was that Appleton's personality was the perfect cover for his real job. He seemed to be just a happy-go-lucky young assistant political officer without much of a future in the finicky, careful world of the foreign service.

Appleton wasted no time. "I have long been aware," he started, "of the excellent rapport you've established with key members of the local press here, particularly with the *Courrieur*. I realize how much effort you've put into currying Bestoso's favor, if you'll excuse a terrible pun." A roar of mirth, and then, "So it is not easy for me to share some news with you. Originally, of course, the *Courrieur* was founded while Landrovia was still a French colony. Ever since then, even after independence thirty years ago, the board of directors has remained in Paris. Now, I promise you that this was none of my doing. Frankly, if they'd asked me, I would have said no. It would be gilding the lily, since you've already gotten so close to Bestoso. By now I guess you have deduced what has happened, eh?" Appleton shuffled his feet, but Jenkins just stared at him.

"Okay, here it is straight. My people have bought into the board, and they have a commanding majority."

Jenkins whistled. "What the hell did they do that for? Maybe they doubted my friendship with Bestoso was transferable to a new PAO?"

"They don't leave anything to chance," replied Appleton without really answering. "But you mustn't forget that Bestoso has no inkling of this, and please don't give him one. Obviously you can never even hint to him what has transpired in Paris. . . . You know he's so damn honest and objective in his brand of journalism, I wonder whether, even if he did stray from the party line in Paris, he would accept guidance. I'll bet they'd have to fire him. Perhaps that's how my agency's masterminds have thought this through; they just want to be sure."

The three men dropped the topic at that. It had become a fait accompli, however they viewed it. But Holmes was mulling over how many of Jenkins' obviously solid contacts could be transferred without damage. He remembered his own rage when turning over his list of opinion leaders he had gotten close to in his last post. His successor PAO had sneered, "You can give me all the names you want; you can spell out who does what in this country and how to deal with them, but I might as well tell you to save your energy. I'm gonna do it my way."

Holmes shuddered as he recalled the vacuousness of that PAO. Yet ruminating further, he saw that the best means for protecting a good investment in contacts must be to lengthen the tours of USIS officers. No matter how hard I try, Holmes told himself, it will be years before I equal Jenkins' value to the United States in this country.

As if sensing his concern, CIA's Appleton patted Holmes on the shoulder while they filed out into the embassy corridor, "Say, I hope you'll continue our interagency lunches on Tuesdays, even when we get rid of Jenkins!"

"You bet. I look forward to them."

Back at the PAO's residence, Jenkins and Holmes lingered over a beer after their showers. They were due at dinner with the binational center director and the co-chairman of the Fulbright Committee—cultural affairs officer, Hedrick Cutting. The other co-chairman would be their host. Jenkins' wife and children had already returned to Washington to be in time for the fall term of school. Holmes' wife was traveling with a stopover in Ankara to see her parents. They had no children. He had met and married her in the Turkish city on his first tour.

As he continued briefing Holmes, Jenkins neared the end of

a long series of items: hints, warnings, and scheduled events. "As to visits," he grinned, "you'll be swimming in them. Tomorrow I've assigned Bakst to escort three congressmen on the House Agriculture Committee. He's got to take them to a kind of county fair near the mountains. For two weeks, a task force of the U.S. Sixth Fleet will be on a goodwill visit down at Starbeck. You're slated to go there and meet with the navy public information officer to cement preparations were set up for a parade, a reception by the mayor, a speech by Admiral Simpson, the task force commander, not to mention protection for sailors who can't handle the rotgut they'll drink in some of those dives down there."

As Jenkins went on patiently, Holmes was trying to figure out how all the activity fit into the post's country plan. This document was updated each year by the PAO and served as standing orders for the post. In a word, it laid out what USIS would do to advance the United States mission toward its goals in Landrovia and what resources would be devoted and how. Holmes wouldn't forget the objective: to "persuade" the government and people of Landrovia that the national defense treaty with the United States was vital and that compared to the Communists' client state of Tuberdad on the northern border, Landrovia's future was more secure and promising thanks to its alliance with the United States. Number two was to remind the government and people that it was essential to supply Landrovian troops for the United Nations Middle East peacekeeping force in the southern Arabian Peninsula.

USIA's desk officer back in Washington would collaborate with VOA's Landrovian programs chief and the editor of the regional wireless file to provide stories and commentary to buttress the post's efforts. Washington, or regionally based agency correspondents, would file USINFO telegrams that USIS Cleartown could offer Landrovian media about troops on maneuvers with the United Nations peacekeepers. Photographs would follow. The U.S. Department of Defense would furnish film or printed features of U.S. military might for a secure peace. USIS Cleartown would try to place these materials with the press and Landrovian leaders who might write or speak of ties to the United States.

Jenkins wound up his briefing. "Well, Ben, that's about all, You can hit me with questions tomorrow."

After dinner and the shadow play at the binational center, Holmes finally snapped off the light in his room. Some thirty

Typical USIS Post

1. Its composition:

> Ambassador
> Country Public Affairs Officer (CPAO)—USIS Chief
> Deputy PAO (in large posts)

Information Officer	Cultural Affairs Officer	Field Operations Officer
Runs press and publications contacts with local, U.S., and foreign journalists	Runs exchange programs, cultural presentations, library; co-chairman (often) of BNC(s), binational center(s).	
		Branch Public Affairs Officer(s) (BPAO) Operates branch post(s).

2. Its place in the country team:
   Ambassador—Chief of Mission
   DCM   —Deputy Chief of Mission
   Head of Political Section
   Head of Economic Section
   Senior Military Attache
   USIS Chief—CPAO
   AID Chief
   CIA Chief of Station

   The country team serves as the ambassador's executive and advisory board.

hours had passed since he'd arisen from his bed in Washington. As expected, jet lag kept him squirming for three or four hours before deep rest took over. He had drilled himself to profit from insomnia, and in the black night he pondered the inchoate task ahead.

First, he reviewed facts about Landrovia. This one-time French colony had retained close connections with its former metropole. Nevertheless, it had gone nationalistic, emphasizing its own language and customs. Only the enticement of free training for its pilots and naval officers plus inexpensive American arms had inveigled its president into a military pact with the United States. Despite this treaty, the Communists had not given up. Landrovian's oligarchic regime suffered some instability which encouraged Communists to bore from within rather than try another Afghanistan-type of takeover. Its geographic position made Landrovia strategically interesting both to the Soviets and the United States. Socially and economically, Landrovia ranked high among semi-industrialized nations. Within its borders were blended half a dozen indigenous tribes, with a high education level in and near urban centers, but dwindling to near illiteracy in the populous farmlands nestled among the foothills of the northern mountain range.

The present rulers had not been able to harmonize the disparate ethnic components. Therein lay the roots of instability. Too many indigent farmers had moved to the cities. Like Puerto Ricans in New York, they added to a discontented nonskilled labor force with 50 percent unemployment.

What should USIS do in such a country? Jenkins and his team had won acceptance by the movers and shakers of the capital. Branch PAOs had sunk useful taproots in their domains. But Holmes suspected USIS had not cut beneath the Paris-trained elite. Holmes had detected one vital weakness in his fellow Americans. Only Jenkins, Cutting, and himself were fluent in the national language. Second, the year-round heat meant Landrovia was a hardship post, where tours were limited to two years with a maximum repeat of two. So probably few Americans would ever stay long enough to master the language.

Although the Washington files indicated USIS Cleartown to be industrious and active, Holmes guessed it would be months, maybe a year or two, before he could be confident his USIS program was on track. Glimpses Jenkins had afforded him suggested effectiveness, but he sensed shallowness and more than a touch of self-deception. What he had seen was calculated to make the post look good according to American standards. But what was happening in the minds of the Landrovians? With that conundrum, Holmes fell asleep.

CHAPTER 11

A Nation-Building Post— Fiction

THOMAS JEFFERSON FORBES FELT NO RESENTMENT over his assignment as country public affairs officer in the hardship post of Linolo. In fact, he was elated. He understood and eagerly embraced what USIS would be asked to do there, though neither the agency nor the State Department had any specifics in mind as yet. They expected him to case the situation in Linolo himself and devise a formula of operations on his own. The prospect of scouting another exotic culture excited the explorer in him; this sort of challenge had drawn him into USIA in the first place. The chance to start a countrywide USIS program from scratch appealed to his creative nature.

In two months this African colony of thirty million disparate tribespeople was slated for independence from its European masters.

The United States government stirred with nostalgic memories of its own struggle for independence. This revolution was proceeding more peacefully, but American observers feared Linolo's level of education and administrative infrastructure might be inadequate to survive a premature cutting of the colonial umbilicus. So did the mother country, but Linolians alternately rioted in the streets of Karth and pounded their fists at the negotiation table in Europe to show their impatience.

The Americans were poised with their postnatal policy for Linolo. They would offer to help the fledgling state become a self-sufficient, integrated, militarily secure democracy. USIS would be charged to spur the citizenry to espouse and strive for these goals. Forbes guessed this would be a tall order, but he was optimistic. His similar experience in Asia would stand him in good stead, and the agency promised to be generous with people and materials when he had determined the post's requirements.

CIA sources indicated that Moscow's aim was simpler. The Communists intended to indoctrinate Linolo not so much with Marxist ideology as with the idea that the Soviet Union could be a strong friend and potential ally.

As colonialism played its final measures that year, the two superpowers warily circled Linolo in a political game of musical chairs. When the colonial tune stopped abruptly—and the moment was imminent—each giant hoped to grab a seat close to the rulers of the infant nation.

In Washington the State Department briskly prepared itself for Linolo. It revved its gears to upgrade the existing consulate in Karth to a large embassy, which would soon be needed. Linolo occupied a patch of Africa about the size of Alaska, and its mineral wealth combined with other natural resources meant busy intercourse with the United States.

The department designated as ambassador a career officer noted for his cool courage under pressure: John Littlefield. Quickly he searched for officers to man his country team. After picking a deputy, his next selection was Tom Forbes. He didn't wait to see who USIA would suggest. He wanted Forbes. They had been together in Alexandria the day in 1956 when Israeli, British, and French forces launched their simultaneous offensive against Egypt. Forbes had won his admiration for exploiting what few psychological opportunities that war provided. No easy feat, since American allies were the aggressors and the Egyptians were furious.

The outlook for Linolo was ominous. Anarchy threatened, since the country was composed of a dozen tribes, each of which felt only enmity for the others. They were not bound by either bilateral or regional loyalties. The territory lacked traditional or political cohesion. The home government had held the colony together by a police army which often resorted to brutality. No one believed the incoming indigenous regime could maintain discipline. The metropole had scheduled an election before independence to produce a parliamentary administration. Still, the transition from dependence to sovereignty was happening so fast that everyone involved knew that turbulence lurked immediately ahead.

So Littlefield picked Forbes as PAO for the same reason the State Department had named him ambassador: an ability to react rapidly and improvise soundly in fluid and dangerous circumstances.

Littlefield threw his weight around USIA a bit to spring Forbes from the mundane headquarters position in which he was mired. Days later Forbes left his wife and four children to finish out the school year and hurried to Linolo.

The U.S. counsul, Griffith Peerson, received him in Karth with mild interest. Forbes sensed Peerson hadn't quite allowed himself to accept the imminent end of an era. The next day he made another astounding discovery. With independence only weeks away, nobody in the consulate knew any Linolians other than servants, clerks, and a gendarme or two. The political officer had extended his hand to some budding politicians among the natives the preceding year and had earned a poor efficiency rating for his pains. The counsul had warned him against such contacts. Diplomats were supposed to deal only with the colonial government.

Such restrictions could no longer exist, Forbes assured himself, and in short order he obtained the consul's permission to venture out and meet Linolians. A good way to start, he decided, would be to visit the seven provincial capitals where election campaigns were nearing their climax. Out of these contests would emerge the national legislators and ultimate federal executives.

For the next fortnight, Forbes frequented the hotels, restaurants, and provincial assembly halls where electors and campaigners swirled about. He found the human dynamics differed little from the pattern he had witnessed once at a national nominating convention at home. The numbers were less, but the participants exuded the feverish friendliness that characterizes political hopefuls everywhere.

Forbes was surprised that the Africans dressed like Western businessmen, with woolen suits that left them sweltering in the equatorial heat, but looking crisp with Arrow shirts and ties. Ted Cotton, the American salesman for Cluett Peabody, had saturated the Linolian market. Occasionally in the open debates, a tribal chief would announce his candidacy, garbed only in a leopard skin loin cloth and brandishing a hunting spear. One of them brought a laugh as he introduced himself, "Je suis Simba, roi du foret!" (I am Lion, king of the jungle!)

It was a fruitful trip. Forbes exercised a warm, but courteous approach among all these strangers. Before leaving each capital, he managed to srike up a comfortable acquaintanceship with many of the nascent leaders. The Linolians accepted this friendly but diffident "European," the term they used for all white persons. This fact did not go unnoticed by the opposition. One evening while he sat in a hotel lounge sipping a beer with a dozen Linolians, Forbes sensed more than saw a lone European staring at him from a corner table. The man nervously fingered his glass of whiskey. After a half hour of glowering, he suddenly shoved back his chair and strode to within a few feet of the group. Everyone looked up, startled.

"Faites attention à ce propagandiste, ce sale propagandiste Americain!" (Watch out for this filthy American propagandist!) he shouted repeatedly, and then waxed more abusive. One of the Linolians rose, pushed him toward his table, and told him to shut up.

Presently Forbes and several Linolians strolled out on the glassed-in porch to eat supper. Most bulbs were missing from the chandelier, and Forbes could hardly see his soup. Through the gloom he perceived the Linolians still scowling over the scene in the lounge. One of them leaned over and said hoarsely, "Nobody behaves that way with our friends. Would you like us to take care of that rascal?" The man on Forbes' right said, "What we mean is, we would be happy to kill him if you wish."

Forbes swallowed a mouthful. This was critical. He didn't want to stir up trouble, yet the Linolians seemed to be testing his mettle. Was he man enough to dispatch his enemies, or have it done for him?

Finally, he replied: "The fellow was drunk. Maybe he'll apologize in the morning. You must realize I am a Christian, and except in battle, I'm supposed to avoid inflicting harm on anybody."

The Linolians seemed disappointed, and when Forbes said goodnight an hour later, one of them murmured, "If you change your mind, we still want to avenge that insult. Maybe we'll do it anyhow. . . ."

From these beginnings, Forbes developed a touch for communicating with the population. Candor was the key. If one told the truth as he saw it, kept promises, showed some humor and respect, the Linolians were responsive.

As he developed his crash program, Forbes saw to it that these insights were not lost in the written, filmed, radioed, and personally spoken messages that USIS would craft for dissemination.

By the time Linolians were dancing the Independence Cha Cha to celebrate their new sovereignty, Forbes had already sketched out a tentative country plan for USIS. Its goals were, first, to explain the United States in terms that the citizens could understand, relate to their own country, and trust; and, second, to participate in the embassy's overall program for assisting Linolo to become a viable, Western-oriented democracy. This meant showing the government how to employ media and public relations techniques in motivating its own people to build the nation. In short, the information ministry would have to run a domestic propaganda campaign. Forbes didn't share the ironic fact with Linolians that this practice was illegal in the United States.

The activities Forbes envisaged would require more people than his present staff of two American junior officer trainees and six Linolians, of whom one received, collated, and stapled the daily wireless file and another two handled book loans from the tiny collection in the former consulate. One of the trainees selected items from the file and gave them to the Linolian mimeographer, who ground out a bulletin. The Linolian chauffeur hand-delivered this around the city to newspaper editors, government ministries, and the radio station.

Forbes wired the agency to send some hardy Americans to join the post immediately. He specified an information officer, cultural officer, English teaching specialist, field coordination officer, two or three branch public affairs officers and a motion picture officer.

Meanwhile, with embassy administrative officer Bob Light, Forbes tramped around the city until he located the proper premises for USIS headquarters. Light, a veteran of service in other fledgling states, proved to be a superb operator in the current chaos of Karth. When Forbes selected a vast, vacant grocery and two adjacent stores, Light steamrollered all problems, such as missing deeds due to absent European landlords and damage from looting and vandalism. Within days USIS was in sole possession of a beautiful launching site for its potential plans.

Still awaiting personnel, equipment, and furnishings, Forbes and Light traipsed around the spacious quarters designating what function would go where. On sheets of wrapping paper they outlined a large information center with a fifteen thousand-volume library. They nailed cardboard signs on the door to each room to indicate information office, cultural office, press office, etc., and chalkmarked the floor in one huge chamber where machinery would be installed for multigraphing bulletins, pamphlets, and tactical flyers as called for. In one nearby store, they figured where to set up the projection booth and seats in a motion picture theater for VIP audiences. In another store they discussed how to adapt it into a capacious film-lending facility. A half mile away they began negotiations for a vacant warehouse where the binational center could be housed after the expected cultural officer had one day organized a Linolo-America society.

Many USIS responsibilities would not hold still until a full staff arrived, educational exchange in particular. Every day Linolians would besiege the small USIS suite in the overcrowded embassy. They would ask the ambassador for "bourses" (scholarships) to the United States. Letters begging for bourses also poured in by the hundreds from all over the country.

Part of this demand arose out of sheer terror, for chaos did ensue shortly after independence. Police forces attempted a coup, which was thwarted by the recently constituted army. Before order could be restored, vandalism and looting filled the security vacuum. Many Linolians thus wanted to escape to a safer place, anywhere, for any reason. Others weren't eating well, and they believed a free trip to the United States would mean good food, not to mention good times. Forbes and his tiny crew screened these applications, always on the lookout for potential leaders or specialists who could man key positions in the information ministry. Most of them were turned over to the AID participant program to decide who should be trained for other nation-building tasks.

Meanwhile, Forbes had to meet other USIS targets of opportunity as best he could. There were many in the land of Linolo that year. The prime ministers—there were three in eight months—announced shifts in policy to journalists so often they were ridiculed for "government by press conference." Forbes always covered these appearances, both to inform the embassy and to hobnob with the federal luminaries with whom he would need to collaborate.

While frantically tracking the confused government, Forbes moved to ease his own overloaded schedule. He established liaison with the one European who kept his unofficial advisory position in the information ministry. This man, Phillippe Guernon, had filled many positions both in the provinces and in Karth under the colonial governor. Unlike many of his countrymen, he had interacted with Linolians sensitively and thoughtfully. He had come to care about the fortunes of the Linolians. At the ministry, everyone from the top down listened to his advice. The information ministers, who kept being replaced along with the prime ministers, in turn accepted his counsel gratefully. Respecting their tender but inflated egos, Guernon kept in the background and kept his snickers to himself over their many mistakes. When alone with Forbes, however, Guernon would gossip a bit about his Linolian "superiors."

Guernon deduced that the Americans, Forbes in particular, wanted to guide the Linolians into building a healthy republic. After a few meetings with Forbes, the two developed a close friendship. Thereafter he became Forbes' guide to the information ministry's interstices.

The ministry was a technically excellent device for urging Linolians to develop their own country. The colonial governor had employed it for the same purpose. He had left it intact for the young government to use as its own internal propaganda instrument.

This fully modern mechanism of communications came equipped with everything but television. Its radio network linked Karth to the entire population through relay stations in each of the four provinces. A rich and sophisticated panel of recording machines was available to tape broadcasts in advance and then play them disc-jockey fashion from the Karth studios.

A liberal supply of cameras and production paraphernalia lay ready for producing documentary films. These would be added to the large collection of films left in hopes they would remind the new nation of its revered ex-metropole.

On the payroll were photographers who were untrained but

ready to make stills of any event the government wanted to publicize.

To top off all these advantages were typewriters and art supplies for writers, editors, and illustrators to pump out printed propaganda; but there were no people to produce it. The ministry had become a rudderless ship upon the exit of the Europeans. The Linolians quickly filled all the desks but almost none of the functions.

Thanks to Guernon's subtle influence and to Forbes's familiarity with the ministers and their lieutenants, USIS and its growing crew began to fill the gap.

The newly arrived information officer at USIS told Forbes about his first telephone call from the ministry's press spokesman, who said, "I have a desk, a typewriter, a secretary, and lots of speech texts from the prime minister's office. What do I do now?" The information officer, a seasoned spokesman himself, gradually shared his know-how until his student attained some proficiency.

The USIS motion picture officer brought in a roving USIS cameraman on per diem basis. Then with his opposite number from the ministry at his elbow, he traveled about and photographed road repair teams, factory crews, and the army on maneuvers. The resulting first issue of a series of half-hour documentaries called "Linolo Today," with the imprimatur of the information ministry, demonstrated progress by the government. The film was duplicated into dozens of copies and shown to enthusiastic viewers throughout the provincial capitals and villages.

When the third prime minister had shown that he could hold his position more than a few weeks, the government began to settle down and serve the people more usefully. The information ministry staged a week-long seminar on public communication at the state university. Several USIS officers were invited to come and give lectures in their particular specialties. The meetings were attended by many non-academics and were covered by radio, newspaper, and film. The minister of information presided, under the guidance of the executive director of the conference, Phillippe Guernon.

Hundreds of students, teachers, and technicians were given scholarships by both USIS and AID. In Karth and the provincial capital of Charmon, USIS staged several public extravaganzas featuring Duke Ellington and his band, Holiday on Ice, and amateur athletes who demonstrated American sports. The Peace Corps sent a team of agricultural volunteers. When the threats of secession in some parts of the nation abated, Forbes's USIS was fully implementing its country plan.

All branch public affairs officers finally assumed their posts after dismaying delays. One almost died of malaria. Another lost his nerve and balked at traveling to his post—the ambassador told Forbes to send that man out of Linolo promptly. Insubordination in any section of his embassy might affect the other staff members.

Another BPAO reached his city in good order only to find the USIS premises reduced to a pile of smoking embers, the target of arson. The fourth was blocked at the airport after a Communist-backed cabal seized temporary control of that provincial capital.

Ambassador Littlefield enthusiastically applauded USIS activities, one in particular. Littlefield had been shocked upon arrival to discover that even after Forbes's early barnstorming so few Linolians were known to the embassy. So Forbes hosted a series of stag dinners and lunches in his hilltop house overlooking Karth. Each one was designed to introduce the ambassador to an important segment of Karth's elite. The first brought together burgomasters of the city; the second, the senior college professors and school superintendents; the third, a dozen senior army officers; and so forth. After eating and seeing a twenty-minute documentary film, Forbes would moderate a give-and-take discussion on topics of importance to the guests. Each time the results seemed excellent. These Linolians were opinion-molders, they were hearing from America's ambassador, and they were impressed with what he had to say.

When Forbes opened the new information center more than a mile from the embassy, he borrowed a trick from another PAO in Africa. This was to create an event out of transporting the two thousand books from the original consulate library to the center. The primary school director gave Forbes permission to have two thousand students carry two books each in a single file parade. The Ministry of Information and newspapers were alerted to the event. Led by the Linolian librarian, the students assembled just in time between two rainstorms, and the school band played while the youths marched to the new library carrying the books.

To attract traffic to the Centre Culturelle Americaine, USIS's motion picture officer rigged up a continuous loop projector which threw its pictures on a rear view screen. When he set the screen inside a plate glass window of the center, the pedestrians thought it must be television, and great numbers collected outside to watch. Linolo had no TV then. Some citizens came every day to look at the same film. When they recognized scenes they had seen earlier, like skiers in Vermont (it never snowed in Landrovia), they would cheer in recognition.

Did the USIS country plan succeed in its nation-building goal? Did the people indeed try to integrate their nation, to convert the tribal loyalties into national patriotism? Did their elected representatives keep their campaign pledges for responsible government? Did the parliament and the prime minister orchestrate their awesome new powers for the good of the citizenry? The answer may never be known, for the prime minister closed the national assembly, sent the regional representatives home, and sequestered the senate so that it was allowed to meet but not to vote.

He did all this in the name of national security when the Communists subverted two of the provincial governments and put Soviet puppets in charge. The central government's army soon recaptured both provinces. Now, where governors were formerly elected, they were named as personal minions of the strongman in Karth.

After two years, the prime minister had gathered all reins into his own hands and ran the ex-colony as if it had never been free. When opposition became vocal in any part of the nation, he imprisoned the leader or bribed him with money or position to cease his criticism of the one-man regime.

The dictator's ministry of information served mostly to aggrandize his personal image. Thanks to the efforts of USIS officers and training grants to the United States, the ministry performed this job quite professionally. Forbes removed this goal from his country plan. He concentrated instead on the government, on what independent press still remained, and on the students, writers, labor leaders, senior army officers, and businesspersons. USIS now aimed to show the benefits of alliance with the United States and the West, regardless of what blandishments the Soviet Union might be tendering.

During its close association with the information ministry, USIS had been able to place materials among the ministry's radio, film, and printed output. At one supreme moment, USIA's director, Edward R. Murrow, was interviewed on the national radio program. The American broadcaster comfortably returned to the medium that had made him famous, and vice versa. As he watched his boss sweating at the microphone in Karth—the air conditioning was dead, of course—Forbes thought Murrow might begin his opening statement with "This . . . is Karth."* Of course he didn't, though the cause of freedom was losing again, this time to a modern, somewhat bland tyrant.

The 1950–60 rash of new nations evolving from European metropoles has long since ceased. USIS participation in postindependence nation-building was widespread. It contributed in some measure to hasten civilization in backwaters of the world. The experience is worth studying; it could recur in isolated cases of future revolution.

---

*Murrow first made his name in wartime Britain, starting each CBS show with "This . . . is London," in stentorian tones.

CHAPTER 12

Crisis Posts—Vietnam Included

CRASH! THE FIRST ROCK SHATTERS THE PLATE GLASS front of USIS Anywhere. More rocks, then axes, sticks, baseball and cricket bats knock away the shards so the mob can clamber inside, demolish the window exhibit entitled "Atoms for Peace," and charge into the library to grab handfuls of books which they pile up outside on the sidewalk and burn. Cheers, boos, and chants of "Yanqui, go home!" are heard.

The scene is familiar but dated. Terrorists and demonstrators have escalated their target to the embassy proper. Instead of just rampaging about, they kidnap and murder. No one has wrecked a USIS information center for fifteen years.* When it was fashionable to do so, moreover, USIA people used to take some pride in attracting such attention. It seemed to prove their impact on public sentiment.

In retrospect, one can argue that with more subtle propaganda, USIS properties might have remained intact more often. USIS might have been more influential among the known leaders of unruly groups, who, in turn, would have shown more respect for American symbols and policies.

In any case, USIS has endured and dealt with more compli-

---

*An exception—on July 4, 1987, one bomb exploded at the Thomas Jefferson Cultural Center in Manila causing little damage.

cated crises than the smashing of its centers. Emergencies of all sorts have engaged USIS talents and inventiveness to turn the unexpected into pluses for America. The following incidents required USIS people to stretch their imaginations, firm their upper lips, concentrate on the long, nearly permanent crisis post of Vietnam, and meet a brief military flare-up in the Caribbean. Each of these occurrences should remind the agency that it has failed to prepare its people for the unusual, the dangerous, the unpredictable. As the security of American diplomats decreases overseas, the time is ripe for some sort of training in tactical public diplomacy.

One tense moment in Stanleyville, the Congo, could have led to a prolonged crisis. As it was, no one from USIS was anywhere near Embassy Air Force Attaché Colonel Benjamin Matlick and his wife while they photographed a monument to the dead leftist prime minister, Patrice Lumumba. The PAO (this was me at the time) would have cautioned them. Africans had been severely beating whites for even approaching the monument. Several gendarmes ran at Matlick. They thrust a broom in his hand and forced him at gunpoint to sweep the steps that led up to a framed color picture of Lumumba. American honor was besmirched; the Matlicks would be beaten and then disgraced. Right? Wrong! Mrs. Matlick laughed and asked the police to "bring him home to my house and make him do the chores!" The Congolese couldn't contain their own laughter, and everyone dispersed in a jolly mood. A fine lesson for USIS on how to defuse explosive situations.

At 6:30 A.M. one Sunday some months later in Leopoldville, I hurried out of my apartment for the deserted golf club. My foursome could play eighteen holes before the worst heat if we started this early. As I closed the door the telephone rang inside. Wondering, I re-entered and picked up the receiver.

"There's been a terrible accident. A Congolese may be dead; Carlucci's been stabbed. Thought you ought to know. . . ."

As I queried this colleague calling from the airport at N'Djili fifteen miles from the city I learned more: The Army attache and political officer Frank Carlucci (now U.S. defense secretary) were being driven to the airport to see some VIPs off. A cyclist swerved in front of the sedan and the chauffeur couldn't stop in time. Carlucci sprang from the car to see what he could do for the victim. Carlucci's act was courageous, for it was known that when a Congolese got hurt in a vehicular mishap his neighbors might try to kill the offending stranger. If he stayed in his own car, they would pour petrol on it and cook him alive. Sure enough, an angry onlooker drove his hunting knife several inches into Carlucci's back as he bent over the prone cyclist. A passing bus driver came on this tableau, opened the door for Carlucci, and took him on to the airport where he said ceremonial good-byes to the departing officials. Suddenly Deputy Chief of Mission Robinson McIlvaine noticed blood seeping through Carlucci's coat. Only then did he admit that "some fellow on the road poked me in the back." Later, at the Reine Elizabeth Hospital, fifteen stitches closed the knife hole.

Learning all this, I telephoned Attapol Charles, director of the government radio station, told him there was a tragedy to report and that he should stand by for details. Charles, who had just returned from a "stage" of six months' technical study with the Voice of America in Washington, joshed me when I arrived in sports clothes. "It must be serious, for you to come in your shorts!" As for me, I was impressed to see him on the job so early and on a Sunday. We picked a good man to train, I thought.

I handed Charles the announcement I had drafted and requested that it be included in the morning news broadcast. Charles read it. He agreed this treatment would be the way to avoid riots and protests. The release said simply, "This morning an accident took place on the road to N'Djili. A cyclist swerved in front of a car from the American embassy and was injured." Not mentioning the rest of the incident evidently did the trick, for no one else picked up the story and it died. Carlucci walked out of the hospital that afternoon. The cyclist did not survive.

When the Congo was in total disarray during the 1960 rebellion, we publicized the good works of the U.N. forces as part of our country plan. They had come to quell the fighting and provide needed supplies. People were starving because the food distribution system had collapsed. One day a huge shipment of wheat was scheduled to arrive at N'Djili. U.S. Globemaster planes were ferrying the U.N. food to the airport, and it was then to be transported by open truck back to Leopoldville.

I called on the temporary information minister, Anicet Kashamura. He greeted me with a thirty-minute tirade of anti-American accusations. When Kashamura had finished, I thanked him for his opinion. Kashamura seemed grateful and said, "What are you here for?" I told him we had some news the government might like to take credit for. After all, the prime minister had asked for U.N. help and now because of his leadership, the people would benefit with a vitally needed shipment of food. "Write up the details so we can announce it," ordered the Congolese. Within fifteen minutes the radio began to broadcast the estimated time of arrival of shipment of food and repeated the news every hour.

At the given time, thousands of people lined the airport road with flowers in their hands. Alas, the planes were delayed until two the following morning. The flatbed trucks finally straggled empty into Leopoldville, it was too late to load the wheat. Hundreds of Congolese still waited along the highway. Nobody informed them why the food hadn't come, and the sweet new image of the U.N. turned bitter. They pelted the passing trucks with stones.

In another country where the U.S.-backed government faced a possible coup, USIS was drawn confidentially into the effort to fight back. For eight hours on the critical night, from 10 P.M. to 6 A.M., a small team of USIS writers and illustrators labored to compose three tactical leaflets. At 7 A.M. they had the pieces printed at a commercial press loyal to the government. Government drivers then distributed them by the thousands at about noon, and the local population responded by demonstrating around the prime minister's office. This show of support evidently discouraged the plotters, for the coup never materialized.

When Santo Domingo found itself in the throes of revolt during the spring of 1965, USIS played a bolder, broader, and more overt role. The ambassador had informed Washington that the Communists appeared to be taking over the rebellion. President Lyndon Johnson decided to thwart Castro's Pan-American ambitions and ordered the United States Marines to intervene. They would protect American lives and property and end the chaos and disintegration. They were there to make an island of peace—they called it the security zone—in a sea of war.

USIS plunged in to explain and justify the presence of American troops both to the Dominicans and other Latin Americans who were objecting.

USIA's associate director, Hewson Ryan, gathered a task force of ten fellow officers, writers, and broadcasters and moved into the PAO's house in Santo Domingo, since the revolutionaries controlled the part of the city where USIS offices were located.

At Ryan's request President Johnson himself authorized a contingent of the Army's First Psychological Warfare Battalion to supplement the USIS team. They arrived from their base at Fort Bragg, North Carolina, by air with a sizable array of psywar hardware. They brought mobile printing presses, loudspeakers, radio transmitters, writers, and artists.

Ryan whipped his growing force into action, orchestrating their multimedia capabilities to create a favorable atmosphere in both the Dominican Republic—on both sides of the belligerent lines—and elsewhere in the world.

Although hindered by communications breakdowns due to war damage and torrential rains, Ryan and his collaborators printed leaflets and a newspaper called *Voice of the Security Zone* to explain the U.S. presence. They mounted a tactical radio station with only five kilowatts strength, but its signal reached around the island and was relayed over the Voice of America to South America. TV and press cameramen photographed the troops engaged in such community action as distributing rations and clothes to citizens displaced from their houses by the fighting.

The U.S. Air Force also joined Ryan's public diplomacy/psywar effort by dropping leaflets over the rebel-held center of the city. That performance brought the only casualty. A piece of flak hit one of the military psywarriors in the buttocks, and he was awarded the Purple Heart. Ryan recounts that the leaflets contained U.S. major league baseball news on one side to interest the Dominicans in reading them. The wounded soldier was embarrassed to have to admit later that he had been shot in the rear end while delivering baseball scores.

Like its author, Ryan's instant campaign under mortar fire was tidy, prompt, and persuasive. To what extent his propaganda exercise calmed Dominican tempers cannot be estimated. It assuredly dovetailed into the smooth diplomacy of Ellsworth Bunker that led to a democratic election and return to national stability. Also, the skillful blending of USIS and the military psywar crew presaged the giant joint U.S. public affairs office (JUSPAO), which was organized later in Vietnam.

Indeed, that same April, President Johnson assigned all responsibility for the American psychological activities in Vietnam to the director of USIA. Ryan was made chairman of an interagency psyops (psychological operations) working group, which included officers from the White House, USIA, State and Defense Departments, plus AID and the CIA.

In Saigon, USIS ranks swelled rapidly from a medium-sized post to one of about one hundred fifty Americans, mostly USIS, and some four hundred Vietnamese. As JUSPAO was born that July 1965, military psywar specialists and AID communications experts made up the balance. Within months JUSPAO ballooned to two hundred fifty Americans and an annual budget of $10 million. USIA's Barry Zorthian was asked to conduct this huge propaganda experiment in the laboratory of a shooting war. The White House ordered him, military psywar officers, and AID personnel in Saigon to meld into one team. JUSPAO thus took charge in the longest crisis of USIA's history.

JUSPAO's task was fourfold: to persuade the North Vietnamese that the war was wrong and impossible to win; to urge the South Vietnamese to support their government and drive out the invaders and the Viet Cong; to show the rest of the world that the United States was helping a small nation under attack to repel a foreign invader and maintain its sovereignty; and, fourth, to convince the American public via journalists covering the war that involvement in Vietnam was necessary, honorable, and successful. The last goal of course is not quite legal since Congress has proscribed USIA from propagandizing the United States. This taboo was conveniently ignored for the duration.

Zorthian, an energetic former executive of VOA whom Ed Murrow had earlier urged into foreign service, landed in Saigon running fast. He had to reduce to practical terms the goals of JUSPAO. The first priority was to get the South Vietnamese in the right mood. They weren't fighting very hard in their army or supporting their government very conscientiously, particularly in rural areas where they often aided and abetted Communist guerrillas, the Viet Cong; some, of course, were brutally coerced by the Viet Cong. Second, JUSPAO had to devise ways to weaken North Vietnamese determination to take over their southern neighbor. Finally, JUSPAO had to demonstrate that the South Vietnamese needed America to help repel the hated invader and to aid them to become economically, industrially, and militarily self-sufficient.

Zorthian had to accomplish all this with USIS Americans

who rarely could speak more than kitchen Vietnamese or, at best, bad French. His USIS Vietnamese had a smattering of media skills acquired from their work with USIS since 1954, when Vietnam was freed by the French. A few had been cameramen, photographers, journalists, and traveling minstrels. His American military colleagues came from the Army, where psywar ranked as a low priority route to promotion. U.S. soldiers made wisecracks about winning battles by psychology. A number of them pinned signs over their desks that announced: "When you've got the enemy by the balls, his heart and mind will follow." Other tokens of GI humor were little cards glued to the windshields of JUSPAO's jeeps which said "Don't feed the JUSPAO." The soldiers referred to psywar specialists as "HAMOs," hearts and minds officers.

Despite these drawbacks, some real and some frivolous, Zorthian started the game with high cards in his hand. To begin with, President Johnson himself endorsed Zorthian and the concept of JUSPAO. Second, through personality, energy, and bravery Zorthian captured the confidence of three American ambassadors to South Vietnam, Cabot Lodge, General Maxwell Taylor, and Ellsworth Bunker, as well as longtime field commander General William Westmoreland.

At the beginning, USIA honored Zorthian's every request for logistics, communications hardware and software of all sorts, including television equipment and staffers. Zorthian's demands for people were so great, in fact, that the agency bled its posts everywhere else in the world to satisfy them. Not every employee leapt at the chance to serve in a war zone. Still, most responded gamely enough. Zorthian had plans for all of them. His scheme for blanketing the country with every imaginable kind of propaganda ripened rapidly under his no-nonsense leadership.

The story of JUSPAO's achievements and ultimate disappointment is long and complicated. A few highlights suffice to recall it.

JUSPAO's primary decision was to filter all civilian propaganda through the Vietnamese Information Service (VIS). Under JUSPAO's counsel, VIS personnel took up positions in every village and town of any importance throughout South Vietnam. Behind virtually every VIS operative stood a JUSPAO American. They printed pamphlets, leaflets, booklets, and posters and lent out JUSPAO-produced films; their total information output ran into millions of pieces weekly in a language Americans could not read, write, or speak.

Vietnamese actors, both men and women, toured the provinces in traditional black pajamas singing and presenting plays which sought to spread Saigon's policies throughout the population.

Cultural efforts spilled over from the pre-JUSPAO days, such as English teaching and continuing support of small libraries here and there and the large Abraham Lincoln binational center in Saigon. USIS had always embraced the Vietnamese saying "If you plan for a year plant rice; if you plan for ten years, plant a tree; but if you plan for a hundred years, educate men." Still as he watched the swarms of information personnel rather than cultural persons pour into JUSPAO, Cultural Affairs Officer Arthur Bardos commented ruefully, "I feel like a violinist in an orchestra of kettledrums."

One day Zorthian and General Westmoreland were brainstorming strategies for Vietnam. They wondered aloud how the British expert in jungle conflict, Robert Thompson, had beaten the Communists in Malaysia. They made a brief pilgrimage to see him in Singapore and listen to his theories of counterinsurgency. Zorthian, at least, returned to Vietnam without picking up anything new or relevant.

JUSPAO's psywar campaigns slalomed from paydirt to nil in rhythm with the fortunes of the battlefield. Not so with "Chieu Hoi" (open arms), which sought to induce the enemy to surrender. Chieu Hoi included various types of leaflets dropped by plane, and supplemented by airborne loudspeakers, over both the North Vietnamese Army and guerrilla enclaves. The messages encouraged soldiers to drop their guns and come over to the South Vietnamese side where they would be well treated and given medical attention and enough to eat. JUSPAO added a fail-safe device to this age-old surrender ticket technique. JUSPAO personnel would photograph each defector alongside a South Vietnamese or U.S. soldier and then tell him that the picture would be released over his former military unit "to let them know of his right decision."

The talley of defectors rose from four hundred fifty a month in 1964 to twenty thousand in the first half of 1967. A third of the defectors attributed their surrender to the Chieu Hoi flyers.[1] These were JUSPAO's claims.

Intriguing enticements were wafted toward the North Vietnamese: gift bags of toys and favors to the children of North

Vietnam from the young people of the south. Tiny parachutes opened under cargo planes during Tet, the New Year holiday, carrying these little treasures earthward. In an ugly twist of their own psychological warfare, the North Vietnamese booby-trapped some of these gifts and then publicly blamed the Americans.

Even as JUSPAO projected its propaganda to a widening array of targets, however, a wedge of bad management was fissuring its structure. Zorthian had assumed the media spokesman responsibility on top of his awesome duties as JUSPAO director. Each of these burdens called for a seven-day week. Never one to shirk, he mushed ahead under the double yoke.

He shone as a spokesman, always alert, always knowledgeable. Fatigue never dulled his eye or slurred his tongue, though he got little sleep or rest. Zorthian's reputation among the American journalists soared, and the psyops group in Washington counted on him to stem the tide of negative reporting from Saigon. Zorthian was their choice to play Canute. He stood a permanent twenty-four-hour watch, feeding out data on the war's progress and putting a positive spin on the not so cheerful battlefront dispatches.

But General Westmoreland was saddened by the lack of appreciation at home either for him or for the thousands of GIs who were fighting and dying. He saw that JUSPAO's press efforts were unavailing and said so later in his autobiography, especially in regard to their briefings:

> Daily accounts of actions that seemed much like each other, dull statistics, and the fact that the briefer was seldom personally familiar with the events he described eventually gave the session a bad name. Reporters who had been to the scene of an action would sometimes rise to tell, as they put it, "what actually happened." They called the briefing the "Five O'clock Follies."[2]

The General's view of the press may have stemmed from his psywar attitude. He never really trusted newsmen but realized he had to deal with them. An example of Westmoreland's willingness to overcome his reluctance with the media occurred in mid-April 1968. At a meeting of the Mission Council (this comprised the leaders of the U.S. embassy and the military), Westmoreland gave a brilliant briefing on an enemy attack due to hit around May 1. He admonished everyone to treat his revelation as top secret. "It must remain in this room," he commanded.

Gene Rosenfeld, chief of the Mission Press Center, then shocked the gathering by saying, "The North Vietnamese suffered a terrible military defeat in the battle of Tet, but because the public was surprised by the attack, the enemy scored a psychological win. This time we ought to alert the media, off the record, so they will be clued in on enemy plans. When they attack, the psychological advantage will be with us."*

Westmoreland looked icily at Rosenfeld and said, "I thought of that. And I rejected it."*

Three days later Westmoreland changed his mind, and Rosenfeld did set up a briefing. Army General "Si" Sidle told some thirty journalists from North America, Europe, and the Far East what the enemy was up to.

The results were positive. The North Vietnamese attacked, as predicted, in their "mini-Tet." The media, which had honored the embargo on reporting in advance, gave the U.S. good marks for divining enemy intentions and tactics. So the U.S. and South Vietnam won both a military and psychological victory. Westmoreland, in fact, did use USIA's advice.

Zorthian's personal rapport with the journalists never faltered. Most of them trusted him and sought his company. They kept him up playing poker half the night. Yet they vied with one another to bring the latest American and South Vietnamese losses and ineptitudes before the american Audience.

JUSPAO intensified efforts to get better coverage by the foreign press, but the tenor of reporting remained negative. General Westmoreland, his forces, and JUSPAO bent over backward to arrange transportation and billeting anywhere in South Vietnam for both foreign and American correspondents. Still the journalistic bile spilled forth by the thousands of column inches and through devastating TV coverage.

After Tet 1968, the morale of JUSPAO never regained its early verve. USIA Director Leonard Marks inspected JUSPAO that spring.[3] He asked Zorthian for a look at what was transpiring in a remote hamlet of JUSPAO's empire.

Zorthian tried to deflect him, suggesting that he could set up better briefings in larger centers. But Marks was adamant.

*Author's interview with Rosenfeld, February 1988.

Calling for a map of the country, he shut his eyes and pushed his forefinger down. "I'll go there," he declared, and within hours was interviewing the field advisor in the village he picked at random.

"How's it going?" Marks asked. "Are you able to influence anyone here to go on fighting, to resist the enemy, to show allegiance to the Saigon government?"

"Oh, yes, Mr. Marks. Everything's fine. I believe we're performing the way you'd want us to."

"Come on," Marks shot back, "I'm not going to hurt your record if you tell me something unflattering to the program. What do you really think of our effort in Vietnam, especially here in this village?"

The USIS officer grinned tentatively, "Let's just put it this way, Mr. Marks, I think we're wasting our time sitting in this place. We can't communicate in their language or their culture. They don't care whether we stay around and help them or not. As for me . . . I've got exactly three months, one week, and two days before I can get home and see my family."

JUSPAO's great juggernaut chugged along after Zorthian finished his five years in Saigon. It changed directors and spokesmen and revolved American staffers in and out so fast they barely had time to get to know the Vietnamese with whom they were supposed to collaborate. Their normal tour was one year. If they agreed to stay for two tours, the total was still only eighteen months, split by a thirty-day leave. Bureaucratically, JUSPAO began to lose control as its rural operations were partly absorbed by CORDS* revolutionary support organization. The job was doable if JUSPAO could have been supplied with expert linguists rather than warm bodies on short stays.

During a stint as deputy chief of the agency's Far East operations, I examined JUSPAO in 1969. Traveling by sedan, jeep, plane, helicopter, weapons carrier, truck, bus, and river boat, I observed, assessed, and tried to improve JUSPAO's performance throughout South Vietnam. I saw that JUSPAO personnel were beautifully positioned at the elbow of State Department and military officials running the war effort, from Ambassador

*CORDS (Civilian Operations Revolution Development Support Staff), a mix of U.S. Army and CIA organizations.

Bunker and General Creighton Abrams (Westmoreland's successor) at the national level down through corps, provinces (all forty-four of them), and hamlets. They lived and worked within earshot and range of hostile fire, often barely secure in their sandbagged offices and housing, from the hills of the north to the muddy flatland of the Mekong Delta. Zorthian had emplaced his minions in every strategic spot and supplied them with propaganda paraphernalia of every description. They were for the most part dedicated, industrious, and often ingenious in their efforts to accomplish their mission. But their labors were doomed to a half-baked, almost indistinguishable result. How could they communicate through the opaque wall of language and culture? Almost no one in JUSPAO ever breached it.

There was another reason for failure: the policy JUSPAO had to sell was faulty. The United States had committed a half million men and billions of dollars in material and other assets. Yet we did not intend to win the war in the only way it was winnable: march up to North Vietnam and defeat it on its home territory, or trigger World War III by going nuclear. It was the Korean War all over again. The outcome could be a compromise at best. It is hard to persuade soldiers to risk their lives for a compromise.

One obvious mistake of Washington was to allow Barry Zorthian to essay two crushing full-time jobs: managing JUSPAO and serving as press spokesman. When he concentrated on being spokesman, the management of JUSPAO suffered. Once it was deployed throughout the country, no one ever really brought JUSPAO the attention and expertise from the top it required, though Zorthian and later directors did their best.

JUSPAO's final record merits the same complaint as the overall American effort in Vietnam. It was often irrelevant to the basic wishes of the Vietnamese. Putatively we were there to help them defend themselves against aggression. The trouble was both on the battlefield and in JUSPAO's arena. The Americans did it almost all themselves while the Vietnamese stood alongside like sidewalk superintendents and watched . . . and wondered what it all meant. Former Saigon official and ambassador to the United States, Bui Diem, sees it clearly now:

> The truth is in the millions of Vietnamese families who have suffered the most horrible tragedies, *people who understood*

what was happening to them only in the vaguest way [author's italics]. The truth of this war lies buried with its victims, with those who died, and with those who are consigned to live in an oppressed silence . . . a silence the world calls peace.[4]

As the military tragedy broadened, JUSPAO's strengths waned. When the ultimate exodus swept out the remaining elements of JUSPAO, USIA's greatest test and opportunity became history. The lessons learned, the achievements (few) and shortfalls (numerous) have still to be analyzed, synthesized, and reduced to a usable doctrine in case such a situation recurs.

This vital process has never taken place. When America withdrew from Vietnam, JUSPAO was dismantled and its components returned to the army, AID, and USIA. The U.S. still has not determined whether future JUSPAOs will be mobilized for limited wars. Only one of the three agencies of JUSPAO maintains any state of readiness. At Fort Bragg, North Carolina, the army conducts a school for psychological warfare whose graduates form an active cadre. As for AID, it can instruct teachers of communications skills. USIA can stage its standard information and culture contacts with foreigners, but as psywarriors its officers can't be counted on. None of them possesses the skills to produce hard-hitting propaganda. Actually, critics often skewer them for being too propagandistic in their pursuit of USIA's peacetime tasks. They are not primed for violence of any sort. When it strikes, they have to react on an ad-hoc, call-the-fire-engine basis. But USIA officers haven't learned to be firemen.

In an emergency such as the Dominican Republic rebellion or the Vietnam or Congo insurgencies, the agency must rely on those few who have the natural talent to operate under stress conditions.

A fully competent USIA officer should be able to handle any possible situation in today's unstable world. USIA, or some part of the government, should have contingency plans and personnel to meet crises that may pop up at any moment.

As it is, hardly a year passes when USIS posts don't face obliteration, as in Iran, Ethiopia, or Afghanistan, or diminution and jeopardy, as in Guatemala and Libya. Under these circumstances USIS officers must exert flexibility, ingenuity, and often raw courage. When not forced by war or insurrection to close shop, USIS has to make do in crisis with its four basic tools: personal contact, the wireless file, VOA, and television.

ENDNOTES

1. Thomas C. Sorenson, *The World War* (New York, Evanston and London: Harper and Row), 1968.
2. General William C. Westmoreland, *A Soldier Reports* (Garden City, N.Y.: Doubleday and Co., 1976), p. 274.
3. Leonard Marks, former director of USIA, interview with author, October 1981.
4. Bui Diem with David Chanoff, *In the Jaws of History* (Boston: Houghton Mifflin Co., 1987), p. 343.

CHAPTER 13

USIS at the United Nations and Other Unique Places

THE ANNUAL PROPAGANDA DELUGE WILL OCCUR AGAIN this year at the U.N.'s annual running of the General Assembly. As the American Declaration of Independence pledges "facts to a candid world," the U.N. Charter calls for full airing of all national opinions. None of the one hundred twenty-five members exhibit false modesty. Each pours forth facts, opinions, and polemics to advance its own point of view at the world forum, the handiest launching pad for propaganda available today.

USIA treats the United Nations as an event to be covered by its media. The agency daily pumps out a massive flow of features and reports on all activities of both the U.S. Mission to the U.N. (USUN) and the U.N. itself, for a key American policy is to curry support for the U.N. USIS posts everywhere receive radio and TV tapes, radio teletype news via the wireless file, video recorders, films, pamphlets, and books which explain, describe, and promote the United Nations as a force for peace that all peoples should embrace.

The Voice of America and Press and Publications Service record U.N. news on radio and television tape, on film, and in photo and text. They operate from USIA offices within the U.N. Secretariat building and from booths in the Security Council and General Assembly.

News and features organizations such as Agence France Presse, British Broadcasting Corporation, Tass, and USIA are allowed to have accredited correspondents on the scene.

The U.N. also has its own worldwide information network. It beams radio programs over VOA facilities (at no cost to the U.N.) and maintains information centers in forty-nine countries.

A sorry contrast, however, to the agency's substantial role among other information services in the U.N. headquarters is its scrub team position within the U.S. Mission.

Public affairs at the modern U.S. Mission building is usually handled not by USIA but by a domestic State Department employee, assisted by speech writers and a spokesman for press conferences with both domestic and foreign media. In the public affairs section sits a lone USIA officer. His presence there facilitates USIA knowledge of upcoming pronouncements from the U.S. Mission, since he can alert in advance the agency's news-carrying media across the street in the U.N. proper. Is there a public affairs officer in the U.S. Mission to the United Nations? Most U.S. representatives to the U.N. have picked non-USIA public affairs advisors who safeguard them in the realm of American public opinion. Thus the answer has usually been no, in terms of the mission's impact on the home populations of other member nations. The mission does not admit or employ the expertise of USIA at this prime site for seeking approval of U.S. policies among foreign peoples.

Edward R. Murrow tried as director of the agency to correct this anomaly. He arranged to install a new office in the U.S. Mission, with the portentous title of "USIA representative to the U.S. Mission to the United Nations." One duty was to develop policy guidance for the agency's media output. Other than that the incumbent had to figure out how best to operate without actually being a member of the mission's top management group, which corresponded to an overseas embassy's country team. He also directed the agency's foreign correspondent's center. It was located across the street from the U.N. headquarters. When I filled that spot, I experimented with movie showings to the personnel from other missions and also lunches in which U.S. Mission leaders would brief foreign newsmen. Murrow met the cost of such affairs from his own pocket, so keenly did he want his man to be useful in the U.N. context. USIA looked poor when one of its films, *Three Cities in June*, pictured an unflattering sequence about the U.S.S.R.'s space program. A Soviet diplomat rose stonily in the theater and stalked out without comment. No one in the audience, including me, misunderstood his exit. The propaganda was strident and offensive.

Shortly after that incident, I enjoyed a brief but heady term as spokesman for the U.S. representative to the United Nations, Adlai E. Stevenson. The two-time presidential candidate and his public affairs advisor, Clayton Fritchey, befriended me by granting me entree to the deliberations of the mission's top team. I was also invited to small official lunches and dinners at the former governor's Waldorf Towers apartment. As a boss, Stevenson lived up to his reputation for humor and humanity. A gifted international statesman, he still found occasion to spoof diplomacy, public or private. He described it as a "mixture of protocol, alcohol, and Geritol."[1] A high point of my association with him was drafting an address he gave before an American nongovernmental organization one night in the mission theater. Halfway through the talk, several of his listeners began to chuckle and laugh. The puzzled ambassador looked over his glasses. "I don't see anything funny about that statement," he said. "But if it amuses you, you can thank Mr. Green there in the front row. He wrote this speech for me."

At present, there is still no PAO to focus on foreign audiences from the U.S. Mission. Why does this situation persist? Partly because the mission is physically in the United States, and therefore has to pay more attention to U.S. domestic reaction, something American embassies overseas don't have to focus on. The other reason is that USIA still has not garnered total respect from the U.S. government's foreign affairs community. It remains curious that, at the propaganda center of the world, the nation with one of the biggest, costliest, overt propaganda agencies finds neither the need nor the wish to place even one of its career international persuaders on the mission management team. A larger question also remains unanswered. Is the USIS officer a true professional? If so, how does he prove it? To date there is no diploma to guarantee competence as a public diplomatist.

The UN is not the only locale where USIS functions differently. Communist countries, for example, present hurdles. USIS is not free to establish its standard offices in the capital city or in other locations. Its representatives may not enjoy access to the press, and opinion leaders deliver or mail information materials at their whim. Instead, the usual practice is to permit a press and cultural section in the American embassy. Beyond that framework, the situation varies from country to country.

In Moscow, the Soviets consent to such a section but proscribe most activity beyond the capital city, except at the American consulate in Leningrad.

Andrew Falkiewicz, a former head of USIS Moscow (although that title is not admissable in the U.S.S.R.), remembers that his own work centered around a continuing process of negotiating, executing, and monitoring the latest chapter of the Cultural Agreement. American Ambassador William Lacy first brought this to term with his Soviet counterparts in 1960. Since then it has had to be renegotiated and updated biennially. It has served as the umbrella under which *America Illustrated* is circulated, large exhibits are presented, and performing arts extravaganzas go on tour in Moscow and elsewhere.

The Moscow post also produces a daily news bulletin drawn from the wireless file. It goes to the offices of Tass, Radio Moscow, *Isvestia,* and *Pravda,* as well as the foreign ministry and other government officials, plus the American and other correspondents of the Western press. The only way USIS information is apt to appear in the press of the U.S.S.R. is when Western news or features media run it, without attribution, in their own country. Then a Soviet correspondent may pick it up and file it back to the U.S.S.R. One exception occurs when the U.S. delegation arrives under the longtime U.S.-U.S.S.R. environment agreement. At these occasions the Soviets may even stage a press conference.

Falkiewicz recalls spending long sessions in Moscow pushing for press rights for American reporters. Throughout his two-year tour, he pursued a daily dialogue with the foreign ministry press division chief, Chernyakov. They haggled over problems of coverage on each side. Falkiewicz went to bat for the American journalists, trying to open up additional news sources to them. As a bargaining chip, his opposite number in Soviet officialdom reminded Falkiewicz that the government had contracted with AP and UPI to buy their services for the U.S.S.R. None of their output reappears directly quoted in the Soviet media. Still the Soviets used the fact that they had purchased their services as an excuse to request more scope for their own news gatherers in the United States. As Falkiewicz points out, this topic referred to technical restrictions on Soviet journalists by the United States government in direct reciprocity for restrictions placed on the ability of American news persons in Moscow to do their jobs.[2]

When the Soviets invaded Afghanistan during Christmas 1979, at the same time the Iranians were seizing American hostages, the U.S.-U.S.S.R. Cultural Agreement quietly fell into escrow. The Soviets informally stopped the ongoing negotiations that have characterized the existence of the agreement. Evidently they used this gesture in mild retaliation against American criticism of the Afghanistan affair. The only noticeable cost in terms of USIS activity was that large presentations of performing or graphic arts were held in abeyance. The four Reagan-Gorbachev summits have brought increasing freedom for USIS. Whether this *glasnost* spin-off leads to permanent liberalization remains to be seen.

Other Eastern European nations yield to the USIS presence in varying degrees. In Czechoslovakia following the 1968 invasion by Soviet tanks, the press and cultural section of the embassy in Prague had been permitted little contact with the national media. Yet large cultural efforts have been accepted. American companies have performed the musicals *Fiddler on the Roof* and *Man of La Mancha* and put on several screenings of MGM's prize-winning feature, *2001: A Space Odyssey.*

Even before Poland relaxed its strictures on Solidarity, the national labor union, the government allowed USIS to operate almost a normal country program, with public affairs officers, cultural affairs officers, and branch posts. Though they had almost no channel to the press, the post could freely send by messenger or mail its daily news bulletin. In terms of access to journalists and editors, the PAO has no difficulty seeing them informally at their respective offices or over lunch or a drink.

In Bulgaria, USIS is conceded what might be described as a mini-version of the Soviet program, although compared to Moscow there is only a smattering of U.S. and non-Bulgarian correspondents to deal with in the capital city of Sofia.

Hungary allows USIS to run a program somewhere between the levels of restriction in Poland and the Soviet Union. Yugoslavia is more permissive, and USIS has binational centers for English teaching, full-scale libraries, and a PAO and CAO to conduct a fairly complete program, even calling itself USIS.

In the People's Republic of China, under another family of communism, USIS has recently been given a lengthy tether. It still is named the press and cultural section but operates quite freely under the new agreement signed by Charles Z. Wick, the present agency director. The headquarters post in Beijing consists of eight Americans, mostly cultural officers and their assistants, and twenty-four Chinese.

These are not local employees of the kind hired by posts in other countries. The Chinese government has decreed that the Chinese employees will be provided for, and paid, by the foreign ministry. The USIS then reimburses the foreign ministry. These people are procured through the Diplomatic Service Bureau, which serves all foreign embassies like an employment agency. A client embassy says "we'd like a librarian," and the bureau sends over candidates to be interviewed. Presumably this system makes it easier to screen out defectors before they are hired and to keep an eye on them afterward. It also simplifies the placement of spies, if that's what the People's Republic of China desires.

When Wick visited the post in Beijing to sign the Cultural Agreement and open a painting exhibition, the Chinese government took sharp exception to the coverage of these events by the *Washington Post* and the *New York Times*. It declared that both papers misrepresented the facts and policies of the Chinese government. It laid a kind of demarche on Wick to force the papers to retract and correct their stories. Wick handled the matter calmly and explained to the Chinese that when you pressure a free newspaper to write it your way, it is apt to do just the opposite.

Regardless of such difficulties in exporting its image as it wishes, the People's Republic of China cannot be under any illusions, in view of its own handling of the written word. As David Lattimore, Brown University's China scholar, says, "Remarkably, the Chinese, most literary of peoples, have in this century produced little save propaganda."[3]

The Cuban Communists and USIS have still another sort of arrangement. For nearly twenty years the Swiss Embassy in Havana has harbored a U.S. interests section. Now the section has become so busy and has so many American staffers that it has been moved back into the former U.S. Embassy building. Officially, the operation still ranks only as an "interests section." There is also a USIS PAO on duty, though he is called a cultural exchange officer in the diplomatic list of Havana.

Robert Jordan, a recent incumbent, was forced to work in a very circumscribed environment. He was permitted to maintain contacts in the cultural community of Cuba, particularly with college professors, but he had to go through the foreign office to clear any guests at his office or house, or even if he paid calls on them. He did manage to develop excellent contacts with the University of Havana and he donated a set of books to the American studies program. This gift marked the first movement of American books into that institution in twenty years. Jordan also reported to the agency on such cultural items in the country as music, dance, poetry, and related doings, all performed with a political twist.

USIS struggles to serve in some other odd situations, such as El Salvador, where the PAO Howard Lane moved from the quieter surroundings of Honduras. Lane kept a modest program under way, mostly through exchanges. He sent a number of grantees under the International Visitor budget and a few Fulbright students to the U.S. At present, no American Participants speakers, students, or scholars are journeying to El Salvador because machine guns rattle without notice.

While shooting continues between Iran and Iraq, the United States watches through the American interests section of the Belgian Embassy in Baghdad. As in Communist nations, USIS operates a small press and cultural section.

USIS Luxembourg, however, is both unique and notable. It has only one employee, a Luxembourger. He is Roland Gaul, an able, experienced ex-banker. He is the only host country citizen to head a USIS national program anywhere. The responsible American is the ambassador—at present Jean Girard. She fulfills the public diplomacy function just as Benjamin Franklin and Thomas Jefferson did when they represented America pre-USIA. She does have the wireless file and the Voice of America broadcasts to Europe, advantages USIA's founding fathers had to forego.

Specific USIS program items include American Participants speakers and International Visitor grants. Expenses total about $60,000, of which half accounts for Gaul's salary. That means USIS Luxembourg is the most inexpensive yet well-rounded program extant today.

USIS South Africa is organized like most posts in an extraordinary political climate. Its themes are often in direct confrontation with the dominant philosophy of the country, namely, that under apartheid the white and black people must inhabit South Africa separately. Undoubtedly because of its need to maintain fruitful economic ties with the United States, the government of South Africa shuts its eyes to USIS practices. For example, despite strictures, USIS fully communicates with any and all types of citizens. The post also invites and treats as equals integrated audiences to its lectures, seminars, and motion picture showings. USIS's task becomes harder when demonstrators agitate against South African choirs and soccer teams who come to perform in the United States.

From this sweep of unusual USIS posts it may appear that there are more exceptions than regular operations.

This is true. As relationships of one individual differ with each other person he knows, so the USIS posts must be cut to fit each country in which they appear.

ENDNOTES

1. The author heard Adlai E. Stevenson II say this informally and later he used it in various public appearances and interviews.
2. Andrew Falkiewicz, interview with author, October 1981.
3. David Lattimore in his *New York Times* book review of *The Chinese and Their Revolution, 1895–1980*, October 18, 1981.

CHAPTER 14

Host Country National Employees

THE PAO'S SECRETARY RUSHED IN and announced: "The ambassador wants to see you and he is really upset!"

The PAO hurried to the third floor. As he entered the long office, he could see from the door that he was in for a heavy squall. Before he could say anything, the ambassador waved a sheaf of papers at him. His jowls shook as he rasped, scarcely in control:

"Who wrote this?"

The PAO gave him the name.

"Who the devil's that?" he boomed.

The PAO told him it was a USIS local employee.

"A non-American wrote something for me. The ambassador had accepted forty-two speech invitations and had told USIS to write all the texts. For a four-month period the load was excessive. To produce this much copy, the PAO set up a speech factory. First drafts would be crafted by a pair of able locals on his staff; he would vet their words and convert them into "ambassadorese," the style preferred by the ambassador. The system sailed along until the ambassador demanded three speech texts all at once. The PAO finished two of them but the USIS messenger took up the third as well, just as the local had composed it, without the PAO's edits. The PAO apologized for the error. He pointed out that when talking to host country listeners it was reasonable to get a local point of view into the preparation.

The ambassador shoved the speech back to the PAO.

"Bring me a new draft. I want it to be totally your work. How many more speeches have I got to make?"

The PAO told him twenty-four.

"They are all to be done by you. No one else is to have a hand in them, understand?"

"Yessir."

For an ambassador to behave this way is a rarity. Over the years, however, American foreign service personnel have been known to overlook the advantages of using able employees who are citizens of the host country. In the past, and sometimes even today, USIS and other embassy officers exhibit a weakness in managing "local" staff members. There has been a tendency to treat them as second-class citizens. The word "local" itself connotes a slightly contemptuous attitude. It's a bit like a tourist speaking of the "natives," or college students at Harvard calling their nonacademic neighbors "townies."

Eventually, the term was officially dropped; and in its place American overseas personnel were instructed to say the name of the people, such as Lebanese, Japanese, Bolivians, or whoever. The other option was to refer to them as "host country nationals," or just "nationals."

The nationals on a USIS staff can and should strengthen the program. They are the post's first point of contact with the people they are trying to inform and influence. The nationals fill many roles as chauffeurs, clerks, technicians of all sorts, writers, artists, and so on. As such they can be a built-in opinion sample for testing new ideas and campaigns. Furthermore, being physically and operationally close, nationals should also be the first people to sell on the post's objectives.

Since their fellow citizens know they work for USIS, they are frequently questioned on the American position. Hence, they should be kept up to date on American policy and, more importantly, be made equals in the international push for peace.

National staffers usually outnumber USIS Americans sixfold. If properly handled, they may be potentially strong, loyal partners. In most cases they are.

USIS has to expect that one or more informers for the host government will be spotted into USIS staffs. Even the spies may be helpful if they can report, from their privileged positions, that Americans act behind closed doors just the way they do in public.

Where Americans show disdain and snobbery, the nationals may well react as if they are under the mailed fist of an imperial master or occupation force. The hurt and disgust thus engendered are seldom expressed in front of Americans but, of course, can sour all other efforts to make friends and influence the host country. Dealing with nationals courteously gives a shot in the arm to the whole program.

The role of USIS nationals ranges in style and importance from post to post, depending often on the caliber and availability of staffers among the local population. Take a look at the post in Israel, as I recall it:

> Our USIS shop included embassy space, a library in Tel Aviv, information center in Jerusalem, and a reading room in Haifa. We were four Americans, twenty-three Israelis—who backboned our operation. Most of them were experienced and trained in their USIS tasks. Through them, we offered library services; a book-mobile for rural areas; a film-lending and projection capability; cultural exchange processing; a labor newsletter; a weekly general magazine that paid for itself; and the wireless file—all with minimal American supervision.[1]

Laos, before it succumbed to the Communists, was different. The USIS nationals lacked education, practical or academic. Their listlessness deadened the post's efficiency. In fact, in the 1950s and 1960s, the PAOs found it necessary to import third-country nationals to operate at all. Thais came in to repair and maintain jeeps, projectors, and mimeograph machines. Skilled refugees from the People's Republic of China were recruited in Hong Kong to join the Vientiane staff. A movie actor from Manila came to produce documentary films. The Laos served as clerks, janitors, and drivers. The PAO's driver made extra money fighting as a Thai boxer in the evening. In that "sport" the contestants use both feet and fists, and some mornings the driver would arrive at USIS with painful facial evidence that he won very few fights.*

*These Laos recollections are the author's as PAO 1955, 6.

One incident exemplifies the Laotian mind-set on work. The PAO had ordered one hundred bulky packages to be moved into a storehouse before the rains came. They contained almost a half million pages of pamphlets, leaflets, and booklets made in the agency's regional printing center in Manila. But weeks passed and the packages remained outside. At last, the skies clouded. The monsoon was at hand. Still the only response the PAO evoked from his relaxed Buddhist employees was "Oui, monsieur, immediatement."

So he borrowed a trick from the navy known as "all hands evolution." He lined up all the Americans and Laos staffers, with himself at the head. A truck stood ready outside. He picked up a box and everyone followed suit, walking to and from the truck until the loading was complete. At its destination one mile distant the truck was unloaded in the same fashion. That night the first torrents fell only minutes after the supplies were locked safely in their new warehouse.

The Laos took a jaundiced view of this procedure. One staffer said to the PAO that white foreigners should never do manual labor in Laos. "That's why you got sick," he said. "Also," he went on, "you should never have shot that Ghekko lizard with your air pistol. Hurting Ghekkos brings bad luck." The Lao may have been right, mused the PAO the day he was medically evacuated from his post.

On their own, the Laos sometimes did well. For example, a river boat captain was hired to run the post's "floatile" unit. This was a flat-bottomed river craft, which ranged up and down the Mekong River stopping to give movies at villages along its banks. Elsewhere, with a motion picture panel truck, a Lao employee was assigned to a territory in the south. As a combination driver-projectionist, he screened USIS films for thousands of citizens near the town of Savannakhet. Then another USIS clerk, jealous of the fieldman, told the branch PAO that he was charging and pocketing fees from his audiences. On being quizzed, the fieldman proudly confessed. The PAO asked him not to continue the practice.

In countries with a multitribal society, USIS may encounter a built-in cultural block. The trouble is that nationals of different tribes don't always like each other. As PAO in the Congo (now Zaire), I experienced the cutting edge of this problem.

In setting up our shop I placed the senior Congolese, Albert Botumbe, as straw boss of his fellow countrymen. He accepted this role, until one day I wanted one of the Congolese to take on a particular task and asked Botumbe to pass the word. He said fine, but the job wasn't done. When I checked with Botumbe he finally let me know that the man in question was a member of a different tribe and therefore refused his order.

So I assembled all the Congolese and said I could understand their difficulty but that we were all part of the same team and that everyone was subject to instruction from the supervisor, American or Congolese. After all, I pointed out, "We Americans are from different tribes from any of you (the implication being that they took our orders without question)!"

They laughed and agreed to give it a try. Efficiency improved, but not much. It proved simplest to have members of the same tribe divided according to function under each American officer. USIS's portion of this tribal obstructionism paled in comparison to the difficulties faced by the prime minister and his government. There were more than one hundred seventy five indigenous tribes when the Congo declared its independence in 1960.

Where there is a wide political divergence with the host country nationals, such as in Communist states, they are not asked to assume substantive responsibilities. Chauffeuring and clerking become the limit of their involvement in the country program. The Soviets hire no locals in the United States for their diplomatic establishments in Washington and elsewhere. Not even American drivers gain access to the official cars. The recent Marine imbroglio of sex for secrets in Moscow has resulted in U.S. adoption of the same arrangement for its embassy.

Any person must consider the possibility that taking money from another government may sully the integrity of his own citizenship. Like a mercenary, one may risk not only health but reputation when employed by foreigners. In Vietnam, some USIS and other embassy nationals discovered in 1975 that they had sacrificed everything, including their lives, when the Communists drove out the Americans.

By definition, there is nothing dishonorable or dangerous about nationals joining USIS posts. However, what should a loyal national do when he disagrees with the American policy he is asked to promote to his fellow citizens? Since Americans do the personal contact selling, the question is mostly moot. If a policy split between the United States and the host country widens too much, then USIS nationals can resign. This seldom happens in non-Communist states, not because they slavishly concur with every American aim, but because they have a regular job, with regular pay. Also in most national staffs the majority supports an amicable understanding with Americans.

ENDNOTES

1. Article by the author, "Adventures of a PAO in Israel," *Foreign Service Journal*, June 1980.

PART IV

Road Blocks and Possibilities

Chapter 15

Obstacles to USIA

AFTER AN AMERICAN PHILHARMONIC CONCERT in an Eastern European capital, the USIS officer and a visiting congressman from Brooklyn* repaired to a bistro. The congressman chaired the Foreign Affairs Budget Subcommittee. In this role he served as the legislative watchdog of State, USIA, and other agencies. On his annual junket abroad, however, he behaved more like a pariah dog. This was looking like one of his nights to howl.

After four double cognacs, he was getting out of hand. An unobtrusive black man standing at the bar suddenly came under verbal fire from the politician. The PAO managed to shush him and calm the stranger, who was reacting to the abuse. He invited him to sit at their table and make friends with the congressman. He's got jet lag from his transatlantic flight, explained the PAO as he drew back a chair. He now recognized the guest as a top official from Zanzibar in town for a convention. The PAO murmured to the congressman that this was an important person. For a while the politician sulked quietly. Then suddenly he slammed down his glass and recommenced insulting the African, ending with "and foidemore, who ever hoid of Zanzibar anyway!"

---

*These references to congressional misbehavior are based on actual fact; names have been withheld to avoid needless controversy about dead individuals.

Such congressional pecadillos were once more frequent and flagrant than they are today. As with the above, they might be perpetrated by the same legislators who called USIA unnecessary. Occasionally their antics were more serious, like the senator returning from an agricultural mission to the Soviet Union. He made a speech before Middle East VIPs and extolled Communist collectives at the expense of free enterprise farms in the United States. Local newsmen consoled the PAO in that country for the damage to America's good name.

When that senator toured Israel, he was counseled by his USIS escort to observe the ethnic customs. The senator kept his movie camera running as they motored among ancient and modern sites until they reached Nazareth. As in Jesus' day, women still carry water on their heads from Mary's Well. The senator was urged to refrain from photographing them since it would offend their modesty. Heedless, he ordered the driver to stop. A willowy maiden was swinging gracefully toward the group, a four-foot urn perched on top of her rich black hair. As she drew even with the car, a rattlesnake-like whirring startled her. Seeing the long lens aimed at her, she wrenched aside. Fluid slopped down the jar, over her face, and soaked her white robe. The USIS aide said quietly, "That's the first time one of those girls has ever been seen to spill water." Being deaf, the senator missed the put-down.

Agency chieftains, too, have been known to embarrass their field officers and sour foreign public opinion. Some years ago, the PAO in a large country of Asia Minor was justly proud when he arranged to have the USIA director speak over a prime time radio broadcast. He prepared some fitting remarks for his boss, brought him to the station, and introduced him to the president of the network. Within minutes the director was talking to the whole nation. After a polite enough beginning, he declared, "The first thing your government must do is get your airline to run on time. I am exhausted from arriving here at two o'clock this morning!" No joke intended, no light touch, just that leaden statement. The PAO took out his amulet and began to pray.

Another hairshirt for USIA is the continuing skepticism with which many career foreign service officers view its mission. Their attitude resembles that of the licensed physician toward the witch doctor or snake-oil salesman.

For instance, a *Foreign Service Journal* article by William C. Dawson complains that though "we are the most talked-about and read-about society in the world history, we still choose to employ eight thousand Americans and foreign nationals to further publicize ourselves."[1] Like some other FSOs, Dawson obviously does not accept the notion that USIA can do more than get America mentioned abroad. These men refuse to see that the agency is in business to inform and persuade foreigners and to advise American policymakers in advance as to the impact their decisions and words will have on the opinion of foreigners.

The agency, and the administrations it serves, chronically suffer from the failure of cabinet members and the Congress to harmonize their policy pronouncements. Ideally, different views held in the State and Defense Departments and the National Security Council should be thrashed out privately until finally approved by the president. One seamless policy would be much simpler to sell abroad. As it is, foreigners can observe the internal dynamics of democratic government played out under the microscope of constant press coverage. USIS must do the best it can to explain the latest adjustments and switches. These are available to USIS via the wireless file and VOA. Confidential telegrams add guidance on how USIS should play the latest shades of policy as expressed by the president and lesser leaders. Democratically formed policies can't be sold as a permanent package because they are always in a state of flux. This fact, of course, is one of the most potent rationales for maintaining the USIS apparatus in some two hundred cities strung about the world.

A more fixable failing is the lack of foreign language fluency among agency officers. After Lederer and Burdick's *The Ugly American* was published in the 1950s, Congress was inundated by constituents asking, "Why can't our foreign service people speak the language where they go overseas?" Congress responded with more money for the Foreign Service Institute. For years, State, USIA, and other foreign affairs agencies had available to them more language training than any of them could, or would, absorb. USIA did exercise this opportunity and now boasts hundreds of officers with moderate ratings in one or more languages. The trouble is, very few can read, write, and speak in any tongue but English *fluently*. The joint U.S. public affairs office in Vietnam suffered seriously from this basic lack. Great language-teaching efforts have been made since Vietnam, especially in the hard languages like Japanese and Chinese. In some cases, the officers to be assigned in such a country are sent to study there for six months to a year before they start their working tour. This practice is most encouraging and needs to be pursued, along with lengthier tours, if officers are to attain their full potential. USIA should also sponsor more courses to teach English to English teachers; this will further lower the language barrier.

What about training for their expertise as information and/or cultural officers? With the advent of career officers, the agency has developed a bunch of generalists who can't excel, or even be proficient, in any one communication skill. The often colorful, and sometimes useless, "characters" left over from World War II days have all retired now. Except for the occasional lateral entrant who is a top-flight writer, editor, cartoonist, broadcaster, college professor, or artist, there is a shortage of trained communicators. The agency deals with it through on-the-job training. This is not enough. Recent short courses by the Wick regime do attempt to prepare field officers before they leave Washington—a good beginning.

What about the deep-down requirement that USIS people be persuaders as well as mere information spreaders? Are the FSO doubting Thomases possibly right that the agency is unable to move public opinion abroad? Shouldn't the agency set up machinery to train and promote officers who can actually influence foreigners?

In the late 1960s, USIA let me inaugurate education of this sort. We staged a seminar in New York in which a top magazine publisher, radio broadcaster, and advertising mogul shared their know-how with some young officers. But the agency didn't repeat the experiment. One can argue that a good public diplomatist, or propagandist, is born, not made. George Allen, Charles Thayer (former VOA chief), Edward R. Murrow, and a number of other agency luminaries have clearly influenced foreigners. Yet none was ever trained in that direction. Those who have it, alas, are not always recognized by the bureaucracy in which USIS people must survive and be promoted. Too often officers rise, not because they can move foreign public opinion, but because they can con a soft-headed supervisor into writing a good fitness report. The rating forms should be recast to include space for measuring this valuable quality, so hard to come by, so vital to the agency's mission.

When people join the agency, what do they learn? Something about the language, culture, and history of countries to regions where they will serve. *Nothing about how to inform or persuade them.*

Of course, Franklin and Jefferson went without training too, but they knew already how to reach people. Propaganda in practice is like parenthood: people are faced with the task and do it without instruction. Some excel just naturally; others try and bumble, but the job gets done somehow, with multiple error and frequent tragedy. So also with propaganda. USIA fields hundreds of officers to spearhead its mission among foreigners, with not a wisp of schooling in sales, promotion, advertising, or public relations; all of which are components of the task to be done abroad.

I have cited USIA's constant quest to be psychological advisor to policymakers; yet who is qualified to do this infinitely tricky job? Certainly not a know-nothing political appointee whose experience has only oblique relevance to the job of communicating with foreigners through a bureaucracy that is equally strange to him. Certainly not in his early months at USIA.

There is some logic in giving up and splitting the agency as now suggested by Senator Pell (see chapter 18). Perhaps the federal government should accede to the popular distaste felt by most Americans for international propaganda. Why should any administration risk its reputation among voters by fighting to maintain an unacceptable function—at least in the minds of voters? The answer is similar to that arrived at in the case of the CIA. Americans don't like to think about the need for an intelligence agency either, especially if it has a dirty tricks division, i.e., covert actions.

Take the human body as an analogy: the hidden parts are not necessarily unacceptable; they certainly aren't unnecessary. They are dealt with by clothing, which is improved by fashion experts to the point where the cover-up becomes dressing up. Propaganda, intelligence gathering, even covert action are as vital to the safety and survival of a nation today as are the "private parts" of a human being.

Yet if we are to spend up to a billion dollars for an information program every year, surely we should be finding ways to make the operators of that agency as expert in persuasive idea communication as in the mechanical expertise needed to operate such modern communications technology as radio and TV broadcasting and wireless file transmission.

Public diplomacy is taught as a course at the Fletcher School of Law and Diplomacy. It was launched by former Ambassador Edmund A. Gullion when he was dean at Fletcher. It is available for USIS personnel to attend, at least on a sabbatical basis. The trouble is, Gullion concedes today, that the curriculum concentrates on cultural approaches to the task of USIS with virtually no substance given to the techniques of advocacy.

One move that I suggested twenty-five years ago has always been rejected; that USIS officers be allowed to attend whatever training is given at the Central Intelligence Agency in the field of black propaganda—the kind that if discovered is harmful to the perpetrator. Although USIA should not and does not engage in this form of psychological manipulation, its people should understand it and how to cope when the opponents of the U.S. engage in it. There is barely a trace of the training that achieving such capability certainly requires. On-the-job learning is virtually the rule of thumb.

This is not because there is a dearth of how-to books on sales, advertising, and promotion. There are college courses in communications and use of the media and countless books on how to public speak, write press releases, conduct public relations, sell reluctant prospects in every commercial field, run advertising campaigns, or promote through multimedia programs any idea or product known to man.

What's missing is the determination to train America's official propagandists on how to do their job: which is describing our country and culture and policies to foreigners so as to get them on our side where possible or at least to understand us, if not always to agree with us. The concept is not really inimical to our national ethos. After all this description fits quite cleanly the requirement of corporate public relations, without which any modern giant of industry would be considered both by its stockholders and the general public to be poorly dressed in the marketplace and public opinion of consumers, potential and actual.

When a new administration takes office in 1989 its leaders should think about this weakness in the nation's public diplomacy apparatus. It will be difficult to correct since practitioners of the old way of doing things will object.

Other changes are long overdue: integrating the Radio Free Europe and Radio Liberty networks with the Voice of America, for example. The foreign listeners certainly are aware that all three are U.S. government stations. No one is fooled any more by their different names. They could be continued in any case, just like Radio Marti to Cuba, which is part of the VOA already, with no confusion or problems resulting.

The Soviets are busier than ever with their own information and disinformation programs. Their glasnost campaign is taking myriad forms and is directed at opinion leaders particularly in Europe. Recently at a meeting in West Germany, I am told, Soviet speakers were conducting a seminar to explain the changes in the U.S.S.R.; the listeners were visibly impressed. Someone from USIS suggested to a State Department officer that it would be a good idea to distribute a recent Department of Defense pamphlet showing the military threat of the U.S.S.R. The USIS officer argued that this would be a good time to show the audience that glasnost was fraudulent. The State Department officer vetoed the suggestion, fortunately, for two reasons: the pamphlet was based on 1983 figures, and the timing was terrible. The audience would be shown by this act that the Soviets were trying to be peaceful while the Americans were jingoistic. Although it needs to be validated, this story is another indication that USIA needs to teach its people their chosen profession.

As this is written, a modest effort to train people in advocacy has begun under Granville Worrell, a former top advertising executive from New York. USIA hired him over twenty years ago as a "hot shot" in the Ed Murrow recruiting effort. He was brought on board to assist John Chancellor, then VOA director. The administrative bureaucrats took so long to process his papers that Chancellor had returned to NBC News before Worrell arrived.

Another long-term question is the budget. As the federal feedbag diminishes, USIA has been rationed along with other government departments. USIA's official, expenses-paid advocate and counsel—the U.S. Advisory Commission on Public Diplomacy—has risen to defend against cutting programs and numbers of personnel. But is it really axiomatic that more is better? Ambassador Ellis O. Briggs found the productivity of his mission to Czechoslovakia increased after the Czechs ordered its size reduced by 75 percent. Neither Franklin nor Jefferson asked for more Americans to be stationed in France during the 1780s.

Agency director John Reinhardt calculated that the cost of keeping an officer overseas was about $1,000 per day. That was ten inflationary years ago. The Advisory Commission is in a position to raise such questions. Its members might, if they are persistent, provoke answers that could streamline the agency's operations for smaller budgets.

Anti-American Communist propaganda provides USIA's biggest obstacle, and raison d'etre. To measure the Soviet effort in rubles is impossible, however, since much of it may be done through intermediaries. "Disinformation" is the "in" word for secretly placed, nonattributed materials that are intended to harm people, groups, or nations.

USIS Athens had a taste of disinformation in 1977. Someone sent several newspapers a forged press bulletin. The release contained insulting criticism of Prime Minister (now President) Caramanlis by President Jimmy Carter. It might have caused trouble except for an alert Athenian editor. He told the PAO, "I don't think the bulletin's from you, since it came in the mail, and you always deliver yours by messenger."

"That's right," affirmed the PAO. Whereupon the paper ran an exposure of this forgery attempt and complimented itself on being alert enough to catch it.[2]

To present a full estimate of Soviet information campaigns is beyond the scope and intent of this work. But the daily Foreign Broadcast Information Service presents a running picture of the constant worldwide radio effort by the Soviets and their satellites to misrepresent and denigrate the United States. A daily reading of Tass, Isvestia, and Pravda leads to the same conclusion. The Central Intelligence Agency's 1978 report to the Congress contains plenty of details regarding "Russia's Massive Campaign to Blacken U.S. Image."[3] To defend itself against USIA-type themes like democracy, human rights, and capitalism, the Soviet Union employs other means beside its constant overt and covert propaganda. For example, in 1970 the U.S.S.R. fired its opening gun in a battle that still rages over the question of a free press for Third World countries. The Soviets noted that Article 19 of the U.N. Charter was safeguarding the open flow of information. The Soviets then proposed that "states shall be responsible for all of the mass media under their jurisdiction."

Since 1970 this concept of state control of information has been debated in UNESCO (U.N. Educational, Scientific and Cultural Organization). It is called the New World Information Order. No decision has been reached, but a number of the Third World nations have tacitly accepted the Soviet point of view by sequestering press freedoms on a piecemeal basis. Leonard H. Marks, former USIA director and a leading champion of independent journalism, warns that even now "less than 25 percent of the nations of the world enjoy a free press."[4]

It is clear that USIA, which has a major stake in this issue, should, can, and does report how the struggle is going for press freedom. An agency that counts on disseminating truth to accomplish its mission cannot idly watch it disappear from the world.

ENDNOTES

1. William C. Dawson, "A Question of Numbers," *Foreign Service Journal*, October 1979.
2. M. William Harantunian, interview with author, October 1981.
3. *U.S. News and World Report*, August 7, 1981, pp. 42–3.
4. Leonard H. Marks, a speech to the American Bar Association, New Orleans, Louisiana, August 10, 1981. Marks, a former USIA director, is general counsel of the World Press Freedom Committee.

CHAPTER 16

Missed Opportunity?

IF THE UNITED STATES COULD BECOME "AMERICA, INC.," in the mold of nineteenth-century Britain or present-day Japan and Germany, USIA could act as its advertising agency. Those countries set a pattern of government and business partnership by which they prospered.

The Department of Commerce is supposed to facilitate and promote the nation's overseas business. In Washington the service has been criticized for inactivity. The commercial officers assigned abroad have been mostly economic experts. Rarely have they been able or inclined to promote U.S. goods and services, develop new business, or improve the climate for American construction or manufacture. Neither have non-USIS foreign service officers. As a result, U.S. embassies are not noted for supporting American business. Recently, this situation has begun to change for the better.

There remains, however, an inherent antipathy between the foreign service, including the USIA officers, and their commercial fellow citizens abroad. Indeed, it has been a tribal no-no for American businessmen and foreign service personnel to collaborate. Some deem it as reprehensible as incest. Prejudice in each camp has been vicious. Businessmen sneered at State Department "cookie-pushers," who in turn snarled at the uncultured boors of business. Reversing this tradition, America might improve the nagging negative balance of trade.

USIA could contribute. Foreign governments are showing the way. Great Britain, for example, is once again pushing mercantilism, using the BBC to hawk United Kingdom products. Canada, Germany, Japan, Holland, Scandinavia, and France are all using federal agencies to pursue aggressive export policies. They are unhampered by domestic legislation against monopolies or internal hostility between their foreign service staffers and industrialists.

A logical locus for such collaboration in the United States would be between government propagandists and commercial marketers. Men of goodwill have tried before. In the mid-1950s, corporate America gave generously to the "Crusade for Freedom" and its putatively private propaganda arm, Radio Free Europe (RFE). One trouble was that the patriotic businessmen believed RFE was private, whereas in fact the CIA funded and monitored it. Why dupe fellow Americans who in good faith were trying to promote a worthy cause? This experience with Uncle Sam alienated many businessmen and deepened their distrust in government.

Yet efforts to link arms went on. In the late 1950s, USIA set up a liaison office with private enterprise. Its purpose was to solicit business gifts and services for the agency's overseas propaganda and people-to-people programs. The procedure called for USIA to concoct joint projects and then convince company officials to implement them in harness with the government. One plan was designed to allay anti-United States sentiment in Latin America. USIA and business would explain U.S. policy, as partners. The approach seemed practicable. USIA had branches throughout the continent, and American firms had already organized the U.S. Inter-American Council (USIAC) to deal with corporate unpopularity.

The plan called for corporations to distribute USIA materials that would cast the Norte Americanos in a more likable light. USIA would furnish films, radio tapes, pamphlets, press kits, and books. The middle management of both sides agreed to cooperate. A meeting was scheduled for USIAC board members and USIA director, George V. Allen, a brilliant diplomat and publicist. He had been U.S. ambassador in five countries. Allen and the USIAC notables needed only to exchange pleasantries and grant their approval. But this was not to be.

Ten industry nabobs collected outside Allen's office early. Their mood was upbeat. I went to call Allen. His face was dour. "Tell them to wait," he growled. I looked at the bare desk, empty room, and quiet telephone but kept mum. I had no clue to his sullen mood. Although he and I were to become good friends, I couldn't understand then that he was in the grip of the traditional feud mentality between our foreign service and business.

Finally, he emerged and offered a minimal smile and tepid handshake. The tycoons reacted to the freeze with perfunctory grunts. Woodenly, they okayed the agenda, but I realized they would simply forget to follow through with the necessary orders to their underlings. Sure enough, the project was born weak and died a few months afterward.

USIA had better luck with another private enterprise group, the Business Council for International Understanding (BCIU). John Habberton of New York became the tireless shepherd of BCIU. After White House approval, the BCIU and USIA collaborated on objectives. Once they were outlined, USIA went outside the usual foreign service luminaries this time (1959) to assure a successful launching. Douglas Dillon, undersecretary of state for economic affairs, was consulted. As a former investment banker and ambassador to France, he enthusiastically endorsed the program for drawing together diplomacy and commerce:

1. Form a school headed by a professional diplomat where business personnel slated for foreign branches of American companies would receive several weeks of cultural and political familiarization with their country of assignment. This would be a kind of diplomatic "charm school" to avoid awkward behavior due to the "culture shock" of strange surroundings.

2. Before leaving for a new overseas post, top Embassy officers, including the USIA public affairs officers, would visit the home headquarters offices of American firms operating in their country of assignment—pick up useful knowledge of their aims and problems. In this way these officers could be valuable official allies of American companies.

Next, presidents of several companies consented to sit with Secretary of State Christian A. Herter and officially bless the program. He was a political appointee, not biased against business. While corporate heads waited for the secretary, a frightening moment occurred. Deputy Undersecretary Loy Henderson, a veteran and distinguished foreign service officer, temporarily took the chair in a large formal room of the State Department. He glumly stared at all these invaders from the marketplace, when their spokesman rose to explain their position. This tall, raw-boned president of Republic Steel might have fought bare-knuckled during his younger days at the steel mills. He and Henderson glared at each other. In his talk, he called the former ambassador "Mr. Loy," perhaps deliberately. Henderson's fists clenched, and he reddened.

At that moment Herter arrived, delayed by agonizing arthritis which forced him to shuffle along the long corridors of the department on a metal walker. Soon his warm personality charmed the gruff visitors, and they went away pledged to the BCIU scheme. It functioned fruitfully for almost twenty years under the guidance of John Habberton.

But despite the usefulness of BCIU's ongoing twin activities, they affect only a small percentage of people and organizations engaged in America's international trade. Although business had benefited from these relations between business and diplomatic personnel, most people in each category have probably never even heard of BCIU. What should be done? It would help to expand the number of business people and families attending BCIU's school at American University and also to boost the quantity of diplomats and information officers getting briefed at the headquarters of U.S. international firms.

In 1969, Director Frank Shakespeare accepted my suggestion that USIA's powers should be harnessed for the promotion of American exports. Year in year out, USIA has several thousand American and host country nationals in place throughout world markets. Daily, they disseminate news, features, commentaries in every medium, and keep up personal contacts all to influence opinion-molders and ordinary citizens. The powerful VOA broadcasts to hundreds of millions of foreigners. What a fine multimedia mechanism for touting American goods and services to consumers everywhere! In principle, no new money, equipment, or people are needed. The promotional mechanism has already been installed. Only the message needs be altered.

Shakespeare gave me the go-ahead. My first stop was the assistant secretary of commerce charged with facilitating business abroad. He was enthusiastic about USIA pitching in. His subordinate chiefs, however, had to be roused from sleeping at their enormous desks in their king-sized offices. They were amicable, but uninspired, either with their mission or with USIA's offer.

USIA's area directors were also flaccid. At that time, all of them had the same mind-sets as State Department FSOs. Told that the agency was going to do something for business, they asked "what the hell for?" Unfortunately, without them nothing would happen. Basically they operate USIA. Even with the director's backing, their objection won out. The idea was dropped.

The concept bounced back sporadically and weakly in ensuing years. In 1972 the agency circulated a long-winded directive that field officers should understand and explain American economics policies. Tucked into this twelve-hundred word paper were these promising phrases: "Among the new services and products the agency plans to provide posts in coming months are: policy statements on USIA's role in the promotion of U.S. exports, encouragement of foreign tourism and investment in the U.S., and cooperation with U.S. private enterprise abroad."[1]

But this instruction never materialized into meaningful action. To date, the objective of promoting U.S. business has never been inserted in any USIS country plan. Unless it is put there, no resources will be allocated to it.

In 1974, USIA Director James Keogh ordered USIS posts to distribute a periodic list compiled by the Department of Commerce called the New Product Information Service. It was better than nothing.

For thirty years the Voice of America has called attention to the American marketplace with a series named New Products USA. This is of limited value, however, since it only mentions newsworthy products. USIA distributes some product descriptions but only if deemed timely for overseas news media.

Now that America's preeminence in world diplomacy and trade has dwindled, ideas like New Products USA should be reviewed and revitalized. Those with some existing forward motion, like BCIU's school and get-acquainted sessions, should be accelerated. An order requiring USIA to promote American exports should be dusted off and implemented with real commitment.

ENDNOTES

1. "USIA and the New International Economic System," USIA CM-2152, October 30, 1972.

CHAPTER 17

Reagan's Man

AS RONALD REAGAN'S PRESIDENCY NEARS ITS END, even his critics still agree he is the "great communicator." Logically his communications agency should be excellent. Is it?

The answer is surprising and has two parts; both are complex and both concern the man he picked to head USIA, Charles Z. Wick.

Wick came to Washington unknown, but within months he achieved notoriety both in the capital and the country at large. His case history is a reverse of the usual federal political appointee. Normally, such people arrive with their reputations intact, their hopes high, and their abilities unquestioned. In time many of them prove to be weak, disappointing, even corrupt. They return home, tails between their legs, their names sullied, and hopes dashed. Wick, on the other hand, got into trouble immediately and then miraculously recovered.

He entered the administration with a varied dossier: lawyer, piano player and bandleader, millionaire businessman, film producer, actor's agent, and Republican fund raiser extraordinaire who had just staged a glamorous inaugural for the new president.

Whereupon he burst into almost instantaneous failure. The press revealed that he was furtively taping his telephone calls, spending thousands of unauthorized funds on a security system for his rented house, traveling abroad excessively, and insisting on first class in planes and hotels. Also he hired numerous young relatives of friends and political connections in a brazen display of nepotism (dubbed Kiddie-gate by some wags). Then he angered key congressional figures when they questioned his conduct of office. Even his $1,200 suits came in for comment, for their cost, not style. Some detractors in the agency and on Capitol Hill saw him as a petty tyrant and buffoon. Perhaps his abrupt and different style bothered them. Neutral observers say when he calls attention to poor performance by staffers he always seems to have cause.

At his maiden speech before the USIA alumni association, half his dinner audience left in a huff before he finished. I was present and thought the behavior of my former colleagues was atrocious. Mr. Wick's speech was unexceptionable in content, and if his delivery was mediocre we still owed him the courtesy of hearing him out. Still, it added another event to a series that left Mr. Wick with scarcely one official friend in Washington.

But that friend happened to be president of the United States. A wily employee of the agency writes the two most important pieces of information released annually by USIA are: "On Christmas Eve Mr. and Mrs. Charles Wick dined at the White House with President and Mrs. Reagan; on Christmas Day President and Mrs. Reagan lunched at the house of Mr. and Mrs. Charles Wick."

The president loyally ignored those who called for Wick's head. "Let Wick be Wick" seemed to be his reply. Free to continue, Wick plunged ahead and more than justified his champion's confidence.

Now Wick is marked as the man who took a run-down agency and transformed it into one of the most prosperous in this administration. He began his tour as a flop and is winding up as a Reagan appointee who can claim success.

Physically Wick seems strong, with a rugged jaw, hard, flashing brown eyes, and a good crop of hair set on a muscular, square build some inches under six feet, looking younger than his sixty-nine years. His manner is direct; he speaks in short takes and likes to leaven conversation with one-liners, usually outrageous puns. USIA troops report him to be a prodigious worker who likes to follow details personally. He delegates almost nothing. He can be harsh in pursuit of his way, which he generally gets. Indeed the remarkable series of changes and improvements in his stewardship at USIA stem directly from him.

Forgetting the furor of his early days at USIA, one can trace the determined course he has plotted. When he took over, it was a propitious time to ponder the agency's record. What's past is not necessarily prologue, but new broom-wielders should at least glance over their shoulders before beginning to sweep. They should consider Santayana's dictum that those who cannot remember the past are doomed to repeat it.

In this respect Wick would not be dissuaded from his ambitious plans by agency troglodytes warning that these ideas didn't work on "our watch." His attitude was healthy, despite Santayana. He was right not to wallow in the neurotic naysaying of those who tried and failed before him. His positive, take-charge approach has brought the agency belatedly into computer age technology and persuaded the Congress to fund it.

The first good sign was Wick's willingness to act forthrightly and brush aside bureaucratic brambles. He started with restoring the agency's former name, USIA, and resisting the temptation to badmouth the foolish decision to call it USICA.

Next he cabled his officers in some two hundred posts overseas to solicit their criticisms and suggestions for improvement of the agency. Any good manager wants to interact with his lieutenants directly, especially if they are so far-flung. To Wicks' astonishment, the AFGE union (Association of Federal Government Employees) challenged his missive. The union threatened to sue him unless he withdrew it and promised not to talk to his people that way again. AFGE argued that he was stealing its prerogative to air grievances. Wick resisted; the argument rankled for a while and then evaporated.

Wick then extended his territory to high ground in both the State Department and White House. He attends the secretary of state's regular 8 A.M. policy session and is accorded a place at the National Security Council table whenever it confers on matters concerning public diplomacy. Most important, his longtime, close association with the president has guaranteed his access whenever he has sought it. This advantageous positioning did not wither and vanish as it did with earlier directors.

Would Wick's favored relationship protect the agency from the fierce winds of budget reduction? He did not wait to find out. His characteristic reaction to the agency's shrinking allotment of personnel and dollars was . . . attack! If the agency were to be denied the resources on which it grew fat in the past, Wick meant to replace them from other parts of the government and from reservoirs of volunteerism in the private sector. He quickly launched two broad campaigns: enrolling volunteer cadres of experts in numerous walks of life, which he termed the private sector initiative; and, under a presidential directive, preparing a multimedia, international, hard-hitting crusade supported by several government agencies, which he called Project Truth.

The private sector initiative lined up chairmen of individual advisory committees for New Directions, Books and Libraries, Radio Engineering, and Radio Programing. Officially approved charters guide the functions of these committees, which are envisaged as informal members of the agency's planning team. Additionally, Wick enlisted a kind of unpaid militia to contribute time and talent directly to the agency's programs, at home and abroad. He drew these operational committees from labor, sports, television, feature films, public policy foundations, press and publications, museums, arts, and the Chambers of Commerce. It taxed the ingenuity of both the agency and private sector to devise a modus operandi for these public spirited individuals.

The constant and finally fatal flaw in President Eisenhower's People-to-People effort was the dearth of tasks that the various committees could usefully accomplish, especially those from private enterprise.

Wick shrugged off this worry, saying that his scheme would prevail because he personally was "committed." Indeed as a proven winner in the tough arena of commerce, Wick did not designate heads of these committees and let them loll idly about. He rode herd on them by frequent meetings. He arranged for them to travel abroad as speakers in the agency's American Participants program. Most important, he picked people who took their assignments seriously. Each year Wick releases news of good works and gifts these volunteers have given to USIA's mission. The list is impressive and grows steadily.

Project Truth took a different path, starting in the agency and then being partly spun off. At its inception Project Truth had a brave goal, authorized by the National Security Council: USIA was to coordinate a vigorous information campaign outside the U.S. to project accurately its character and its foreign policy. A principal task was to refute misleading Soviet propaganda and disinformation. Another was to highlight the Soviet threat to stability and security of countries and regions and to publicize unacceptable actions like the takeover of Afghanistan and the use of chemical warfare. At the same time the campaign was to stress the common moral, spiritual, and cultural values that bind the United States and its allies. Finally, the campaign was to remind the world that America is committed to peace and arms control but will pursue these goals from a posture of strength.

All this seemed déjà vu to USIA's old hands. In large measure it was. Basically, Wick made a hasty, incomplete effort to cut new furrows in public diplomacy. His presentation on Capitol Hill met resistance and disdain. As a consequence, Project Truth melted down after a year or two. The idealistic themes went into the National Endowment on Democracy. This private organization was formed in 1983 to strengthen democracy abroad; President Reagan's speech on the subject in England led to its creation.

The feisty portions of Project Truth were added to USIA's other programs. These included three new "weapons," as Wick liked to call them: a monthly "alert" to publicize the latest defamations by Soviet propaganda; telegraphed rebuttals to all posts of specific Soviet disinformation and misinformation thrusts; and a news-feature service as a streamlined, pro-capitalist, anti-Communist addendum to the wireless file.

When it began, Project Truth emerged as a slam-bang return to the Cold War, with legions of public diplomatists striding everywhere at once to a martial beat. Of course, it is valid to say that the Cold War never ended. Detente as introduced by Nixon, Ford, and Carter never existed. America dropped out of the Cold War but the Soviets didn't. The new administration, along with the electorate that put it in power, was frustrated by years of trying to placate the implacable adversaries of America.

Wick was firmly in tune with Reagan's spirit—we, the good democracies (always including a few rightist dictatorships), and they, the evil empire of the U.S.S.R. USIA would now fully reflect this outlook. No longer would the U.S. stand mute in the face of Communist vilification. No longer would the nation compete shyly in the idea marts of the world. It was time, in the Wick-Reagan partnership, for America to speak up.

"Speak Up America" describes USIA's rallying cry since Wick launched his stream of vigorous initiatives. The best known to Americans was "Let Poland Be Poland." This treated the world to a sample of Wick's "Hollywood" approach to public diplomacy. It was a telecast of events on the "Day of Solidarity with the Polish People" which President Reagan promulgated January 30, 1982. The one-and-a-half-hour video was produced by a Los Angeles firm and then broadcast worldwide by satellite. Approximately fifty countries signed up to receive the presentation. An estimated audience of three hundred million has viewed it, though most foreign networks may have rebroadcast only small portions of the ninety minutes. VOA also carried it to a potential total of one hundred million listeners, in thirty-nine languages. The telecast pictured four of the fourteen Solidarity Day rallies held in the United States under the sponsorship of the AFL-CIO and the Polish-American Congress. It also projected other rallies abroad and included statements by world leaders, scenes of life in Poland to contrast the hardships of martial law, readings of freedom documents, and appearances by noted artists.

Wick made good his intentions about volunteerism by enlisting contributions of major American corporations to defray most of the half million dollar cost of the spectacle.

By special permission of Congress, "Let Poland Be Poland" was aired on public broadcasting channels in the United States to a mixed reception. First, the title was ambiguous—one commentator remarked sourly, "Whatever that means. . . ." Many critics felt it was boring, foolish, and too flashy. But no one took serious issue with the idea of redressing the indignities that have been foisted on the Polish population. Wick had demonstrated that he and the president were determined to promote freedom in the face of tyranny, at least of the left, if not of the right. Furthermore, they would take hoopla techniques from their shared background in motion pictures and exploit them with the latest broadcast devices.

It should be noted that Americans' response to this performance was irrelevant. What counts is how this sort of program affects foreign viewers. Those who saw it could understand clearly that the Reagan administration doesn't hide its beliefs.

Carter's cowering tactics and occasional petulant retorts over Afghanistan had led to diminished respect among America's allies. But now the Europeans expressed alarm over Reagan's hard-line policy, and this program in particular. One sophisticated Swiss pundit switched off his set, he said, when the military dictator of Turkey began touting, in orotund phrases, democracy in NATO.

In any case, "Let Poland Be Poland" didn't formulate policy. It merely expressed policy, and that is the task of the agency. What the total foreign impact was no one really knows.

Meanwhile Wick turned his energies to beefing up the agency's TV capability. Following the October invasion of Grenada in 1983, he set about expanding existing facilities and programs into a satellite television network he christened Worldnet.

This service is an amalgam of news, commentary, and features that USIA sends abroad over the air to foreign networks, with tapes for cable systems, and through dishes into American embassies. It has cloned domestic morning talk shows with a daily two-hour live broadcast called America Today. Technically it is so smooth that the lay audience would find it hard to differentiate from the look-alike commercial programs in the United States. Substantively its presentations are considered bland in comparison, but they make a good try at being topical in presenting prompt renditions of the latest happenings in the United States.

Worldnet's brightest star is the interactive teleconference which is staged live with one-way video from the United States to the foreign audience, and two-way sound. This is normally picked up at an American embassy where foreign journalists along with experts of various sorts discuss important issues with American spokesmen, such as the secretary of state or treasury or whoever else is appropriate. The conferences are unrehearsed and thus present American's open society at its public best. Since November 3, 1983, Worldnet has conducted more than three hundred fifty of these teleconferences, and they have a multiplier effect since foreign media writers report them in their own newspapers and network television.

Worldnet now offers daily service between the United States, Europe, Africa, and South America, the only network to do so. Mr. Wick is probing ways to extend it further. From the beginning he has personally overseen Worldnet, and no decision however small is left to others. He can take credit for its extraordinary growth and for the bargains he has negotiated to keep its price tag relatively modest—4 percent of USIA's total budget. For 1988 that comes to about $34 million. He has managed, for example, to get up to 90 percent reductions from commercial satellite rates and through installation of TVRO (television receive only) dishes on U.S. posts and embassies. Most remarkable is that, through the sales efforts of USIS officers, Worldnet can be seen in some 25,000 rooms of 121 hotels throughout Europe through closed circuit. Worldnet's reach is lengthening daily.

So is Wick's list of initiatives. Each year he announces a summary longer and more diverse than the last. Wick orchestrates the agency's media like the bandleader he once was whenever the administration engages in a major event. From him, USIA's old pros have learned how to squeeze the maximum out of each happening: presidential summits, the air raid on Libya, the rescue in Grenada, the Soviet-American missile control accord, to name a few. When the president or anyone else accomplishes something, the outpouring of publicity from USIA recalls Hollywood's huckerstering of stupendous, colossal, you-name-it movies of the 1920s.

For twenty-five years VOA's operating machinery has been steadily deteriorating with little more that a patch here and there to keep it going. With Wick's prodding the Congress soon approved a $1.3 billion renovation. Bureaucratic slowdowns and delays in negotiations of new transmitter sites are impeding progress. But despite controversy, the VOA is already airing its programs in forty-four languages through its new $1 million computerized control room in Washington across the street from USIA headquarters.

Since the early 1960s, successive presidents have been goaded by the intractable Castro's anti-American tirades. The Cuban community in Miami felt that their friends and families at home should hear the American side of the story. Senator Paula Hawkins of Florida and others introduced legislation to create a radio station for this purpose. Senator Hawkins insisted that it be made part of the VOA. When the law passed, Charles Wick's hard driving hurried the station into service a scant two years later. It was named Radio Marti after the Cuban patriot. Under the new law it began broadcasts to Cuba in 1985 to provide news, commentary, and other information on events in Cuba and elsewhere to promote the cause of freedom in Cuba.

Meanwhile, Wick pumps out more and more initiatives. Already the most creative and innovative director of USIA, he has also become the most durable, now in his eighth year. To highlight just a few more of his accomplishments is necessary before assessing his remarkable record.

Reflecting his own tastes, Wick launched the Artistic Ambassadors program. These are musicians who have won acclaim as they travel from country to country teaching and giving concerts.

Next he began to modernize one of the agency's vital engines of public diplomacy—the wireless file. It has long suffered transmission defects. The receiving teletype machines frequently brought forth garbled copy. This bothered a post awaiting the full text of the president's latest foreign policy speech. The press officer had promised copies to the foreign office, several local reporters, and the prime minister, who was about to make his address devoted to relations with the United States. In came the feverishly awaited copy, and half of it was unreadable.

In the past, the file was sent by high frequency radio broadcast, which is subject to disruption and distortion from atmospheric conditions. Wick's improvements should soon deliver the file errorless almost 100 percent of the time. Transmission linkages will differ from country to country and depend on a mix of satellites, telephone cables, telecommunications companies, and the old system over the VOA and ITT.

Wick is now upgrading the file to the level of major American newspapers and commercial wire services. He will automate the production of news texts to avoid cost increases and still continue to meet tight deadlines. Texts will be written and edited originally on computer terminals and then transferred electronically to the field. The computer will also store and retrieve wireless file items for quick reference, for use in other parts of the agency and for archives.

On October 16, 1987, Wick inaugurated the first phase of his new version, which he aptly called "The Express File." This is lengthier and goes seven days a week to twenty-six media organizations in six capitals: London, Rome, Brussels, The Hague, Copenhagen, and Ankara. Wick said proudly that this service will instantly deliver its contents which are "factual rather than sensational, informative rather than dramatic, comprehensive rather than terse."[1]

The VOA will also profit from these improvements with text-editing machines to print broadcast scripts and reduce lead time on news stories and commentaries. The VOA system will permit simultaneous use by a large number of writers and editors. Texts will appear on small screens and in print, just as they do in modern daily newsrooms of commercial media. The equipment also will provide an automated archive of VOA broadcasts for access throughout the agency. Wick has expedited these changes, which were started before he came on the scene.

Other Wick innovations are using advertising abroad to increase public attention to VOA and Worldnet broadcast schedules, opening another foreign correspondents center on the West Coast, expanding USIS to islands in the Pacific rim, putting overseas two hundred thousand more American books per year, and installing a new system for teaching English.

The list of transformation by USIA continues. We have discussed enough to see why the agency has now risen to a level of admiration by the press and support by the Congress not seen since the days of Edward R. Murrow. From the Peck's Bad Boy of public diplomacy, Charles Wick can now bask in some well-earned, if grudging, respect, even from his early critics. Former Senator Fulbright concedes that "he didn't do as much damage as I thought he would."[2] Senate Foreign Relations Committee Chairman Claiborne Pell says privately, "I like Charlie Wick. I can trust what he says."[3] Publicly he stated, "I congratulate Charles Wick on the truly excellent job he has done and is doing."[4]

Even the *Washington Post*, source of so many anti-Wick stories early in the administration, has chimed in with praise. *Post* writer John M. Goshko reported that the agency has become "the largest and most technologically adroit propaganda apparatus in the world."

Other congressmen important to Wick have become supporters. Dan Mica of Palm Beach, Florida, for example, forced Wick to reinstate the West European medium-wave VOA service which had been cut to save funds. House Foreign Affairs Committee Chairman Dante B. Fascell has congratulated Wick for restoring the agency's technical machinery.

But what about the target audiences? This is a question the Congress always asks. Are you getting the taxpayers' money's worth? Wick has tried to answer it by letting Americans hear about USIA's achievements. To this end he furnishes press stories galore about overseas doings of the agency.

This is always a dangerous route to follow. How can the agency brag about influencing foreigners without risking their wrath when they hear about it? How can a lover publicly describe his conquests and expect to be able to repeat them? The answer is obvious. It was demonstrated during the early

1950s in a Scandinavian country where USIS distributed pamphlets and books about the advantages of a free labor movement. These printed pieces purportedly enabled a candidate for president of the shipworkers' union to defeat his Communist opponent.

Lobbying the Congress for a larger budget, agency people cited USIS's part in this election of the anti-Communist unionist. News of this credit-taking actually got back to the country in question, and USIS lost acceptability there for years afterward.

Having said that, it must be admitted that President Reagan shows that there are ways to boast safely about USIA abroad. In his speech to the fortieth anniversary of the U.S. Advisory Commission on Public Diplomacy he described a Cuban named Ricardo Bofill, a former Communist who has been listening to Radio Marti. Bofill is now president of the Cuban Committee for Human Rights. He wrote as follows, said the president:

> It seems to me that there will arrive a moment concerning the situation of Cuba . . . , when it will be necessary to speak of the time before and after the broadcast of Radio Marti. The ability to answer the monologue that Fidel Castro has sustained for nearly twenty-six years . . . has finally arrived.[5]

Although he has yet to finish his tour as director, it is timely to ask, What hath Wick wrought? One retired officer says that he is flamboyant, self-aggrandizing, and sacrificing everything for Worldnet; he goes for the sizzle rather than the steak, a showboater; but now he's settled down to a much more serious view of his work with less tendency to grandstand.

Another officer still in the agency says that though he still doesn't talk the language of Washington foreign affairs brahmins, Wick has demonstrated that he has an intuitive idea of what USIA is all about and has brought enormous efficiencies along with the technological innovation. As to field officers, he certainly gives lip service to their value as the vital final step in reaching target audiences.

Marvin Stone, Wick's present deputy, is the perfect management foil for him. "He's the entrepreneur who makes things happen for the agency in Washington and abroad," says Stone. "My job is to stay here quietly and mind the store." Stone, former chief executive of *U.S. News and World Report*, is highly respected in the agency and elsewhere. Wick and Stone now run a machine that is restored, polished, and accepted by the foreign affairs community as never before. This is truly the golden age of USIA.

ENDNOTES

1. *USIA World*, January 1988.
2. Senator J. William Fulbright, informal chat with author, September 1987.
3. Senator Claiborne Pell, informal chat with author, September 1987.
4. Senator Pell, remarks before the conference on Public Diplomacy in the Information Age, Department of State, Washington, D.C., September 16, 1987.
5. Presidential address, same conference.

CHAPTER 18

The Future—Uncertain

A QUARTER OF A CENTURY AGO the Communists' temporary government in Stanleyville on the Congo Riger, headed by Antoine Gizenga, was disbanded. Shortly thereafter the USIS public affairs officer from Leopoldville (now Kinshasa, capital of Zaire) visited the city and reported:

> Two odd traces of the Communist high tide remain in Stanleyville—youth group members, much wooed by the Communists, still call each other "Camarade"; and they reminisce about the thirty Russian girls that came to Stanleyville to prove the Communists are not racist like the Americans. The Stanleyville youths sneer at this obvious ploy, but admit they enjoyed the girls.[1]

Today Zaire remains non-Communist and Communists continue to spray the world with propaganda. Recently their latest bit of disinformation surfaced in Africa: they "leaked" the story that agents of the CIA and technicians of South Africa had jointly concocted a lethal gas that will kill blacks but not whites. PAOs in USIS posts throughout Africa have been busy dousing angry reactions from those who believe the tall tale.

USIA's role is to speak up for America against the continuing Soviet assault on its reputation and policies. Edward R. Murrow saw it in shining garb:

> Where men are curious and minds are seeking, where desires are eager and dreams are near bursting, there you will find the

men and women of the agency. If any part of American life had
been entrusted to tomorrow, surely it is the job we try to do. We
work with the future, and seek to implant upon the hilltop of
challenge the imprimatur of what is best in these United States.[2]

There remain nitty-gritty matters for USIA planners today,
never forgetting the idealistic underpinnings espoused by
Murrow and his followers.

First, how can the agency absorb the vast gains in satellite
technology? Leonard Marks points out that a single satellite's
capacity has increased fifty fold in the past generation. Fiber
optics will mean another quantum jump in communications.
Quoting the *Scientific American*, Marks claims that if the full
capacity of optical fiber is exploited,

> the entire present telephone voice traffic in the United States
> could be carried on a single fiber. The contents of the Library of
> Congress could be transmitted in a few seconds. We have appar-
> ently discovered an inexhaustible medium for communication.[3]

Marks warns, however, that except for about nine industrialized nations most of the world's people do not and will not
be able to profit from all this for years to come. At present
numerous large countries including mainland China haven't
even built a good telephone system. So Marks urges USIA to
step up its use of radio and books. The Soviets are outperform-
ing the U.S. propagandists through their radio and book programs, according to USIA research. So it would seem they
agree with Leonard Marks. This isn't to say that the agency
should stop improving and extending Worldnet while figuring
out how to harness fiber optics.

Meanwhile the agency should correct its language disability
as well as the weakness mentioned by Deputy Director Stone.
He has noted that with FSO generalists in the management
slots (under the political appointees), professional communicators are missing: people who can produce a radio or TV
show or write a press release or design pamphlets and magazines. Present restrictions on lateral entry of such trained cadres are steadily incapacitating the agency.

There is a new cloud on USIA's horizon: Senator Pell and
others in Washington have suggested dismantling the agency
and inserting its components elsewhere. Pell sketched out his
scheme before the U.S. Advisory Commission on Public Diplo-

macy and shocked members of USIA in September 1987. Wick sat silently as Pell's plan unfolded: put the cultural elements in the Smithsonian Institution, the political and policy newspeople in the State Department, and create a BBC-type organization out of which the Voice of America can operate separately.[4]

Months have passed since Pell threw this hand grenade. Not a whisper of his proposal has hit the media. The battle to come—and it will—should center around the issue of whether to let the agency go from strength to strength or once again to try to stuff the omelet back into the eggs, as had been done so often in the past. No part of government has been restructured so often and moved around so often as USIA.

Some like Pell's dismemberment idea because it would remove the USIA as a single target for those Americans and foreigners who don't like "propaganda." Artists and academics who travel in exchanges would no longer worry that they're sent abroad for strictly political ends. The State Department could finally recapture its freedom to speak for itself and not have to deal with an advertising and promotion entity they can't really control. USIA officers who are in the foreign service principally to get a shot at rising to ambassador would be encouraged. A high official in the VOA told me, with a grin, that eighteen hundred of the two thousand employees of the VOA would be delighted beyond measure. They have been struggling for independence for over thirty years—their only success so far has been their location on Independence Avenue in the District of Columbia.

Pell's speech didn't elaborate the ramifications of dismantlements, such as how to manage USIS in the embassies and consulates and how to keep a trained cadre of speakers, writers, and architects of country programs.

Pell did say that the present specialists in USIA could be moved to a new personnel "cone" (as the State Department calls its categories of people) in which they could pursue their profession.

The principle objection, it would seem, stems from Murphy's Law, paragraph I: If it ain't broke, don't fix it.

USIA has from the beginning been a dream that was trying to come true. The fact is that in our pluralistic society it will never come perfectly true. There is too much residual prejudice against the practice of propaganda. Furthermore, everyone who has ever served USIA has his/her personal version of what it should do and how.

My own view is that an integrated USIA should continue to function as long as the U.S. government endures. In a competitive and risky world, the U.S. must speak up in a clear and confident tone. The past eight years have seen the agency grow stronger than ever before. Despite its faults, USIA should be given the chance to consolidate its new gains, not to be rent asunder.

The country needs it, and its supporters in the Congress, the ranks of USIA employees past and present, and others will insist that it stay in business, as is.

ENDNOTES

1. "Psychological Counterinsurgency," author's research paper at U.S. Naval War College, Newport, RI, 1963, p. 37.
2. Quoted in "USIA World," March 1983.
3. Leonard H. Marks, remarks before the U.S. Advisory Commission on Public Diplomacy, Washington, D.C., September 16, 1987.
4. Senator Claiborne Pell, remarks at same meeting.

Index